I0590486

The King of Erotica
Earlier years
Larry Wilson, Jr.

<u>*GOD First!*</u>

Love You.

Love you more than you LOVE anybody!

O   p   t I m I s m

Life   *D*   *the white man is against*
                R   *ME—Umm, NO!*
                E
OBAMA!!   *A*
                M

Liberty   *Perseverance*

Safe Sex   *Drink Responsibly!*

Wear Condoms (Janet don't JAM without JIMMY!)

Your dick isn't your MANHOOD!

Use birth control

You make it you raise it, bitches.

You help make it you teach it, Niggahs!

Be a man!

Don't throw it in a dumpster

Your FAMILY will hurt you before your FRIENDS!

Ladies, your brain isn't in your pussy!

I BUILT THE KING OF EROTICA PUBLISHING LEGACY BROKE, HOMELESS, BEING BASHED, BEING TALKED ABOUT, INCARCERATED, ON AND OFF PAROLE, SUCCESSFULLY REHABILITATING MY GODDAMN SELF. ELEVEN YEARS AGO CORRECTIONS OFFICERS SAID I'LL BE BACK. ELEVEN YEARS AND 3 PUBLISHED BOOKS LATER I SAY I HAVE SUCCEEDED. I MADE IT AND I WAS MADE IN DADE, BITCHES!

‡KΦΣ3

V.I.P—

‡
H
Σ
LiŞt
ΣditiΦn

Limited Release

Barnes and noble.com and amazon.com

Published by ‡.Ķ.Φ.Є. Publications
Goulds, Florida.

BOOKS BY DAPHAROAH69

The King of Erotica 1: The Throne (out of print)
The King of Erotica: The Throne's Special Edition
The King of Erotica 2: The Crown
The King of Erotica 2: Special Edition

ANTHOLOGIES

The WSN Network
Mocha Chocolate
Voices From Within

PHAZE PUBLISHING

The Diary and the Strap

Coming Soon.
The King of Erotica 3:
The Sword

V.I.P—
The List Edition
Limited Release

╫.Ḳ.Φ.Є. Publications
PUBLISHED BY LARRY WILSON, JR.
GOULDS, FLORIDA.

ISBN# 978-0-578-01060-1

COPYRIGHT © BY MYKHALE RIVERA (MY GOD DAUGHTER)
AND LARRY C. WILSON, JR.

FRONT AND BACK COVER
BY LARRY AND JOHN WILSON ®
MAKE UP ARTIST: JASMOND WILSON
ALL OTHER PICTURES BY JAMES NEWTON, KEY WEST, FLORIDA

LIBRARY OF CONGRESS CATALOGING-IN-PUBLICATION DATA
HAS BEEN APPLIED FOR.

PUBLISHER'S NOTE:
THIS BOOK IS A WORK OF FICTION. NAMES, CHARACTERS,
PLACES, INCIDENTS ARE EITHER THE PRODUCT OF THE
AUTHOR'S IMAGINATION OR ARE USED FICTITIOUSLY, AND ANY
RESEMBLANCE TO ACTUAL PERSONS, LIVING OR DEAD, BUSINESS
ESTABLISHMENTS, EVENTS OR LOCALES ARE ENTIRELY
COINCIDENTAL. WITHOUT LIMITING THE RIGHTS UNDER
COPYRIGHT RESERVED ABOVE, NO PART OF THIS PUBLICATION
MAY BE REPRODUCED, STORED IN OR INTRODUCED INTO A
RETRIEVAL SYSTEM, OR TRANSMITTED, IN ANY FORM, OR BY
ANY MEANS (ELECTRONIC, MECHANICAL, PHOTOCOPYING,
RECORDING, OR OTHERWISE), WITHOUT THE PRIOR WRITTEN
AND SIGNED PERMISSION OF BOTH THE COPYRIGHT OWNERS
AND THE ABOVE PUBLISHER OF THIS BOOK.

TABLE OF EROTICISM
CUM TASTE PERFECTION:

V.I.P:

POEM:

THE SHORT STORIES

When all the lights blow and the wind change
And your pockets draw lint and your heart dies asunder
And your friends become mortal enemies and your family talk
And the birds fly south and the waves part...
In the end all you have is yourself. So learn
To live with you before God calls you home.
Friends, family and material things you can't take with you.

±Ķ∅ËIII

I always aim to entertain folks through my work and images without trying to impress you. During the creation of this project (let's be real I raise the bar with these books) I was homeless. Going through it in ways I never understood or asked for. There were nights I couldn't sleep. There were people I went to for help and they wanted to fuck me in exchange for room and board. Initially, I was going to pay out the ass for a photo shoot or maybe call Steve Shires, who took the cover for the first two books but I opted for a more laid back, stripped down to the bare essentials approach with a friend of mine named James and a one-time use camera. I went to Key West for a few days to get lost in the simplicity of the city. Dancing up Duval Street, almost puking at the name Crabby Dicks restaurant (wondering who would name a restaurant two names that should never go together: Crabby. Dicks.) I then went out to Clarence S. Higgs Beach to get lost in the gorgeous waters. I marveled at the pelicans and inhaled the salty water and reminded myself that love begins with me. That all the problems I had began with me. That I should never let people touch or mold my spirit. Key West reminded me that sometimes less is better. Which is why I present to you the V.I.P. version with simple photos of me in Salvation Army clothes and an entire future in literature at my beck and call? Love you all.

Pharoah69

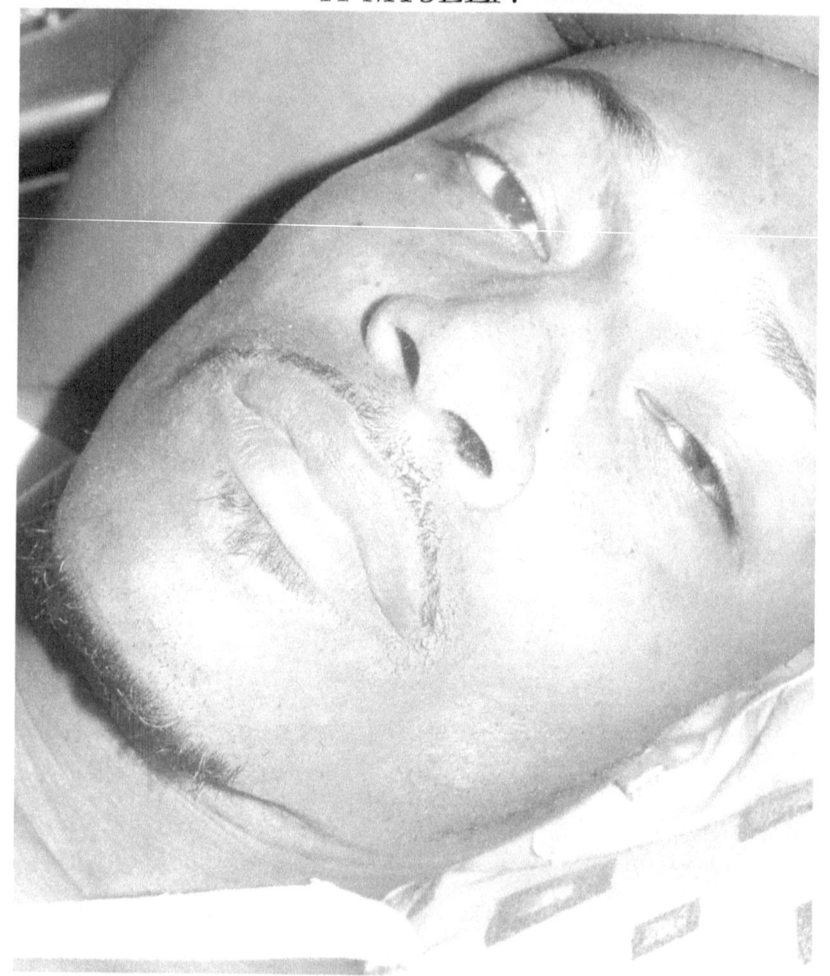

LARRY WILSON, JR.
OWNER AND C.E.O.
⳨.Ҟ.Φ.Є. PUBLICATIONS
GOULDS FOREVER!

RUN TELL THAT, HATERS!

The List:

To my family and friends in Goulds, Florida City, Homestead. I did it like I said I would ya'll! To my teachers at Goulds Mobile, Pine-Villa (Miss George, Miss Went, Miss Mike), Bel-Aire, Cutler Ridge Middle, Southwood Middle, Boyd Anderson High School and Southridge Class of '95: because of your time I am educated. Thank you. To those battling Cancer, Breast Cancer, H.I.V., diabetes or Kidney disease. I pray for you. For my Lance Armstrong Army of Friends. For all the starving and sick babies in the world. God loves you and I do too. For those living in poverty: Be strong! Chandra McCray (Sister). Tyrone Payne (Lil Brother). Kelvin Brown (Brother). Big Brother Larry Lott. All the men and women I know on LOCKDOWN. I do this for us. Marlon Rolle. My Sweetie Pie Easter Moore (MY BOO) Alvina Harris. Queen's Angel. Caramel Shay. Latoyia Shipp. Christopher McCullor. Millicent Courtney Ware (Weekendbooks.com). Barbara L. McCray (Mama). Artevia Wilson (Brother). Lonnie Wilson (Brother). My best friends Carlton Bragg, Vanesso Louis, Damian Campbell and Arica Campbell and Adi Todman. J'Anthony Hilliard. My Greenroom Barber Shop Homies: Landis Wordly: my Barber and friend for over twenty-three years. C.J. Douglass Freeman. Cool ass Albert Strachan. Marcus Johnston. Clint Harris (Florida City). Yvonia Payne. Demos Yannikos and Nikki. Shelly Garrett. Daffney Merritt. Rachelle and Katina Martin. Angie and Sherry Henry. Bianca (Lyric). Shantae McCray and Markeisha. Iona "Yonna" Gaines. My Pine Island Niggahs: Low and Kenny and Shawn. Granddaddy Luther McCray. Alma McCray. Katara Rolle. Marah and Darious Peterkin. Jermaine Graham. Tamera Oliver (Best friend/Confidant). Miss Bling Da Bling Diva. Miko Evans. JL King. Luther (RICKY), Michael Wayne and Wendell

McCray (MY UNCLES). Aunt Kelis. Steve Shires (Photographer and friend). Michael Albetta. Nancy Hanna. Robert Hamilton. Liliana Marks. Kim Jordan (sister). Jose Bravo (my favorite Chico), Todd Norris, Ofelia. Demetrius (best friend) and Starling Mozell. Sonji T. Watson (cousin). Ramone A. Hodges II. Nick Baugh. Janis McCray (Auntie). Heather Consuela (Barbados). My BIG LOTS crew: Ana Rodriguez, Maria, Carmen, Deanna, Donna, Mercedes, Robert and I know I'm forgetting a few of you. Damn. Don't kill me! To: Chantel Rogers. James McCray. Jenita Lawhorne. Shirley Milton. Clarise Kilpatrick. Punkin. Tisha Shelton. Auntie Keysha Shaw. Nujilia Brickhouse. Yolanda Lucas. Dean Smith. The Ogre Poet. My Pink Bunny Rabbit—Marcella Cross. Lori Ann Vieth. Queen Michelle. Mark Bohn. Jesse Jackson. Christy Noel Fedderson. My cousins Jamilla Harvey, Cornbread, Luke Evans, Nene, Debbie, Chris, Cambrell, Corey, Kim Harvey and Jesse and Grant. Jay and Frank (NHB) Bobby Nottingham. (HEY AUNTIE!) Debra Brown. Carissa Brown. Jamie Dailey. Renel Jordan. Cathy Harris. Chip. Willie Boyland. April Howenstein. Amanda Dowell. Danielle Mainor. Hans Bidon. Sarah Tomlin. Nate the Great. Vicky Bynum. Matthew Anders. Quincy Lathan (I love you). Shaundria Parks (sister). Barbara Parks. Auntie Judy. Tarod Brown. Patrick Davis. Akima and Meka and Frederick Rolle. Nakita Rolle. Arlette Rolle. Felecia Trotter. De'rick Bristol (My brother). Gregory Sargent. JadaRae. Dennard Fluker. Charles Arnold. Jennifer McNeill. Sandra Hansborough. Natashua Green. Immanuelle Jerome Franklin. JP (Dramatic) Morgan. Lil George and family. Tori Way. Jennifer Hennessy. David Jackson. My nieces mother Kasey Hernandez. Andre. Chantelle Hall. Marshall Latimore. Kari Morrison. Rosa McCray. Keishla Jones. Rayne Wissman. Audrey Michelle. Reduell Crowder. James Newton. Tamereka Cassimere. Priscilla (Elliot) Dowdell. Linus Spiller.

GÅLLER̴Ỳ

Ø

F

Å

ĶING

My life

       Ain't your life

      So talk! TALK! Go ahead, talk.

I   don't   care what you say about me!

        Judge me

             Then fuck yourselves

         There's one Larry C.

My last name "Wilson, Jr."

           Need not apply.

My Daddy abandoned me

      I was 17 months old.

          Does that make me

        Worthless?

I am *something*, baby.
Whatever it is release it.
People talk about things
They don't understand
So I'm going to give their dumb asses
A come-stained manuscript
A stage play
Plywood to build the theatre
A ghost light, props;
Cheap wardrobe, my old shoes
My bed, a pissy mattress
My socks, an old Army jacket
My old insignia that is of no use
And a mirror
Am I smoke?
I am something, Baby
whatever it is *say* it.
Touch my lips to find it
rock my seas, resift the sand
Give me at least one wave
Then put it up.
And never look at it again

Am I air?
No.
I'm a Blotch mark.
I'm whatever you want it to be, Baby.
No, seriously
I'm a complicated mess
I'm sexy, ugly
Something.
Look in the mirror to find it
I'm tall, skinny
Something.
Whatever I am God made it, Bitch.
I'd rather do time then
Disclose your panties and boxers, Snitch.
My Mama's coochie pushed out
A WARrior!
My Daddy's dick didn't spit very far.
Mama's clit told it, "Come here, baby."
And when it came it wasn't man enough
To stay.
I eat pussy to remember Daddy
I rub my nuts to remember
Them…
If you *hate* it pray about it
You want it…give me a call
I got bills to pay, hold up your wallet
Keep an eye on the Word, Baby
A finger on the Bible
A foot in Georgia
The other foot in Florida
The state line between your legs
Your ass on the cracked pew
Your skin misconstrued
Worship two masters,

DAPHAROAH69   16

Three acres
And a mule.
Something's better than nothing.
Right?
Tithes and collection plates
Has become the Pastor's stale mate
At the end of the day
I whip out the lotion and masturbate
Safest damn way
To duck incurable STD's
Spell it A-B-C
1-2-3
Break it up, mold me
Taste me, drink it
Pull it
What is it?
Smoke? No. Mirrors? Ah.
Trickery!
I fucked the earth
And got nothing but a dirty dick.
Instead of the "N" word.
It's something.
Isn't it?
I'm a ghetto Niggah
Full of Ghetto Tronics
A Man of Color they say I am
Hmm, I don't look like the color blue.
Goulds is in my blood
The Village on my teeth
Across the Tracks I am
Something, right?
Chocolate City in my nipples
Sugar Hill upon my feet
Across Allapattah would be my

Come-stained sheets
I'm a married man's wedding ring
And his wife's ailing bouquet
Both of them said my name
Let's not talk about my confidence
It's something, anything
Nothing like the Sun rise
Kiss my lips
Call it experience
Touch my eyes: Nose
Something.
Niggahs try to be thugs along the block
Then once the sun set
They fuck each other
The instant my clock tick-tocks!
The one that *spots* a gay man
Is a gay man
Takes one to know one
That's something, right?
Explode my mountains—teach me
Give me the grade—with a red pen
Progress reports—the lawyer's retorts
Offer a rebuttal—Niggah, drop the gavel
Declare a mistrial—Do something…
Your Goons and Goblins are watching.
I'm fine as hell,
Or so they say
Something
What is it?
Nothing
I'm a gay man's dream, a lesbian's clit
a dyke's tongue
a butch's tit
I'm a transsexual's wig,

DAPHAROAH69

a fag's death wish
a bum's Old English
In a 32 ounce bottle
I'm something,
Right?
I'm a bisexual's mistake
My mother's Greatest Achievement
Dressed in a black sheep.
I'm daddy's nightmare
He forgot to wake up
Misuse of his seeds
I hide behind photos
My eyes tend to mislead
I play musical beds
I touch to tease
I touch rods
And cop pleas
Braiding pubic hair
Blowing backs out
APB's all over my sheets
Rap sheets across my lips
I'm a lesbian's clit
I'm sexy, ugly
Something
Anything, nothing
Blurry
I'm
The Gallery of a King.
They don't make 'em like me!
There's only one
And he's a lyrical beast
A bitch in the sheets
Something…
A soldier in the streets

Nothing.
26 years ago at Pine-Villa Elementary
Mrs. George taught me
To spell my name.
L-A-R-R-Y
She handed me a dictionary
My foot in Georgia,
The other one in Florida
My ass on the pew
My eye on the Bible
My wallet in the air
My bed behind me
The pastor on stage
Handing out five collection
Plates.

THE SHORT STORIES

V

I

P

A
@
L
Σ
X

AŇDRÏA

*"**G**od is trying to tell you something. God is trying to tell you something!"*
I sang with the rest of the church, fanning myself because it was hot in here and the air conditioner was broken, as always. Well, I was actually lip-synching. My lips quivered like Whitney Houston overdoing it in the "I Will Always Love You" video. No one noticed. The stained glass windows were so dusty I had to twitch my nose and breathe in deeply to stop myself from sneezing. My sinuses were bitches with attitudes; my allergies were their Niggahs with stronger attitudes. Fake flowers were hanging from every corner of the room. It smelled old in here and the furniture looked so 1930's. There were too many ghetto-acting people looking like they were trying to take part in some secret popularity contest. I swore. Half of these weird, lame black people

wore their *Sunday Best* like every Sunday was Easter. *Grr*, I wasn't in the right frame of mind. My period was on and I was a month behind on my phone bill. And to add insult to injury, somebody defrauded my debit card; my car insurance was taken out of my account twice and State Farm was going to get burned to the ground if my money didn't get credited back.

My stupid-ass sister Tracy ate up all the food out my refrigerator and claimed "The aliens must have ate it, big sister, 'cause I was in Orlando…" My light bill went up fifty dollars this month. And right now, Mama was aggravating me. *I should have stayed home.* Mama jabbed me in the side with an old, bejeweled finger. I jumped out of my skin. I was ticklish, shit! Her floral hat was hiding her tired eyes and she kept telling me something negative about everybody. All I wanted to do was go home, *play* with my pussy because its mine, *drink* a V8, smoke a cigarette and play phone tag with my home girls.

"Aalex…what kinda dress is Sister Mary Fake wearing?" she whispered conspiratorially, holding her *Songs* Book, pretending she was praising the Lord. "She knows she needs to go home and hang her curtains back up. That dress looks like the curtains dangling in her dining room." She eyed Sister Mary over the book with calculating eyes, rocking from side to side, bumping into me. I just looked at her. I didn't have a song book. I knew most of the songs by heart.

God is trying to tell you something! G-od is trying to

teeeeelll yoooou something!

God these hags need to shut up! And who in the hell is that trying to be the next Kathleen Battle with the Opera singing? Jesus!

"Mama—I don't know and I don't care."

She sucked her teeth. "Why would you wear red pumps with a pink dress and green Mother of Nature hat with red roses around the brim and white roses across the breast area?"

"She's Haitian, Mama. And Haitians love vibrant colors."

"And they have pet cats, but that's beside the point."

My mouth fell open. "Mama! Stop being prejudiced!"

"I'm not being prejudiced! Stock in Cat Chow has dropped. And look at Brother Vanload. He's devoid of any type of common sense. He needs to call 1-877-Segal-88 and find a cure for his schizophrenia."

My mouth fell open. "Mama...*please*...!"

She challenged me. "Mama—please my *tail*, girl. I heard something about him. I wonder how that white girl is doing."

I shook my head, gritting my teeth. "God, Mama—sing!"

She licked her tongue at me. "Ha—daughter, stop lip-synching..."

This was going nowhere. I danced a little because the choir and the little church band were going to town. They sounded pretty good, except for the Opera Singer. She was the one person in the church who had to be seen and heard…Oh, snap! I knew who was singing now! Brother Vanload's wife, Sister Betty! I heard that she broke up with her husband *seven* months ago. She then took him back and he bitterly left her for a white girl; the white woman cleaned him out, taking his car and all his money, used him and talked bad about him, spreading his business all over town. The church wasn't the same. These church folk bashed him so badly he briefly left the church and lived life in a very reckless way. Rumor has it that he went back to Betty and he turned around three months later and had an affair with a closeted homosexual male in her bed while she doing over time at the Laundry Mat. Then the gay dude committed suicide in her kitchen several minutes later by stabbing himself repeatedly in the stomach because he was in love with Brother Vanload and didn't know he was married and he just couldn't deal with it. His death splashed the newspaper (briefly) and was the product of the news for all of three days. Vanload hasn't been the same since.

And Betty was still married to him! *Preposterous*! He either has the best dick in America or they made it right with God because they were back in the church, where we accepted them with open arms. But *enough* of that. Thinking about my own life overshadowed church. I was already drained. I stayed up half the night doing Mama's weave-and-finger wave hairdo. She claimed she was broke but she was the neighborhood Cookie Lady. She had hot sausages, Reese's Pieces, Snickers, name-brand sodas, Airheads, Mars Bars, potato chips of assorted brands, etc. She wasn't broke. She just didn't want to pay for the hairstyle. I bought the bonding glue, the human hair, the accessories and the perm kit. That shit cost me over two hundred dollars from Deco Drive. And she pissed on my hard work by wearing a hat to church? Forgive me Father; I knew not what I just said. I have been going through a lot. Men were full of crap; women were full of *more* crap and claimed I wanted their men! No woman in my neighborhood trusted me with their men. And they were right! They couldn't blame me if the men wanted a dose of the funky stuff between my legs. I didn't turn down free head. Not me! If a man wanted to suck my pussy then Hey, get your knees dirty. My Daddy had been a piece of crap for years.

I missed my Pap Smear test the other day. Martin Luther King's birthday was last week and I didn't go to any festivities because I was a scorned woman so celebrating men was out of the question. I looked exhausted, and so did my black dress. I was dressed like I was going to a funeral as opposed to serving the Good Lord, but even *He* was praised at funerals. I guess my period sliding down my womb was indirectly being celebrated. And this corroded church! Over the years this place has gone through various changes and different Pastors. The pews looked mildewed. You could actually smell it. Sister Hag, an old dean bat, kept spraying air freshener toward the dirty ceiling fans (that spun with this hideous creaking noise that made my skin crawl), and I was reminded why I loved being home so much. The carpeting was torn in huge areas. Let's not go there about the baby roaches scurrying here and there…the bathrooms looked like sex-houses…smelled of sex every time I went in there. Sister Gray played the hell out of that abused-looking organ in the front of the church, and she played one melody for every song we sang in here. Now for real, the "Yes Jesus Loves Me" melody didn't sound good with "God is Trying to Tell you something" from *The Color Purple* movie, but these stupid church members managed to pull it off *every* Sunday.

Nonetheless, I clapped my hands, faked a smile, stomped my toe on the clawed feet of the pew and I wanted to scream from the excruciating pain; but I smiled again, ran my hands over my hair and felt sweat running down my back to the crack of my buttocks. The Pastor's fat wife, Pricilla, was prancing around, fanning herself, helping people sing, giving out song books, being nosey and trying to be seen. And when the tramp came over to me she stood right by my side, handing me a song book. Mama was snickering. I wasn't amused.

"Here, Aalex." She was whispering in my ear, her hot breath taunting my ears. And they weren't happy about it either. "It's not good to lip-synch. Ask Ashley Simpson."

I did what Mama did—I rocked to the up-tempo music and bumped her big self into the aisle. She stumbled, falling on the floor, dropping books about her. Inconspicuously, I patted my hair, smiled, popped my chewing gum, refusing to look at the Pastor's Wife who was no Whitney Houston and waving my hands in the air.

"Hallelujah!" I called out, and someone members of the body answered my calling by saying, "Praise Jesus. Hallelujah! Yes, Father!"

I then waved at a few people I *knew* I hated with a passion and winked at a few men I did the wild thing with; I lowered my face and patted my ponytails when Frank glanced at me. My legs drummed together like pistons.

Frank! He ate me out so good in the church bathroom last week I almost went blind. Pushed my legs back on that cracked toilet in the Men's room and went to town.

His tongue was so deep in me I thought he was probing for my pulse. But when he gave me that pathetic little six inch whatever you wanna call it, I felt like I was being tickled to death so I faked an orgasm, pulled up my panties I bought from the flee market, on sale, mind you, and danced back out to the body of the church like I was Mother Mary and came off looking like Jezebel.

And that was the problem. I was always doing something out of the ordinary, something normal women wouldn't do but most women *weren't* normal, especially when that time of the month slapped you in the face with cramps you could hardly deal with. I didn't take church seriously; this was something that stemmed from my childhood.

My parents were yo-yo participants, here one minute and gone the next. Poof. Like the wind.

Mama glared at me. I could tell she was upset that my mind was everywhere but in church. "Aalex...Aalexandria?"

I looked at her, annoyed. She stared me down, then cut her eyes around the church. It took a minute to realize that I was the only one standing up.

Everyone gazed at me with eyes that seemed to tear my clothes off.

I had a big butt and some of the fellahs either licked their lips, elbowed someone sitting next to them and nodding at it or they smiled at it.

I gushed, covering my mouth. "Oh, sorry. I'll sit down now."

I tucked my dress under my behind and attempted to sit down.

Pastor Thompson, a very tall, ugly man with breath that reeked head aches and migraines, smiled at me with checkered teeth and said, "Since you're standing up, go ahead and give your testimony?"

"Huh?"

"Tell us something, anything."

"The bank debited my account twice."

"Funny. Tell us something revealing, something that makes you Aalexandria."

Why did I roll my eyes at him?

He clapped his hands with the rest of the members of the church, trying to encourage me. I didn't feel like being applauded. I wasn't going to give a testimony. Not me! Not today! I *wasn't* a child. They needed to go and taunt someone else. Now why didn't I stay home like I started to?

Why did I come here? Lord! It starts. "Testimony?" I said, swallowing what I really wanted to say. I wanted to run. I was being put on the spot. My best friend Gertrude Prescott-James was snickering. She sat behind me. Silly woman! "I don't think so, let someone else go first." My stomach growled. Dang it, I didn't eat breakfast. Hell, I haven't been eating that much lately.

"Come on, Miss Cummings," The Pastor went on, toying with me, clearly enjoying my uneasiness. "You have been attending this church off and on for years. We're like family."

You people aren't my family! "I think my Mama is sitting next to me—"

Frustrated, Mama slapped my lower leg, chastising me and I got mad.

"Don't *embarrass* me," she snapped, covering her face in shame. "Church, I don't know *who* she is."

I glared at her, trying to sway public opinion.

"*Yes* you do. You were in labor with me for 10 hours. How do you not know who I am? I guess you're catching the bus home."

She was appalled. "Girl, please. Me? Catch the bus?"

Some people were laughing. Gertrude kept mumbling something, fanning herself but I ignored her. Out of the blue some woman blurted out, "That's what happens when you spare the rod,

you spare the child," and I looked at the hotdog-
eating-bitch and pointed at her.

"Don't get slapped in here!" I told her, eyeing
her down. "…If you spare the Crisco-oil you
spare the cup cakes your big ass ate and ballooned
to a size hot air don't appreciate, nosey trick!"

She tucked her chin back, with her mouth
hanging open. Kids were laughing, "Mama, she
said *spare* the cup cakes," some little boy said,
laughing his eyes out and his Mama hid her face
behind her flyer and all you saw were her shoulders
quivering.

I had enough. "I'm not giving a testimony! Are
you crazy?" I had a change of heart. Time to
dismantle this gossip fest my church has become
over the years. "Ok, fuck it, maybe I will say a few
words."

There was so much shock and embarrassment
from my cursing that the church was rendered
speechless. No one said anything.

"All right. Let's testify. I, Aalexandria, do
solemnly swear to tell the truth, the whole truth
and nothing but the truth, so help me God because
half of you are full of complete crap." The gasps
and looks of disdain filling the church was mind-
blowing. The Pastor held the podium, not uttering
a word.

"I have been giving one hundred dollars or
more to this raggedy-looking church for years,
even when I don't attend. A lot of other people in
here give money. Some of the freaks in here give
the money just to *give* it. Out of obligation instead

of selflessly, and the A.C. is still broke, half the men in here I fooled around with, some of them are married and their wives are so promiscuous it's *ridiculous*. And I say ridiculous with emphasis on the word '*dick*' spelled with it."

A few of the Elder women, with their fancy asses, jumped up to their feet and tried to walk out, shaking their heads. They were talking shit under their breath. I eyed them with a smile.

"Don't run. Nah. Don't leave."

Hesitantly, they paused at the door. One of the ladies had on a flower dress, with an ass out of this world. Another had on a pants suit, too much weave and too much-make up. I mean why did her black ass have blush on her cheeks, making them look rosey? That kind of shit was for white women. And every time she walked or moved you'd swear a herd of horses galloped on her scalp. And the last of the Let's Leave Crew had on a white dress and blonde hair that did nothing for her black face (and I mean it was blacker than tar) and the other clung to her Bible, rubbing her pearls.

"Let's be real. Take a look at those three women back there. When they joined the church they were recovering crack heads and fledgling prostitutes. They sold it all over town."

They ducked their heads behind their purses.

I went on. "And now, years later, they are trying to run up outta here because I've had enough of the phony shit going on in this organization. God said come as I am. Well, damn it. I'm one pissed bitch. This isn't church. This is a popularity contest. Look around. Tommy, Ralph and Sean Combs will be pleased. And ya'll are so damn nosey. Always in somebody's business like your business made the NASDAQ and it don't even make sense! Oh, girl! Guess who's sucking who? Sister Lee's son is so gay he seems happy. Chile, the Pastor got a leprechaun dick! And let's not even go there about his breath."

A deafening roar of laughter filled my ears, nearly made me go deaf.

"…His breath is so stank the dead says, 'Please, put some water on *that shit*!'"

Boy did the church go up in laughs. The Pastor lowered his head, put his hand a few inches from his mouth and he blew on it, snatching his head back a little.

"Yea, its stank, Pastor. Do I recommend Crest? With mint, 'cause plain Crest will be like using water with no soap when you stank as hell. And Sister Whatever-your-name-is." I looked at her old ass. "If you spray that air freshener one more time I'm going to spray it under your arm pits because the flies keep winding up dead when they fly within a foot of you. Get my drift. Anyways. I'm scorned today and I'm cramping, so if you will excuse me, Pastor, may I step down from the bench? I gotta call the bank and see if they credited my money back, and my sister better buy me some more food or I'm going to put some Nair in her hair—"

I was heading to my car, up the aisle, shaking

some hands. "Girl, you're so crazy," said Gertrude, hugging me and I wanted to run. And with that I strutted my stuff out to my car, with Mama running behind me, cursing me from here to Africa.

When I turned the key in the ignition, Mama, snapping on her seat belt, said, trying to act like she's still angry, "What you said about the Pastor was despicable, wrong and you don't cuss in church. But did you see the way that head snapped back when he smelled his own breath?"

"I thought he got whip lash."

Mama made whip-lashing sounds.

"I've been holding that in for years."

"Did you have to tell the Air Freshener Lady to stop spraying it? With the way it smells, I thank God for every whiff of heaven he blesses me with."

"The smell of vanilla with mildewing furniture and funky curtains isn't my idea of heaven."

"I guess you got a point."

Mama and I laughed all the way to her house.

So I could drop her behind off and pick up my phone and make another doctor's appointment

Scratching my left tit, I thought about my life. Pulling on my cigarette, the smoke blasted into my lungs, giving me a head rush. I needed to cut back on smoking and drinking. I gave up on joints a long time ago, even though sometimes, when I was mad, I still got high. I got high all through college. I weighed more than 160 pounds in school; because the more weed I smoked, the more food I ate. Weed made you hungry and I supplied that need. When I wanted a man to eat my coochie real good, I'd give him some weed. And by the time he puffed it all away he was famished so I'd open my legs, pour some good parmesan cheese on my clit and told him, "Bone Appetite!"

Since I've graduated and cut back on the weed 98 percent, I was back down to a size 8.

And with *that* in mind I think about who and what I stood for. I munificently live, breathe, eat, crap, piss, screw and suck my Independence. It was all I had as a woman, as a Black woman. Don't confuse the two.

There was a difference between being a woman and being a *black* woman. When it came to women's rights and wanting us to be equal then I was all for women empowerment.

But once those white bitches became salt I was then a black woman, competing with them, jumping over hurdles and proving that I may have to work harder than white bitches but damn it I was a black woman and hear me roar, bitch.

I loved my feminist attributes so much I was obsessed with it.

It has me tenderly possessed, like I was Carrie Ann in *Poltergeist.* I looked forward to my PMS days.

I called it *"Poor Mama's Shit!"*

I loved the malediction of it. I embraced it whole-heartedly.

Most women ran from it like scared little girls, but I was steadfast.

If I didn't run from men then *why* would I run from Poor Mama's Shit?

If I had thirty arms, hands, fingers, feet, ankles and toes I still couldn't accurately count the number of men I screwed, sucked, swallowed, pussyfooted, propositioned, sissified, stabbed, tricked, manipulated, robbed, nurtured, played with and pissed off trying to find love or some rare form of it. And here I was, standing in my bedroom mirror, thirty-one years old, bitter, angry and alone (even with a boyfriend) still trying to convince myself that I *needed* a man. Men weren't men anymore. Give me a man from the 1930's or 40's any day. They were gentleman. Home trained. They knew how to speak to women, they didn't yell, scream or talk down to her. While I looked over my gorgeous body, hungrily puffing on my cigarette, I recalled the times I cooked and stole for men over the years, and they weren't necessarily my "boyfriends."

God, men surely could lie. I just couldn't understand it. So I started lying to them. Getting off on it, really. What gets me was that they talked shit, walked around being macho, macho man yet in the sack they couldn't last for ten minutes. So I started masturbating. What they lacked between their legs I made up for with my fingers. Men seemed to come faster than speeding bullets and I didn't look like Mama's Gun. I used to get so frustrated with sexless, inept men that I used to throw a tantrum, throwing my dishes into the walls, screaming, venting and just going crazy. But I haven't been doing that lately because every time I do, there goes the police. The first time I'd shattered my dishes was when I got tired of having phone sex with Don. I tried to tell him nicely but he wouldn't listen. I mean really. What straight man you knew would rather fuck me over a phone then put my pussy in his face? Where was Arsenio Hall when things made you go *Hmm*? Then he called me all kinds of bitches and whores. I got so mad I shattered every plate in my kitchen.

I guess the neighbors were worried or thought I was being raped or something 'cause the cops banged on my door and when I answered, red-eyed and angry, my hair disheveled, they rushed into my condo, looking around, guns drawn and I put my shaking hands on my hips and snarled, "What the heck are *ya'll* doing? Did I invite you in my house? Don't make me snatch my goddamn hair rollers out. Took me an hour to part my bushy hair!"

"We got a call from your neighbor…is anyone else in her with you?" asked a tall, bald-headed jack ass cop who looked at me like I was lying.

I got in his face. "The neighbor needs to put a *dick* in her mouth and shut the fuck up! *Always* in my business!" I screamed, walking past the cops and across the hall, pausing before her door. I pounded on it to make a point. "Stay outta my motherfucking business, Ho!"

I waltzed back into my place, snatching my rollers out one by one. My blood boiled like a pot of cheap rice. "Get out!" I yelled at the cops. Fuck the police. With their crooked asses. "No warrant, no entry! I shattered my own dishes 'cause lying men, looking like you, pissed me off now GET OUT!"

I never saw three male cops run so fast in my life. "That time of the month," one of them said, closing the door behind them. What? Oh, no he didn't! I snatched the door open and yelled, "Yea, time for your little dick ass to go have plastic surgery and learn how to please a woman in the bed."

His mouth fell open and when he turned to face me I slammed the door closed.

Enough said.

Then from that I graduated to CD-sex. I'd put on some Maxwell, take out my huge black dildo with the small ribs and bang myself into AN EARTH-SHATTERING ORGASM. A good nut was like a Power Drink. Once you got your high you would crash and be more depressed than you were before you bought it. I was in a rut. I just felt like I couldn't live without a warm man lying next to me, stroking me, talking to me and telling me everything was going to be alright. It seemed like I was going to die alone. I had wanted a good man, who wasn't on parole, who wasn't an ex-convict, who didn't have

fifty damn kids from fifty damn clueless bitches
and who didn't live with his Mama or
Grandmother, claiming he was nursing her or
saying he had a home but his sister suffered lung
failure and he had to give it all up, move back into
his Mom's house and take over everything. Lying
motherfuckers! What a coincidence he did all that
shit after meeting me. OK, dumb ass. Men didn't
want a woman with a ready-made family but they
thought they were going to barge into my place
with three kids. Eating up my food and twirling on
my ceiling fans like my house was Disney World.
Chile, *please*. Take you and your damn babies to
another bitch because Aalex wasn't having it.

I then played the Ride or Die chick you heard
about in the rap songs and washed their cars trying
to be Mariah Carey in the "Lover Boy" video. I
was dressed in the little Go Go Gadget Hoochie
Mama shorts, trying to give men an illusion. And
those Coochie Cutters, a name I gave my tight,
skimpy shorts because I was forever digging them
out of my crotch, always gave me rashes. I think I
was the reason stock in Vagisil and Summer's Eve
went sky high, as many times I ran to the store,
depending on the stinky cream and the douche to
heal and clean me. But these men. Jesus. Let's not
talk about the violence. Lord! I stabbed and shot at
so many men (and a few men shot back at me and
I wasn't intimidated) I lost count after four; I've
testified for and against men in court, especially
Bernard and Clive—the man who almost ruined
my entire life. I sold and held their drugs for

months, sometimes stashing zip locked bags filled with weed or cocaine in my vagina or rectum…very uncomfortable.

I fought any female that flirted with them; allowed my house to be their little get away from a world that hated them. I was naïve then, so confused about love. I thought I knew it all, Miss Aalexandria, whose pussy pounded harder than Miami Bass. Couldn't anybody tell me a thing about the male penis, men, hustling and making that cheddar? The first time, with Bernard, who I loved with all my heart (known him since high school) I told myself, "Hey, I been to college and graduated, so why did I sink to an all-time low by getting a drug dealer for a man?" I still didn't know. I really couldn't talk because I sold drugs when I was 15, trying to survive on my own. Right after Daddy crushed my ego and my inner beauty, and I had to survive while going to counseling all at the same time.

But as far as getting a dope head for a man, something was better than nothing, I figured. So I took it…him *and* his little dick. My girlfriends warned me that he was no good.

What has he done for you lately?
He was cheating on you.
Girl, you can do better.
He stood you up.
Chile, guess what, he stood you up again!

But I figured they were jealous. I had that Janet Jackson attitude.

"*Yes*, Honey! I. Love. Him! He is Fine!"

And wound up with the police constantly pulling me over and harassing me.

Be that as it may, after four months of hell (and bad sex) and vowing to never date another dope dealer I quit him and told him he could pick his shit up off my porch when he got to my place. I didn't care if the crack heads stole it.

Not my problem.

I was single for three months, until Clive sought me out.

I wasn't going to even think about Clive right now. It was just too painful.

I called a plumber. But every plumber I called talked down to me because I was a woman instead of talking *to* me. They tried to flirt. Get at me. Take me out. Gave lewd remarks.

Hell, it wasn't my fault they made a career out of fixing toilets! Not my problem!

"Are you sure it's the toilet that's broke?" said a representative from Fix Your Stools.

"Nah, I think it's the shower head, dummy, what do you take me for?"

"Damn, Mama. Why you so mad? Ain't got a man? How about I take you out for dinner, *your* treat—"

I hung up. Niggah couldn't talk proper English anyway.

Grim-faced, I called Stay Fixed Plumbing.

Another man answered the phone.

"Good day, my toilet's broke. I need your service."

"Is it just the toilet?" he asked with an attitude. His wife must have left him.

"Yes."

"Anything else?"

Jesus! "No."

"Any other problems in the bathroom?"

Lord! "I. Said. *No!*"

"When was the last time the sink gave you problems?"

"What?" I sat on the couch, holding my forehead. "Fuck the sink! It's the toilet, goddamn it!"

"When you're done cramping, call me. I don't have to deal with your attitude. And watch your mouth. I'm *not* your child. You don't cuss at me, bitch!"

"*What*, bitch?"

"*You're* the bitch. And I own the company. So don't even think about calling my manager. I *am* the manager."

"Man you need to grow up. This isn't good business. How are you gonna curse out the woman who has the money to keep you in business."

"Did I know you yesterday?"

"Well, no."

"Well then, that means my business was afloat before I met you. So it'll stay afloat after meeting you. Your money doesn't make or break me."

He hung up on me. I sat back and stared at my TV.

I called Brother's Fix It. That was a stupid ass name for a plumbing company.

"Hello, yes…this is A'alexandria. My toilet is clogged up. I've done everything that I possibly could to unclog it. I need some assistance."

Another damn man. A black man. The worst kind.

"Most *certainly*, sexy."

"I'm *not* sexy. I just want my toilet fixed."

"Damn. Fat girls need love too, I guess. Got a man?"

That was it.

"Yea. I got one. He told me he fucked you in the ass last night, fag boy!" And I bammed the phone down. I'll do it my damn self!

Aretha Franklin taught me that.

A few days later, after getting nothing accomplished, I decided to go to the Home Depot. About to pull my hair out from frustration, and still mad because my bank was playing around with my money, I needed to find someone at the store who knew how to get toilets fixed.

My toilet broke and my business was floating around it like my bathroom was waiting to be raided by toilet paper. I couldn't even call a reliable service.

If it wasn't one thing it was another, I swore. A bitch couldn't get ahead and stay ahead for nothing.

If I had the ability to turn into a white woman

from a seedy family for six months just to get a house, car and save some money and then had the ability to change back to the black woman I was and keep all I achieved as that white woman then I would do it in a heart beat.

I called my insurance company. I smoked a cigarette waiting on someone to answer the phone. It rang and rang and rang and goddamn rang. It was business hours, so someone needed to answer the damn phone. Finally, I got the automated service. *Figures.* These companies were so impersonal. I pressed a series of numbers, sat through three different menus, smoked two more cigarettes, my stress level at an all-time high; and when a representative finally got on the phone I said, "When are you guys going to put my money back on my account?"

"Your name is?"

"A'alexandria Cummings."

"Ahlexandria?"

"Yes, that's how it's pronounced."

"Account number?"

"Um 5-4-3-2-1-bass, bass, bass, bass," I joked, but I was serious as hell. "You know who the hell I am. When are you going to credit my money back?"

"I need the proper account—"

"Listen. Is your name Hank?"

"Yes."

"The very same Hank I talked to four times now? You should know my account number by heart. You guys took out two payments of $130."

A large gush of air. "Oh. *You.*"

"Yes, *me*, Hank! I only pay $130 a month for my car insurance. *One*, not two! And you claim you have *no* record of it."

"We don't, A'alexandria Cummings."

"…I have my bank statement showing me in my goddamn face that your company took out $130 twice on the same day. I'm taking ya'll asses to fucking court. I want my money!"

"Can you fax us the bank statement?"

"Why yes, Hank. And when I do, cancel my insurance. I don't *want* it anymore. I'll call goddamn Geiko and deal with the lizard!" I hung up, faxed him the bank statement and grabbed my keys and purse so I could go to the Home Depot.

On the statement I wrote in plain goddamn English, "I'm taking you to court. You'll be hearing from my lawyer."

Thank God for the Home Depot! The first guy I ran into was just what the doctor ordered. His name was Hector and he had what those plumbing guys I called didn't have: quality customer service. He was a sincere Cuban with macho qualities and he *knew* his shit. He told me he'd been employed there for three years. Once I shook his hand I knew it wasn't just All State that gave me good hands.

"I'm A'alexandria, by the way Hector."

"Nice to meet you. What is exactly wrong with your toilet?"

"It's stopped up. I used the plunger but I was just plunged into more frustration because when I flushed the stool again, the water ran over." And created in my mind a scene that took place once before in my Mama's bathroom. With a beheaded Barbie doll.

I shuddered just thinking about it. *Girl, let ir go. It's the past. You're a grown woman now.*

"I tell you what. I know you don't know me. But I'm a struggling college student. If you can show me where you live I can fix the toilet on my lunch break. I get an hour and I go on break in a few minutes."

I debated. "Sure. No problem. Where do you want me to meet you?"

"Hell, just browse the store and give me a few minutes."

Handsome. Good vocabulary. Fluid speaker, I liked that, but I never fucked a Cuban and I never will fuck a Cuban. Simple as that.

And I had my reasons.

We pulled up in my drive way and I cut the ignition, grabbed my purse and pulled out my keys. After I unlocked the door I led him to the bathroom. I was embarrassed he seen the inside of my toilet.

"My brother did his thing on my toilet. And I told him it didn't work," I lied.

He started laughing, covering his mouth. He had a very youthful appearance. "*Goddamn,* A'alexandria!"

We cackled. He fixed my toilet in ten minutes. I was impressed. I was glad to see that he was good with his hands. I felt that all men should be good with their hands. That way I wouldn't have to fuck up my nails doing work men should be doing. Men were cursed by God to plow the fields. Not me.

After he flushed it and I had my toilet back (thank the Lord!), I propositioned him.

"How about we go and grab a bite to eat?"

"My treat," he said.

"No," I went on, giving him forty dollars for fixing my toilet. "My treat. I really appreciate what you did today. Let's go to Red Lobster."

His eyes sparkled. "No bullshit?"

I patted his shoulder. "It isn't like you have never eaten there before."

He stared into my eyes, a sad expression clouding me over. "I haven't. Can't afford it."

"Are you playing with me?"

"I'm serious. I've never eaten there before. A long time ago I wanted to, but I just never really cared to go there…"

I kissed his cheek. "Well today is your lucky day. Wash up, you can use my bathroom." I pointed to the small closet. "Towels are in there, soap is under the sink. And I'll be waiting in the car."

"Thank you, A'alexandria. Thank you a lot."

"No sweat."

I closed the door behind me.

We talked about everything under the sun. He asked me how many siblings did I have and I was sad for a moment. I had two sisters, both younger and a big brother who was locked in a mental institution. He was a paranoid something, whatever the term was called. My cold-hearted Daddy had him locked away. I probably shouldn't have been opening up to a man I didn't even know. I knew nothing about his life. But I guess I didn't give a shit. If I kept it simple it would be simple. Hector was cool as hell, a really down to earth type of man.

He said he was born in Cuba and nineteen long years ago his family boarded a life-threatening boat (when he was five years old) and fled, in search for freedom and hope. They found it and prosperity in Fort Lauderdale. It took him three years to learn English. And he did a good job of it. I was impressed. I was normally biased about Cubans because they took our jobs and drove on our roads like they owned the freeways, always got in accidents, were the rudest people I'd ever met; they made everything so hard to achieve by requiring that you be bilingual in your own English, American city, blocking decent black folks from achieving gainful employment. And Hector single-handedly just changed my entire view I had about Cubans.

"So, A'alexandria. Do you have a boyfriend?"

"Yes. His name's Marion. We just met, actually. Been talking off and on for about three months or something like that. He seems really cool."

"Sounds really cool. How did you two meet?"

"On the chat line. He's a lawyer, or so he said. I was like, yeah, right, a lawyer on a funky, sex-driven chat line. But he was. A very successful one at that. I'm not going to lie, I like it. I never had a career man of that magnitude before."

He grinned. "And now you do?"

"Yes. I love it. We've talked all hours of the day and night when we met. We'd get on the phone at about 10 P.M. and talk until 5 A.M."

"Goddamn!"

"I know, right? We never thought about time. Never even looked at the clock. Time ceased to exist. In the beginning, we were both pressed for time. We talked, but we didn't talk, you feel me? But for the past two months or so we've been bonding. Even when I'm at work, I talk to him on my cell phone. I'd sit on the toilet and just talk, talk, talk. I haven't introduced him to my friends yet. But I will."

"Well good for you, Beautiful. How did you two hook up?"

"He asked could we meet and I said *yes*. I told him where I lived and he pulled up in a red, flashy Benz that made every head in my neighborhood turn. He was debonair, tall and one of the sexiest men I'd ever seen. He looked like pussy was sent to him in the mail everyday. I couldn't believe he was unattached, but he was. He told me good looking men get a bad rap, people figure because they're so beautiful they can't possibly be alone, lonely or sex depraved."

"That—I can agree with."

I raised my brows. "Do you have a girlfriend?"

He smiled really big. "Yea. And I have a boyfriend."

I chocked on my strawberry martini and my throat burned. He sat back in his chair and just smiled at me.

"I'm sorry," I apologized.

"It's no big deal. He's sweet, masculine, and compassionate and we both go with women who don't have a clue. I'm on the down low, in the closet fixing all the coats and shirts and I only come out when company leaves. I hate being this way, living a double life, but I got two daughters and a five year old son who adores me, looks to daddy for all the answers and I don't want my lifestyle influencing him to be the way I am."

"I could certainly understand that. But what about H.I.V.? Have you been tested? Have your partner?" I put my hair in a ponytail.

He thought for a few seconds. "Yes. We went together when we met, and after we dated for six months. We're negative, thank goodness."

"Yea—thank God!"

"Thank Goodness, I don't believe in God."

I was silent for a moment.

"Why not?"

"He made Castro. And my father."

We got something in common—I detested my father. And I wouldn't be retesting anytime soon!

"Well, no offense, but if he made Castro and your father then that means God is real, don't you think?"

"How's your lobster and shrimp that's no longer steaming." We smiled at each other.

"I don't know. How are your potatoes and fried fish?"

"Taste like chicken."

After our meal I took him back to work. We agreed to hook up again in a few days.

"But only if Marion lets you," he reasoned respectfully.

"Chile, Marion will be—"

My cell phone rang.

I held my chest. It was Marion. His ears must be burning.

I answered.

And I didn't like what he had to tell me.

"You're going to Acapulco? Without me? You're going with your family? What am I supposed to do? Meditate until you get back?" I asked him, discombobulated as hell.

"I'm only staying for a week, A'alexandria."

As if that makes it better, Creep!

"Am I going to see you before you go?" I asked, flustered, getting a head ache. I couldn't breathe. Why was I feeling like this and we only been talking for a few months?

"Yes. You will." Marion promised.

"Why am I having trouble believing that?"

"Look, we're not married."

"What? You've never spoken to me like this before!"

"I apologize. Anyways, I'll be leaving—"

I hung up. I guess his Kodak moment was wearing thin. Niggahs always put their best foot forward when you first met them and slowly, as the weeks peeled away the layers, they turned out to be something I'd never seen in the beginning. Turned out that the good foot was the bad foot and the bad foot all along. As Cyndi Lauper sang, "I see your true colors shining through."

Hector stared at me, getting out of the car. "Having boyfriend trouble already?"

"Yep," I said, rubbing my forehead. "Big Trouble in Little China."

"It's going to be Big Trouble in Acapulco if he goes. Do you know how many fine women are over there?

I glared at him and he started poking fun of me. Felt like I knew this man all my life. Strange. "Well, Gee Whiz! *Thanks*, Hector!"

"Something isn't right in the honey about what he just did to you, Aalexandria. You're a sweet woman. Don't settle for limes when you need apples to maintain your sweetness. You'll turn out bittersweet."

"What a lovely thing to—"

He leaned up to me and kissed my cheek. I held my breath. He then kissed my lips, tongue action and I was wet. Our tongues danced together in complete harmony but then I had a gross image of Hector sucking his man's dick, swallowing his nut and eating his asshole and I pulled back and said, "Whoa, what are we doing? You need to get back to work."

"I'm sorry for that. I don't know what came over me. It won't happen again." He looked embarrassed and I wasn't trying to embarrass him. "I don't know why that happened?"

"Because you're a lime, threatening my sweetness...thanks for fixing my toilet. We'll talk soon."

When he got out and closed the door I had never driven away from the Home Depot so fast.

Sometimes. I didn't know. What to do with myself. I've made so many bad choices in my life. I needed to work on myself. I got everything a black woman could want. And I was still being ungrateful. Still jealous of bitches who had more than me. I never thought about the women who didn't have what I have: A mother. A degree. A career. A condo. Money. My health. God. A 401 (k). A retirement plan. A man. That was a lawyer. And a car.

With that in mind I had to go and work on someone who pissed me off earlier.

And, yes, I had a major bone to pick.

I made a detour on the way home. Traffic was a bitch. It was so hot! A Cuban man cut me off before I could turn on the upcoming block and I had to cuss at the top of my lungs to calm myself down. Where were all these people going today? I went to a service center and parked by a Ford F-150 pick-up truck. When I got out of my car the heat nearly made me get back in it. Was I in Phoenix, Arizona or Florida? I closed the door, hugged my purse, sashayed into the building (I called it the Diva walk) and paused at the receptionist desk. It was cool in there. A few customers networked with other staff members. I was looking for someone in particular. I looked around coolly, noticed the fake hanging potted

plants and Two Live Crew's "Pop that Pussy"
played loud. That's a Niggah for you. No respect.
Very stylish in there for a plumbing company,
though. I was just about to leave when a
handsome brother, about 6 foot tall, stopped me.

He extended his hand. "I'm the owner."
Bingo, I thought. I had my man.

"And your name is?"

I gave a very heart-warming, sexy smile, leaning
back a little so he could get a good look at my sexy
legs and my tits and bubble ass. "They call me
'Sexy.'"

He smiled seductively, looking me up and
down, cupping my hand like I was a fine
piece of crystal.

"*That* you are," he said, brushing off his work
shirt. Said "Ken" on the tag. He was rough-
looking, weather beaten but had some dangerously
sexy looks.

"No, I'm *Sexy*, the one you talked to on the
phone earlier when I called about my broken
toilet? Fat girls need love, too? I'm the fat girl!"

His face turned another color. "That was *you?*
You're too fine—"

"Too fine? Duh. I *know* I'm fine. Talk that
mess now, like you did over the phone."

"Look, bitch. You're a sexy broad! But don't
think you're going to punk me—"

Time to stop office activity. "You are a punk! Real men don't talk to women like that."

He had fire in his eyes. "And real women don't talk to real men like that!"

"You're right, Webster!" I insulted his ass.

He flipped the bird and put his hands on his hips, angrier than a drunken sailor.

"You aren't a real man," I went on, getting cocky.

"Webster? Do I look short to you?"

I didn't wanna go there. Should I go there? Should I put his ass on blast? Yea. Hell. Yea. I. Should.

I pointed at his open zipper. His little pecker was hanging out. Embarrassed, he shoved it in his pants and zipped it up. I wanted to laugh. He was beet red in the face.

"You can't stay ahead of the game with that little dick. Cute, but too Webster-ish for me. I like Muhammad Ali, you feel me, baby? And you got a flip mouth. Good tongue action, my brothah. The wise woman always said if he got a little dick God made up for it with his tongue. Stick it out, let me see?"

His co-workers found this hilarious. I did, too! Homeboy wanted to run out the room but his pride kept him nailed to the floor. "Maybe my pussy can give it an anatomy lesson while it finds Pearl Harbor. Give your stank ass something to do. You can't be getting any pussy 'cause you're too uptight!"

"You would know, wouldn't you? You don't

know me from a can of paint."

"I don't have to know you. But you aren't going to be talking to me any kind of way."

"Bitch, spare me."

"I got a spare dick in my trunk, if you need to use it."

There was so much laughter I had to laugh. He looked around wildly, not believing his minions were making a fool out of him. His eyes were red, his mind was racing, and I could just about hear his heart.

He exploded. "All right, slut, get out—"

I stopped office chit-chatter when I slapped the Niggah so hard he fell back in his chair. I picked up the coffee pot and dumped the hot liquid on his dick and he screamed in pain, brushing it off, looking retarded.

"Since you're the manager and the owner, tell your brother's to fix your dick, bitch!"

Feeling a tad bit victorious, I spun on my heels, Diva Walking out the office with my mind on my paycheck and my other hand on my hip, flicking the ashes from my cigarette.

"And you have a nice day," I went on, as the creaking ironed door closed behind me.

"May God bless you *and* that little dick."

DOMESTIC

V
Ì
Ø
£Σ
N
©Σ

I originally wrote this for my blog on Myspace for Domestic Violence month. Since people figured I was all about Erotica, little did they know that Erotica was a writing style I picked up to make a quick name for myself. But it's not all I'm about. It's been a little minute since I wrote a short story. Since I'm always writing new things and finding new ways to grow I put a twist and a spin on this Domestic Violence story. I wrote this fresh off the dome, took me about twenty minutes to finish and now I am publishing this in the V.I.P. Edition:

The KING of Erotica

DOME
S
TIC
VIOL
ENCE

C lad in a floral dress and my hair piled atop my head, with a few loose curls falling in my face, I felt like shit. My name was Quality Reynolds, a woman who was lost within herself. I slowly drove my car over by a row of sky-high bushes and I cut the engine. I needed to get a tune up because this Dodge Intrepid was a monumental piece of shit. Seriously. There wasn't a parking space available and I didn't care. I had more pressing matters on my mind. Sucking in air, I listened to Whitney Houston's "Saving All My Love," Post Crack Whitney, before I killed the engine. Hearing songs like this made me miss the good ole days. Snatching up my purse, checking my make up in the mirror, I got out, my heels sinking into the muddy area, and I began cursing.

"Shit. My pumps and stockings...messed up!"

Disgustedly, I was shaking my head.

"Damn it. Now. What. Am. I. Gonna. Do?"

About to face extenuating circumstances beyond my control, I looked at the entrance of this place and I closed my eyes, the little sunlight left slowly turning into the epitome of a gorgeous sun set. God decided to splash some pink and light oranges across the clouds like a canvas. I marveled at the beauty of the earth with a flutter in my heart. But that was short lived.

On second thought, I got back in my car and drove around the back of the medium-sized building and parked by some oak trees. Why, I wouldn't know. I just didn't feel comfortable with my car out of my sight. I paid good money for that ride and no one gave me a damn dime towards it.

When I saw Daddy I smiled, opened the trunk and pulled out a lawn chair. I brought his favorite Vodka. I knew it'd been a long time since he took a hefty swig of the good stuff that, if used dangerously, would bring out the bad side of you. And Daddy had a drinking problem. Maybe I was playing with fire, knowing full and goddamn well I was going to get burned. It took a while before I could gather my thoughts. Daddy and I didn't exactly end our relationship on good terms. So why was I bringing his grouchy ass some Vodka? Why was I here trying to mend fences and spend time with a man I barely loved? Or did I love him at all?

Hesitantly, I said, "Hello, Daddy...It's me."

I set the bottle and two glasses on the ground. Getting on one knee, the slight breeze blowing my hair, I poured him a shot of Vodka and handed it to him.

He just looked at me. He refused to take it.

All righty then! "I have something to say. I *doubted* you. Yes, I was wrong."

I set his glass in front of him and poured me a

small shot, killing it instantly.

"I never understood why you never forgave Mama for talking about your grandmother, your deceased grandmother…"

I stood up and walked to the trunk of my car. I pulled out a thick green comforter. The last thing I needed was for grass to start irritating my skin, considering I took good care of my body.

I looked back at Daddy.

He looked dead into my eyes.

I spread the comforter a few feet in front of Daddy. I sat on it, the moon beaming as the rest of the sunlight gradually vanished. Sweet ole Pops. A few tears streaking down my face because I'd been talking to him and the only thing that responded was the smell of the trees, the feel of the breeze and the pitter-patter of my own black heart. I felt alone. I betrayed Daddy and he wasn't talking to me. Who could blame him? If I was him I wouldn't talk to me, either. So why was I so distraught over misfortunate times such as this? Was the idea of family truly destroyed in America?

No matter what I did he didn't respond. Maybe a little entertainment would do. I took the small boom box from my back seat. Setting it on the ground I then took off my pumps and slid into my ballet shoes, and danced like there was no tomorrow.

I recreated my eight grade recital performance, the one he was so proud of and happened to capture on film and show all family and friends. I twirled on my tippy toes, my arms extended, looking heavenward. I did perfect *petit allégros* and a perfect *pirouette à la seconde*, which was usually done by male ballet dancers.

But he didn't respond to me tonight.

That hurt me more than words could express. So I stopped in the middle of a *battement développé*, sweating. I took a towel from my trunk and dried off. I did my best to control my breathing, wolfing down another glass of Vodka.

Daddy hadn't touched his.

I then tried another approach, because I wasn't the type of black woman to give up on something I wanted. I began singing his favorite songs by Nina Simone. Daddy breathed this woman because she was so hard to decipher and classify. He especially liked the songs "Don't Explain" and "Fine and Mellow." Those were two songs he always played when he was in a very dark mood. Songs he played when, well… I wasn't ready to remember that just yet. I shuddered with hate just thinking about it.

When the singing failed to spark a response, I grew soulfully tired. I have been talking to him for about an hour and after getting nowhere I folded up the lawn chair because I hadn't even sat in it, put it in my trunk and sat back on the comforter.

Wiping hair from my face, I smiled at him.

Nothing.

Come on, Daddy Make this easy for me. "Stubborn ass."

Nothing.

I gave him the puppy dog stare. Always worked.

Not today.

Damn it! *You don't have to be a prick about it, Dad. Jesus! Help me out here.*

I knew I wouldn't get through to him, and now I thought back to a few years ago. When I got a headache at work. My stomach in knots, I clocked out without permission and gunned my car home. A very strange feeling befell me in a way that I'd never experienced before. I had an eerie feeling that something was wrong with one of my parents.

When I got home, I saw an unusual car that wasn't my mother's. Gathering my things, I walked to the front door, put in my key and it opened on its own.

Shit.

Robbers.

I was a bold bitch so I tip toed in heels up the stairs, since we hardly had anything expensive downstairs and I heard muffled noises.

Oh, no! The robber has my mother and father hogtied. I kept creeping to their room, slowly taking off my heels. I set my things on the floor, picked up the cell and called 9-1-1. I should have done this before I turned into Wonder Woman.

"9-1-1 emergency..."

Before I could tell them why my heart was about to pound out of my chest, I saw my father screwing another man.

In a state of shock, a third man had his penis in the man's mouth, grabbing him by the afro. *In the bed my mother shared with him!*

D addy was trapped in a lustful dance. "Make it come outta me, baby!" He told the man, slapping his ass. "…Handle your business! Take my man's dick, take that shit."

The third guy, I recognized from church, leaned over the back of the man's head and spread his ass cheeks so Daddy's nature could slide in with ease. Shockingly stunned, I started vomiting all over the floor. The wrenching echoed through the room like gunshots. The force of the puke startled Daddy. He looked at me and hyperventilated. He was holding his chest, reaching out to me, trying to plead his case.

"Baby…It's not what you think…"

"What?" I painfully screamed, wiping puke from my mouth with the back of my hand. *What about my mother, you sick man? God, what kind of shit was this?* "It's not what I *think?*"

I tried to run at him but I slipped in my own vomit and my chin slammed against the tile. His friends scurried into the bathroom, afraid to come out. "Get out of my Mama's house!" I said aloud, staggering to stand up. I looked a mess. I glared at the closed door. "Get OUT OF HERE, PUNKS!"

I heard a racket in the bathroom, something sliding and then silence. I walked over to the door and tried the knob. It was unlocked. I kicked it

open and ran inside, swinging but my fists caught
nothing but air and the wall. That shit hurt. I
looked around. The window was open and the
curtain blowing.

They'd escaped through the window.

I turned on the cold water and washed my
face, sobbing. My heart burned and my skin
crawled. I felt the bile rising up my throat
and that burned, too. My heart felt like it
was ripped from my chest. I couldn't believe
Daddy was unfaithful to Mama. Worst of all I
couldn't believe Daddy was gay. How long had he
been a homosexual? Was this something new he
was interested in? Had he fucked other men in my
Mama's bed while she was gone? Why here? Why
would he bring that to his family's front door and
in their house? He could have gotten a hotel room
to hide his indiscretions. What kind of man went
back on his vows? What kind of man stood before
God and two families and lied? Who was to say his
heart wasn't in the right place when he first
married? Would it have been different if it was two
women? Would I feel betrayed? My Mama and
Daddy weren't exactly pals these days. She seemed
to do her thing and he did his, which I just didn't
get. Ever since I was a small child I knew I'd find a
man who was as kind and gentle and sweet as my
Dad. I used to show him off at parent P.T.A.
Meetings. I loved him, adored him and would do
anything for him.

Not anymore.

Images of the past slowly dying out of my mind, I just looked at him through the mirror. He was standing behind me, fully clothed, his eyes withdrawn and gone. I didn't say a word. I thought about Mama, who had been faithful to him heart, mind, body and soul. What would this do to her?

"Are you going to tell her?" he had the nerve to ask me.

I turned to face him, seething with rage. "No. It's not my place. *You're* going to tell her."

He mocked me with an evil smile. "Then it's settled. I'm not telling her a thing and if you do I will make your life a living nightmare now fuck with me and find out. Stay out of this. *You* would *never* understand. If you breathe a word to her your allowance will be cut…"

He approached me and took me into his arms, rubbing my back. I didn't want his hands on me. He kissed my forehead.

He went on. "You will buy your own clothes; you won't eat a thing in this house. It's my money that keeps everything running the way it should. Your Mama doesn't pay for shit. But she took a lot from me. She was always jealous of my family. When we married she wanted me to cut all ties and make life all about her."

I looked up at him. "Why are you doing this? What are you telling me?"

He was lost within himself. I didn't know who this man was holding me. I didn't think I wanted to know.

"Your Mama was the reason I stopped talking

to family. For a couple months I turned my back on the very people who always supported me and gave me what I needed. When I found out that was her true intention, I put my family back in my life, rebuilt the foundation that had gotten me to that point and she hated it. She talked down to them. She never let you go to their functions."

"Dad, I didn't care for it…"

"Listen. She did the unthinkable. That's all I'm going to say. And she will pay for it, one way of the other. She will pay."

He'd never threatened me or Mama before.

Now I speak on that eventful day. Sitting out here on this comforter, my legs getting tired. My belly hurt a little bit. He seemed to grow pensive then.

"How could you do that, Daddy? If you knew you loved me then why did you lead her on?"

I desperately waited for him to answer. The long, thick branches of the oak trees surrounding us danced with the breeze blowing off the Atlantic Ocean. Hurricane Karen was out there, threatening the Caribbean and right now that was the furthest thing from my mind. There was a hurricane in my heart. I cleared my throat without being disrespectful.

"Daddy."

I rubbed my arms, trying to keep it together. I was hungry, hadn't eaten in two weeks. Every time I tried to eat I would vomit. I couldn't function at work. I was a nurse at Miami Jackson Memorial

Hospital. But today, before I came to see Daddy I had quit my job. Fuck them. Fuck work. Fuck food. I had my reasons. Reason one being rebuilding the bridge to my Daddy.

"Daddy..." My voice drifted off. I had to try another approach. "Listen, Daddy. I know I've disappointed you. And I know it's going to take some time before you forgive me. I was wrong for what I did. For years I watched you beat Mama and I always sided with her, because I felt a man shouldn't beat a woman. That he had to be repulsive and sick to beat someone he loves. Someone who birthed his child...I even blamed you for keeping your sexuality a secret from the woman you shared your life with..."

Standing up, I lit a cigarette. I didn't smoke Salem Lights, I smoked Kools, but right now this stale cigarette had to do. I felt uncomfortable walking around this wet grassy terrain barefooted, trying to look cute but right now it wasn't about that, it was about making things right with my Daddy.

"I never understood why you did what you Daddy, but *now* I do."

My brows rose, awaiting his approval. It would never come. I stumbled over a root sticking up from the ground. I had to catch myself, my chest tightening. A lump rose from the pit of my stomach. The branches continued to dance. My hair was blown from the pins. I opened my small purse and pulled out a small mirror and I flipped it open, looking over my face. Black rings of mascara were around my sad brown eyes. I could taste my lipstick, I had on too much. I closed my eyes, sucking in the air. I felt the breeze dance across my skin. I heard a shrieking noise and I dropped the mirror and my purse. Startled, I turned around to face a security guard. He was tall and cocky, reminded me of a black Brad Pitt. He gripped his gun and his crotch. Real crummy asshole.

"Oh. *You* again."

He breathed a sigh of relief.

I glared at him, with an attitude. "Yes. *Me* again," I said, really bothered that he would interrupt me and my father's conversation, even though he wasn't talking to me right now. But his eyes were on me, boy did he stare me down. He didn't even look at the guard. I figured he's used to seeing him.

The guard frowned. "Why are you *here*, ma'am? This time of night."

As if, asshole! I'm grown! "I'm talking to my father. We have issues to discuss," I snapped, putting my hands on my hips, trying to pretend like this handsome security guard with pimples all over his forehead didn't scare me.

He had a shit-eating grin, looking me up and down. I felt dirty, the way his gorgeous eyes danced across my huge breasts.

"You and your father can talk another day. The facility is closed. You have to vacate." He looked past me at my Dad with a weird look on his face. "And you have a nice day, Sir."

"At least you spoke to him today."

"Shit, I speak to him everyday! Ever since I have been working at this place I talk to them all. Sometimes I talk to him when I'm going through problems, but he doesn't say anything. He just stares at you, like he's doing now…"

"That's Daddy. *Avoiding* strangers."

"Like he avoids you?"

"You need to mind your own damn business…"

"You have to leave. And I do mean *now*. Pack up your little green blanket, grab your liquor bottle and glasses, your muddy ass pumps and leave…"

"Yes." I leaned over to get my purse. "I'll leave." I didn't feel like getting into it with a young punk.

He was looking at my ass. Men. Could never think without it getting hard and crass.

"Good night, ma'am," he said, walking off into the darkness.

"Fuck him, Daddy. Listen…I was always your little girl. I remember when I was 7 years old. I painted you on construction paper and signed it 'Viola Gray.' You loved that picture. You even framed it. I remember when I was at the table drawing it, you and Mama were arguing over who was going to cook dinner."

Defiantly, I sat on the ground, admiring my Daddy's eyes. You could fall asleep in them. I was smiling through my tears, burning up inside, being eaten alive by fear, rejection and autonomy.

"Mama was very feisty, the way you liked her.

And because of your temper I cringed. I knew you were on the cusp of snapping. And when you hit her and she started to plead and cry I stopped drawing the picture and I ran upstairs, burst through the door with a knife and I cut your leg."

I was shaking now, pulling on the cigarette, hoping the crummy bitch relieved my stress and quite frankly it didn't.

"In sheer pain you screamed and I stabbed you in the foot. I was screaming LEAVE MY MAMA ALONE and she grabbed me and fled the room. I hated you, Daddy! I never understood why you went from this sensitive, caring man who loved chocolate and flaunting his lady to beating her and detesting chocolate and the very fiber of your being."

I was opening my purse, pulling out my blood pressure pills. I popped them and opened the small bottled water and I downed the pills with one gulp. I smacked my lips. I rubbed Daddy's face. He was cold and stubborn. Refused to move. Refused to talk back to me. I loved him, truly loved him. But I let him know *too* late, when he didn't care, when his problems seemed oblivious and non-existent.

"Daddy..." My lips were trembling; I was running my fingers along his arm, trying to get him to talk. It started to drizzle, the atmosphere changing, getting cooler. The wind picked up, blowing my hair like boisterous butterflies. I tried to keep it together but I was slipping.

Slipping…

"I went to the hospital with you, crying. Yes,

Daddy I loved you but I hated the monster that hid behind your gorgeous smile, the demons that took solace in the sparkles in your eyes. You were a people person. Everyone loved and adored you. Your co-workers praised the very grounds you walked on. Even our maids loved you more than anything. The church members would shoot Satan for you but at the time I thought you *were* Satan. I sided with Mama; she was my hero, my strength. Since you left she withered to a nursing home and dyslexia and other medical problems. I went to see her the other day; she looked at me blankly and didn't even know who I was..."

I was kissing Daddy's lips, trying to rub his face...he was stone cold inside, he didn't want me here. It started to rain, my dress clinging to my body, making shapes with my nipples, which were hard and erect. I felt like a failure.

I felt a little pain in my abdomen, it was then I remembered I was four months pregnant and I wanted my baby. I wanted to nurture it and I hoped it was a boy. So I could introduce him to my Dad. I was hugging Daddy.

He was cold as ice.

I died for affection, attention, to make things right. "Daddy! I am so sorry for cutting you. And I tried to tell you this when I was younger, and yes you forgave me, even accepted the drawing. Mama *hated* the drawing; she told me I shouldn't have given you anything, a woman beater. But despite what you did I still loved you. You were my father and I was a Mama's Girl."

Still, nothing.

"*Daddy!*"

I heard a crunching sound behind me. The guard was back. Twigs broke under his feet.

He wasn't happy. "*MA'AM!*" I ignored the guard. "Ma'am, I'm calling the authorities!"

I turned my head and snapped, "Leave us!"

He was stubborn, more vicious than he was before. "I'm serious! I'm going to call the police." He was pulling out his gun, like he was going to shoot me. "I've been telling you for the past two weeks to stop coming here when the place closes but you keep showing up…"

I looked at Daddy with a longing in my eyes.

"LISTEN, DADDY! I am so sorry for killing you, for shooting you when I was 19 years old, last year. Yes, you recovered; yes I was at your bedside. *Yes* I felt remorse. I felt *bad...*"

"Ma'am! I'm going to tell you one. More. Time. Leave. The. Premises."

I ignored him again. Didn't he get the point? I was holding my Daddy but he wouldn't hold me.

"Mama blamed you for ya'll marriage ending. Mama said you wouldn't change, that you were vicious and nasty! I shot you for jumping on Mama. I couldn't take it. She was innocent and pure, always went to church..."

"*Miss!*" The guard took out his walkie-talkie and radioed for the police.

The crackling of the radio and the voice of the

respondent flowing into my ears, I let go. I let it all go. "Daddy! I understand why you beat Mama. I never thought I would, but I understand. She fucked your brother back when you two first got married. She slept with him on your wedding day and faked a back ache to stop herself from going on the honey moon with you. She would sleep with him for years to come. And you found out. And you beat her every time she looked at you. You beat her every time she looked in your eyes and said she'd never cheat on you…she took you for granted. She lost your brother's child when she had a miscarriage.

"She was pregnant from him and made you think you were the father. And you found out. You were putting up a shelf in the bedroom closet when you overheard her and your brother talking about it on your birthday when I was 13. You overheard it all, how they had an affair from the day you brought her home to his family way back in the day…I never knew. I only just found out, when I read your Journal. I'm sorry for betraying your private thoughts."

The security guard grabbed my arm and yanked me up to my feet and I brutally kicked him in the nuts, snatched his gun out of his hand, sorry motherfucker, and I aimed for his heart.

I was talking through clenched teeth. "Radio in and tell them it was a false alarm." Fire in my eyes. I had to talk to Daddy.

He panicked, took the walkie-talkie from his waist and called it in.

"False alarm, damn cats and animals, sorry."

He was about to tell them what was going on and I kicked him in the face.

His flew backward, his back slamming into the huge root sticking up from the ground. He moaned piteously.

I put my foot on his balls, "Are you trying to be Mighty Mouse and save the day?"

"No, please. Don't shoot me; I got a kid, a family."

Whatever, dude. "Yea, yea bitch shut up…I *had* a whole family. I had a…father but I lost him, because of my slutty mother playing the domestic violence Ho for years. She made me think she was Saint Augustine and was really Jezebel R' Us!"

The rain softened up.

"STAND UP!"

Staggering (holding his testicles) he stood up. As much as I didn't want to admit it, he looked good standing there under the moon with his rain coat on, his little golf cart parked off to the side.

I sucked in air, looking at Daddy. "Good bye." I shot the guard in the chest and shot him again in the head, like I had did Daddy, like I did when he beat Mama after recovering from the hospital.

When I shot him the first time.

The images of yesterday rushed into my head with the force of an atom bomb…knocked me to my ass. I was digging my hands into the earth, pulling up roots and grass. Screaming like some sick deranged beast. Maybe I was. I was slipping from reality…Slipping further…

I was remembering the old days. I had come home from a football game to Daddy dragging my mother, who was only 5 feet 3 inches (he was 6 feet tall) through the house. He was screaming at her. Calling her names.

I didn't understand the onslaught. How could a man beat a woman who would do anything for him?

I shook with hate. I wanted to kill him; the pit of darkness opening and the sinister air seeped from my ears and created tears.

Her face was reformed from the way he punched her. The dried blood on her face turned my stomach. A trail of blood was all through the house. The couches were overturned.

The big screen TV. Destroyed. The bar broken into debris. He had cut his face out of the wedding pictures and pasted his brother's face in place.

I never understood it.

Did he think his brother slept with mother?

Preposterous, or so I thought on that day.

He was pulling out his dick and pissing on her. I hadn't read the journal then, never knew it existed. I was outraged.

Why was Mama acting so weak?

Why didn't she fight back?

Did she love him that much? I'm sorry. There wasn't that much love in the world. When a man hit you then it was over. It was time to pack your shit and leave his ass!

was fumbling through my purse…"MAMA FIGHT HIM DO SOMETHING YOU SCARY HELPLESS BITCH YOU DO SOMETHING I'M YOUR DAUGHTER!"

My hand was still in my purse:

I ran up to him.

We made eye contact.

"HI DADDY!"

Sick with an evil rage, I looked at Mama. Her nightgown was stuck to her body. She perspired profusely. She smelled of Daddy's piss and her blood. I shook with revulsion. I tried not to look at the gory scene, but I had to. I just had to. Daddy hugged me.

"Baby, get out of here. I'm a monster. I can't stop…There are things going on here you'll never understand."

"I love you, Daddy…"

Pulling out the shiny .22, I had shot him in the head. His brains splattered across Mama's body below and the wall behind him.

I slumped to my knees, screaming into the air…

et up, Mama…" I had helped Mama off the floor. She took the gun and called the police and said she killed him, couldn't live with abuse anymore. I backed her up. The case was closed; no one really cared about a black family in the suburbs. We didn't even make .0001 of the bottom corner of the newspaper.

And now I looked down at Daddy's grave, the rain stopped. I got on my knees, the dead body behind me staring into the sky. I ran my hands over Daddy's picture, his face...his arms. Looking so good in his plaid shirt, the one I bought him for Christmas, several weeks before I killed him.

I was crying so hard snot stopped my nose. The pains in my stomach were worse. I had swallowed the entire bottle of blood pressure pills and I didn't have blood pressure.

The bottle bared Daddy's name.

"Daddy I'm sorry for killing you! I'm sorry Mama had betrayed you! I'm sorry for thinking you were a monster! I'm sorry for everything. I'm sorry for not believing in you. I have to live with this on my conscious for the rest of my life."

I was hugging his tombstone, the stone cold against my face...I was a wreck, shaking uncontrollably.

"I'm sorry Daddy! Talk to me, *please talk to me, please*...I know what Mama did. She cheated on you and your brother betrayed you. She had three abortions, your brother's seeds. I know Mama poisoned your grandmother by lacing her food with rat poison to rid her out of your life and you found out, but you never told her. Mama killed your grandmother. I know how hard that must have been. You just beat her. Her prison, her sentence was the loveless marriage you kept her hostage in, unknown to the rest of the world. And

for years she told me she didn't *know* why you beat
her. I called her a sorry bitch for not getting out.
But Mama killed your grandmother and fucked
your brother...now I understand." I put the gun to
my head. "And now it's too late. You don't love me,
Daddy! And I don't love myself. If you won't talk
to me here on Earth I'll buy a ticket to wherever
you are and talk to you there…"

I put a bullet through my heart.

She doubled over in pain, the worst pain of
her life, her blood pouring out onto the
grass, engulfing the bottom portion of the
grave...

She was returning to the earth, looking up into
the sky, asking God to forgive her for this
unforgivable sin.

She weakly asked him to talk to her Dad, tell
him that she apologized.

She forgives him for beating her mother, the
murderer, the adulterer...

And as the colors faded and the oak trees
turned into blurs and the dead security guard
turned into ghosts she would never remember.

Her eyes getting heavy, she hugged her Daddy's
grave and she drew her last breath when it once
again started to rain, washing her blood back into
the earth, returning it back to her deceased father
at a graveyard that was closed since 6 p.m.

f

$\pounds$

@

$\S$

H

£

ï

I

G,

'H

⧺

∫

They say flashlights were sometimes everything you desired when it came to the darkness. I, on the other hand, was a man who challenged any and everything I heard. I never got into politics. They were mere scripted occurrences I didn't want to be a part of. I didn't care for Obama or Clinton. Neither one knew I existed. I never sat down and spoke to them. I didn't care for elections, voting and people's rights. The government did what it wanted to do. As long as I got my bills paid then fuck everything else.

During daylight hours I was a straight man with everything together. Good job at the post office, stamping people's mail, putting up with their shit, listening to their problems, becoming belligerent about their antics, looking at their photos (when the line was stretching out the door, damn near to the parking lot) and a host of other shit I didn't want to get into right now. I smiled when there was nothing to smile about and I cursed a bitch out when provoked. Being that I was a 40 year old man I thought life ended when the clock struck midnight on my 40th B-day. There wasn't any posing for the camera now, flick, flick, flick popping with me. Even at my birthday party, given by my 20 year old knock-out, gorgeous son Billy, I didn't pose for pictures. My wife pulled me out to the middle of the floor and wanted to celebrate my big day, and the fact that it was our twentieth anniversary. We got married on my birthday.

I remembered she looked deeply into my eyes, looking sexy in a flowing black dress and her hair swept from her face like our kitchen floors. I swore she aged gracefully.

"I love you," she said.

Amongst oh's and ah's I kissed her back, holding her tightly. "I love you, too."

"Twenty years of marriage. And not once have we *ever* cheated on each other."

I thought about the darkness then. I was faithful to her in the light. But in the darkness, I was a totally different person.

"And I never will," I told her. *The sun's setting.* "I love you too much."

She smiled, trying to trick me into taking pictures.

Now I sit in the darkness. In fact every light in my house was turned off, thanks to the circuit breaker. The moon light shined through the window so I got up and closed the blinds.

I wanted it completely dark.

He's breathing and so was I. This man, this, um...stranger I met on a site called black gay chat. He touched me and I touched him in a way that made him take my fingers and suck each one slowly. He remembered I dipped my hands in cheesecake, which was on the nightstand.

"Mmm, this is good," he said appreciatively, turning me on my stomach and spreading my cheeks. He slapped my booty repeatedly, each smack a little harder than the last.

Smack.

Smack.

Smack!

SMACK! SMACK!

I loved it. "Damn, baby." I was twirling my ass on the sheets. I could still faintly smell my wife's perfume on the pillows.

Smack.

Tears formed in my eyes. "Umm, slap it again."

Smack! I reached for the popper—alkyl nitrates packaged inside a very small brown bottle—on the nightstand, opened it and it made a popping sound, hence how it got its name. I put it under my nose and got a quick high. "Goddamn, baby."

Intensely, time seemed to slow down. I was giddy and spontaneous all of a sudden.

He put the popper under his nose and inhaled repeatedly until he was satisfied. "You like when I…" Smack. "Slap that ass." SMACK!

I was about to lose myself. "Hell, yea." I felt light-headed, my sensuality taking on new heights that had me about to do any and everything he wanted me to.

He wiped cheesecake on my anus. He spread the chocolate rosebud open as well. "Say ah," he says to my asshole, cramming cheesecake deep in there. I felt his warm tongue, slithering like anacondas across bushy terrain. I shivered with delight, never before being eaten out. He dug his tongue deep in there, and like a scoop he dug it out, swallowing it. He leaned up to me and snatched me by my mini afro. He forced me to look into his eyes. But it was *too* dark I couldn't see his eyes. But we felt our eyes, knew it was our eyes and he kissed me, pushing a huge glob of cheesecake into my mouth and we melted into a kiss. My lips were the wicked witches and his tongue was the house that fell on her sister from the East. I knew I was clean downstairs. I didn't eat for two days, I took an enema and I drank some Metamucil just to be safe. Then I used one of my wife's douche bottles, stuck it up inside me, and squirted the vinegar and water. Viola, clean booty for my dude to play in without worrying about getting shit anywhere.

We couldn't see each other. In my mind he was the most beautiful man. In the darkness I could hide my dirty laundry, sheets and sex life. I didn't have to overdo it or explain it. I could be all that I wanted to be. I wasn't a 40 year old in the darkness, with flabby arms and thunder thighs and fat agglomerating around my waist line. I didn't have ugly toes. I didn't have to see my son or beautiful wife, who has never done a thing to me. But I had a high sex drive she could never match, giving me pussy once a week was maddening so now I was shopping my stock options and hoping the Dow Jones came along and gave me ten inches on the boards to stick in my mouth and orifices to keep me rich in pleasure.

He kissed me and I kissed him. He trailed his tongue down the length of my neck and gave me passion mark after passion mark. He said he tasted blood because he was strapping me down, sucking so hard.

I told him, "Remember, I'm married with a son."

He said, "Whatever, you're mine tonight. Tell her a mosquito bit you and you ran out of pink Calamine lotion."
I was under his spell, in a trance. I was gripping his dick, slowly stroking him into deepening moans that pushed me into the abyss of ecstasy.

He straddled my neck and slid his passion in my mouth. I took it like a man, slurping noisily and gripping his booty. Holding the headboard, he humped my face for dear life.

"Damn, baby. Damn, let me get that hot mouth. Damn, shit! Um, yea. Damn, oh my..."

The bed springs sung their praise and my mattress let out a continuous romping sound that had me twirling my hips all over the place.

To my surprise he locked up, his thighs on either side of my face. That dick slid on my lips and tongue.

"I'm about to come. Let's get the first one out of the way."

He exploded down my throat. I gulped it like a power drink. Getting my energy and getting on with it.

The poppers were wearing off so I put it back under my nose and inhaled until I felt the effects.

He wasn't done with me yet. Most men I heard needed two to three minutes to recuperate. Not this Niggah. He was still harder than a battling ram hoping for the walls of Troy, and my ass had those walls on lock down.

He rejected the poppers, he'd had enough. He closed the cap on it, because if wasted on your skin it'll burn. I knew I was going to have a massive headache when I came off this high, but fuck it I wanted to give the mushroom-shape on his dick a head ache.

With a sense of urgency, he was suckling on my booty cheeks. He put some passion marks on them. He was a possessive little fuck but hey, I got what I asked for. My wife never touched me with this much longing and zeal. The pleasure mixed with pain I welcomed. Because when the sun came up it was back to work to talk to a bunch of customers I didn't care for.

I thought about his friend that came here with him.

"Where's your boy?" I asked my lover.

He said, "Probably trying to find his way back to your room in the dark."

We chuckled.

We heard a tussling noise, like someone tripped. "Ow, shit!" came the harsh whisper.

My lover said, "There he goes."

The door opened and he stumbled into the room. He was chuckling, his voice bouncing off the walls. Thank God for the darkness. Then I wouldn't be reminded that I was a married man. My wife was in Greece with my son. They loved to travel, yet never really talked about it amongst their peers. You knew some black folks. The minute you started talking about traveling they automatically assumed you had money.

"Are you ready?" my lover asked.

Wanting to be fucked, I said, "Yes."

My asshole quivered with a longing it had never experienced. My body on fire, my heart raced with sensuality.

The third person in the room, I'll call "Flash," turned on the flash light. Over his face was a white, ghostly mask. On his body was a black robe, tied at the waist. A hood was over his head. Now this was the freaky shit I was talking about.

My friend entered me slowly, gently, his hand on the small of my back. In the doggy style position, I tooted my ass up towards his sweaty pelvis. I was about to die from the anticipation. My colon swallowed inch by inch effortlessly. I was extremely tight. He said, "Your ass keeps pushing out my dick. *Damn*, Pa. You got some tight ass. I can't wait to pop your cherry again."

I was breathing hard, taking each inch over again, climbing the walls and hoping to find the paint he'd wipe all over my face.

My cell phone exploded on the nightstand. The vibration sent it dancing. I looked at the screen and it was my son. I decided not to answer. After all, he was in Greece with his mother having a grand ole time.

My lover felt so incredible, his Old Spice mixed with a little musk tramping my nose. He pulled out of me and fumbled around for his boxers. The beam briefly danced across the underwear on my bed. He took them up and pushed my face down to the pillow. He put the boxers under my nose, and part of them in my mouth.

"Suck on those boxers, bitch."

I loved to be controlled. His manly scent made me shake with convulsions as he caused my hole massive damage, in a good way. Slapping sounds filled the room.

Flash started casting the flashlight, the beam sporadically flickering. He turned in circles, turning it on and off, like a huge disco ball.

Our shadows danced in unison as he finally found the grappling hook in the bottom of my hole and took me out to sea, to dance amongst the sharks and the swordfish.

I wanted to be anchored, so I reached back and spread my cheeks so he could fall in deeper. Location was everything.

He was taking me higher, my ass cheeks jiggling all over his thick stick. Slapping my ass, the shadows made different shapes on the walls, on my family photos, on my mirror, dresser and nightstands. The shadows, big and small, frantic and calm.

He turned on another flashlight, swinging both beams like a circus act that forgot to make flyers announcing they were in town.

How could they?

They were in my room.

He turned me on my side, sliding his nature back into paradise. Holding my leg up, he pulverized my tight hole to the point I heard swishing sounds.

The beams found us, smiled and laughed, touched and teased our skin, letting off the warmth and glow that made candles jealous and the sun envious.

I felt it rising, the bile in my throat. He was too big, eleven inches felt like twenty. I slept with two guys in my 40 years on this earth, never really getting into the lifestyle. The light, remember I had a marriage, a son and an image.

My cell phone vibrated again. It was my son. But I was too lost in ecstasy to stop. My lover pounded the dick deeper inside me. I was scooting up towards the headboard. He was right on my ass.

"I know you're not running from this dick…"

I was moaning out of control, feeling his dick damn near in my gut. "No, baby."

"You're letting a twenty-five year old make you run from dick?"

He was a pro at what he did, I couldn't deny it. He had me stuttering and speaking in tongues.

"Huh, can't talk?" he demanded, turning me on my back and pushing my legs in the air. He drilled me like my ass had oil.

I shook with abandon, a smile playing on my face. He was working it, I could feel my walls gripping and sliding on what he had to offer. We were soaked in sweat, it dropped into my face.

"Damn, Pa. I'm about to burst again…"

"Come inside me, baby."

"I want in on your face…" Shivering, he pulled out, pulled off the Jimmy and came in my face. He was standing over me, one hand planted on the wall, the beams dancing across our bodies. The shadows bobbing and weaving.

e lay spent. Flash turned off the flashlights and remained quiet. I was too tired to ask did he want to join in on the fun. Three's company when the third person wasn't doing anything.

My phone vibrated again and I answered.

"Dad, why aren't you answering the phone?" he asked frantically.

I was alarmed. "Something's wrong, Son?"

"No, Dad. Someone ran…" The phone was breaking up. "…and Mom went inside…"

I was frustrated, getting out of the bed and asking Flash for the flashlight.

He handed it to me. I turned it on and said, "Son, hang up and call me back. I can't hear you. The phone is breaking up."

I hung up.

From the bed, my lover said, "Is everything ok?"

I said, "You two have to go. Something is wrong with my son. He said something about my wife; I hope nothing happened to them in Greece. And I'm over here in the States being unfaithful."

My lover got up and gathered his clothes.

"I'll call you when I get home," he said and we shook hands like complete strangers and he left.

I eyed Flash.

"Didn't you hear me? Get the fuck out, go home."

Flash shook his head "No."

"What the fuck!" I stormed up to him and took him by the neck. I wasn't playing. My phone exploded again. "Get out."

He shook his head "No."

"FUCK!" I answered the phone. "…Son…"

"Dad, someone else just came out…"

The phone died in my hands.

I looked at Flash, trying to keep calm. I opened the dresser and pulled out a pair of sweat pants and put them on. I didn't bother with putting on a shirt.

"Flash. *Look*. This is my wife's house. I was out of pocket for fucking your friend in her bed when she's overseas."

He reached for the flashlight and held it under his face, tilting his head. OK. He was scaring the fuck out of me. What was going on here? Why did I feel insecure in my own home? What kind of man was I?

My son warned me that crazy people were on the internet. Oh, God! I feared my life. Flash slowly turned the flashlight around my room, looking at the hanging family photos. He stopped at the one of my wife.

He reached over and picked up a Sharpie marker from the nightstand.

On a piece of paper he wrote:

She is pretty.

I stared at him, thinking of a way to get to my gun.
I knew I had to do something or he could possibly
kill me. And the last thing I needed was for my
wife to find out my extracurricular activities.

And your son is hot!
Is he gay like his Daddy?

I said, "Flash. Please, get out of here."
He wrote on another piece of paper:

I'm a black belt.
One wrong move you die.
I know your family is in Greece.

Oh, God! My family!
What have I done?

He walked over to the dresser and I
sprinted past him, into the walk in closet
and reached up on the shelf and grabbed
my pistol. Fearing my life, I went back
out into the bedroom. All the lights
suddenly turned on in the house. Did my lover
turn on the switch in the circuit breaker box?
Protecting my family's home, I aimed at him. He
turned and froze when he saw the barrel of the
gun.
    "Get out, Flash! *Now!*"
    I meant business.

He released a large gush of air. Taunting me. A smile. Perfect white teeth. Where had I seen that smile before? I frowned. Abruptly, he ran at me and the gun went off, shooting him in the arm.

He doubled over in pain, screaming.

"*Dad?* What's going on?"

I froze. My son was behind me, shaken. I didn't want him to see the scene that lay before me. But it was too late. "A strange man just left out of our house. And before that, another man ran out of the house. He jumped in a car and high tailed it. What was that gun shot? I'm calling the police!"

I looked straight ahead in a dead silence.

I got on my knees and took off Flash's mask. I hoped the taunting son of a bitch was dead.

No one fucked with my family.

When I saw his face I closed my eyes and sucked in air wishing I was a little boy again, when life was so simple.

When cookies were cookies and a car was a car.

When it quacked like a duck and remained a duck, when Mama was Mama and Daddy was Daddy.

I was shaking so badly I had drool falling from my mouth.

I couldn't think let alone grab a thought. What had gone wrong? What had I done? I knew that damn smile, but it was too late. Flash wasn't Flash at all. Flash was my *wife*.

S he was the one spinning the lights around the room, watching me give a body I gave her in Holy matrimony to another man. Oh, *God*! I shot my own wife! My son raced past me when he saw his mother on the floor, blood pouring from the shot wound.

"MAMA! MAMA! *Who* shot you? Did those men…?"

I shot my wife, Son! I didn't know she was in disguise. What kind of man was I? What kind of man did this to his family over his thirst for the human flesh?

Was I that weak?

What was I lacking in my marriage that I had to bring another man (men) in my wife's bed and destroy her solitude? What will my son think when he finds out?

I backed away from her, shaking my head in denial. Wide-eyed, I sat on the bed, sobbing into my hands. How could I have shot my own wife? She was trying to tell me on her scribbled notes that she was Flash.

She was secretly taunting me.

I thought back to my birthday party. When we danced, our warm bodies pressed against one another. I told her that I *loved* her. That I never *cheated* on her. Oh, *God*. In my heart I meant it but in the head of my dick I had my fingers crossed. Ha, ha. April Fool's. *Fooled* you. No, no. I fooled myself.

The joke was on me.

And for her to see this?

S tunned, my son helped her up. "I'm driving you to the hospital," he said, picking her up in his arms like her knight in shining armor. He was frantic, about to flip out. "Then I'm calling the police. Dad, open the door so we can get Ma out of here…"

I stood up, truly shaken. When he rushed past me she spat in my face. A huge glob landed between my eyes and nose. I let it trail my skin. My son was even more shocked.

She said, "You don't come nowhere near me and my son, you unfaithful motherfucker!" She never cursed a day in her life.

My son was confused. Looking from me to his Mom. "What is going on?" he asked. "Dad, come on…"

My wife screamed, "No! *No*! Get me out of this cocoon! It isn't a house anymore. Get me the fuck out of here now!"

My son fled, carrying his mother without anymore questions. A few seconds later the power went out. It was then I realized that it was my son who turned the circuit breaker on. I broke down into pieces. For some reason I started praying.

God help me. Something in my conscious said, *"No!"*

I screamed so loud I started breaking the mirrors and the walls. I was trapped in the darkness, going mad. She took the flashlight and I had no way down stairs to the circuit breaker box. What's done in the dark always came to the light. But in this instance it took a flashlight to reveal my deceit.

You'd think a 40 year old man would know that by now. Now I lost my family, forever. As I sat here in the dark.

The same person I was in the light.

Weeks have passed by and no call from my wife. I couldn't eat or sleep. I called her parents, nothing. They refused to talk to me. I tried to explain but they weren't hearing it. They lost all respect for me. I drove over to their home. They refused to open the door. I called her friends, nothing. They hadn't heard from her. I knew they were lying. I was about to go crazy. She didn't come for her clothes and she didn't even come for her feminine products.

She left me hanging. I was pieces of a man, not knowing what to do. Despite my deception, I couldn't give up on my wife.

I thought the police would show up at my door to arrest me for shooting her.

When I went to church on Sunday the pastor called me into his office and told me my wife and son withdrew from their organization without giving a reason.

He knew trouble was on the home front. And it wasn't his business. I politely told him and his church to take a hike. He eyed me, giving me a hug. I didn't want him touching me. Hadn't we touched enough when I first joined the church? I still know what his testicles tasted like. When he left I fell on my knees and asked God why. *Free will,* something answered back. *When you got married you were supposed to face the future. Yet you looked back and turned to salt and burned your marriage to smithereens.* I hadn't shaved in weeks, nor did I want to. Inside I tortured myself for destroying my family. They were perfect. Both my son and wife were so beautiful.

And I went out and destroyed it because my flesh was weak.

Monday afternoon the house phone rang. I answered it.

"Hello."

"How are you?"

I smiled. "Hey, how are you?"

"I'm good. I hate to call you with this, but your wife filed for divorce. She cited that you committed adultery with another man. She doesn't want the house, the car, nothing. She said she is leaving that life behind and moving on. Your son doesn't want to have anything to do with you. They asked that you respect their wish, and they wish nothing but the best for you in your future endeavors."

"But…"

The family lawyer hung up in my face.

Ǧ,
Ø
£
Đ

Đ
Ï
Ģ
Ģ
Ʃ
Ř

"**G**irl, you gotta pretend with these men to get what you want," I told BeAnthony at Cedars, a very happening spot in Miami that only a selected few knew about. The dress code was simple: drop your panties and leave your attire, shoes, inhibitions and attitude at the door. That went for the security guards, too. They looked like Chippendale models.

"I know, right," she told me, sipping her Patron, her titties in my face. We were hanging out, trying to kill off the grueling work day we had. We were both court reporters. I was sick of thinking about criminals, which was putting it mildly because half of their dumb asses were fine as shit.

"I'm glad we came here," I said, a few fine men walking past the table with dicks swinging like an episode of Tarzan. I was a size Queen, Honey.

"Me, too, Maxine. I work too much, Chile," BeAnthony chided. I pushed my blonde weave behind my head and looked over my blonde-colored acrylic nails. She took one of my hands and smiled.

"I know you don't wear this to work."

"No, I don't. And this is a wig, Chile." I took it off and my stringy hair showed signs of needing an ultra-expensive perm.

"Oh, Chile. Things are going to be a little easier once you put the wig back on."

I put it on.

"Damn, big difference," she said. "Look, I have been meaning to tell you something."

I gazed at her. She always wanted to tell me something. "What?"

A tall man stopped at the table holding a tray. His dick was a little on the small side but his lips screamed KISS ME. He said his name was George Franks.

He was staring me down. "Are you ladies comfortable?"

Um, my friend and I were talking. Men. I tell you. Half of them thought the earth revolved around them.

Be'Anthony said, "Yea, we are. I would like another shot of Patron. Put the salt on the lip of the glass and bring me the goddamn lime slices."

He was a God. He smiled and my pussy was wet. I was already horny. I rubbed my aching clit and stood up. I kissed his lips and he looked at me. I put my fingers under his nose and he took a whiff. He kissed my cheek and I sucked my juices down my throat.

"Can I finish taking the young lady's order first?"

I said, "I get jealous."

"But you don't know me."

I grabbed his dick and squeezed just a tad.

"Does this have a circuit breaker box? Because I need a fuse in my asshole so you can see my clit."

He kissed my cheek. "Maybe later."

"I have condoms."

I was getting to him. "Then we can do the damn thing after I am done with this order."

"I take it in the ass, too," I said. Ding, ding, ding. Right answer, Bob!

"Ahem," said Be'Anthony, tapping her empty glass. "Can he bring my Patron first? Goddamn. *Shit!*"

We chuckled. He again kissed my cheek and turned, walking away. "I'll be back."

I ran up behind him and slapped his amazing bubble ass. Those manly cheeks jiggled. *Ow!* Damn. Happily, I danced back to the table.

BeAnthony was fuming. "Must you act like a sensational Ho?"

"Chile, I'm single and doing it. And I'm a *whore*. My 'Ho' has the 'W' for a hat and the 'R-E' for Prada shoes. I'ma pricey bitch."

"So are you gonna have a Patron with me?"

I looked at the waiter coming back, looking into my eyes.

"Yea. *After* I sip the magic come from the hole of his dick."

"Girl. You need help."

"No. I need some dick in my life."

"Well, this is the place to get it…"

We were in the back room, dancing all over black silk sheets. The room was an exclusive room. I had to pay about $20 dollars to get inside, but with over $15,000 in the bank that was like two dollars for a lollipop. I had to pay another $300 to have sex.

He was incredibly eating my pussy and making me shiver. I must have come about three times from the warmth of his mouth alone. He loved taking care of his…customer, accustoming this pussy to those lips. The AC was on full blast. The room was a recreation of ancient Greece, complete with pillars and fancy columns. *Some* of them lay about in ruins, mimicking history. I was clad in a silk wrap over my wig and a blonde-colored kilt. It was pushed up over my waist.

He straddled me and slid inside my wet pussy. I was holding his back and biting his bottom lip. His dick wasn't as big as it looked earlier. To be completely honest, it was bigger when it was on soft status. Was that shit even possible? Nonetheless, he was experienced, hitting spots a ten inch dick *never* did and I found *that* amazing. His shaft slid against my clit and I could have died.

He was moaning my name in my ear, making me fall in love. I always fell in love with good dick. He flipped me over and I was riding him and I felt a pair of huge hands on my booty cheeks and I looked back and a tall, sexy chocolate man with a white mask on his face got behind me and the size of his dick was amazing. He spread my cheeks and started sucking my asshole while ole boy grabbed my hips, grinding his dick into me. One was gorgeously fucking me and the other man, I would call "The Phantom of the Asshole," was sucking my chocolate star, going down to my friend's nuts and sucking those, too.

He was bisexual; tasting us both and this was hot. I didn't care what they did. As long as they penetrated both my holes and made me come out my nose then it would be a job well done. He slowly put his stick in my ass, allowing my rectum to absorb it all.

I was being double penetrated for the first time in my life by two fine ass men and I wished it could last all night.

They made me rise and fall as I pretended to be a wave and he was the moon and his love glowed on me and I wrapped my legs around his sweaty waist and he dug me out and I wanted to call George Bush and tell him that this trooper, who was deep in my pussy, was mine.

He *had* to be taken off the draft list and if he said "No," I would wait until Obama was President and I'd tell his ass, "If you draft this one

I will vote your ass outta office during the next election.

You wanted *change, well I (C)ontinuously (H)elped (A)(N)iggah (G)et (E)lected,* now help this pussy."

I must have come out my soul when I had my orgasm.

"Damn, he rocked your world, huh?" asked Be'Anthony, tipsy. Six empty glasses sat on the table and green lime peelings were all over the place. She had hung up her cell phone when she saw me coming. She knew I couldn't stand her men friends because they were young punks.

"He was good, shit." I was floating on Cloud 9 looking for Cloud 16. "Correction. *They* were good."

"You nasty bitch. Were you double-donged?"

I was seething with pleasure. "Yes, ma'am," I said jubilantly. I wanted round two.

We slapped palms. "Do your thang, baby! Do your *thang.* I ain't mad at 'cha."

Be'Anthony rubbed her titties, flicking her tongue in and out of her mouth. Very sexy, if you asked me. I wondered could she do that on my pussy.

She said, "You need a man. A *decent* man. Because we can't keep coming to Cedars."

I was appalled. "*Why* not? Everyone in here is safe."

Be'Anthony waved at a few sexy lesbians who walked by, checking us out. They waved back, looking as gorgeous as ever. Think of Halle Berry, J. Lo and Miss Nasty Jackson flocking together.

"I know, but damn, Gurl. I don't want to be giving up my pussy like this forever."

I said, "Look around, Gurl. Fine men are everywhere. Paradise. Even the rich and the exclusive don't really know about Cedars. We are under oath not to *reveal* its location."

"I hear you." I thought about it. I knew she was right but I was in denial right now. "And if I do get a man I will play the damn role, Chile. He gotta be packing and stacking the change, you feel me and I'm not talking about fifty cent and piggy banks. I will milk him for every nickel and dime. A bitch needs things in life. That's what it's all about. Live good, fuck aplenty and die happy."

"Then go out there and find you a scape goat." Be'Anthony sipped her drink and her cell phone rang. She eyed it without answering.

I said, "Maybe later. I'm about to go out to another place. One that I can keep my clothes on. A bar, perhaps. Probably the one on South Beach. Washington Avenue. The Irish Pub."

"I fucked one of the bartenders in there. They call him Swell and, Chile, his dick did anything but his name...Well, Gurl. See you later."

I stood up and kissed her cheek. I was trying not to remember when we sucked and bumped pussies the other day. My first lesbian experience and I was sure it'd be my last.

Two lonely women together ain't always a good thing.

MONTHS LATER

T he nerve of this man. Trying to tell me that in order to be with him we have to fuck five times a day. Oh, *really*? Let's do the math. I will have a ruined asshole and pussy if I let him fuck me five times a day, seven days a week: 5 x 7 = 35 times a week! Multiply that times 4. I will have my Grandma's curtains for an asshole and pussy in roughly six months trying to please this big dick man who couldn't even suck my pussy right let alone have a little finesse in what he did. And to think he wasn't like this seven months ago.

When we met at the Irish Pub on South Beach he told me he was single, articulate and very available. He didn't have many friends at all because of his profession. When he said he was a doctor I almost fell off the stool but I played it cool because I wanted the fool. His sparkling Phantom keys arrested my attention as well as his clean-shaven face and his threads cost more than everything in my living room with more to spare. He only had eyes for me and every jealous bitch Ho in the establishment accidentally bumped into him, looked at him or tried to act bold and stand in front of me, talking to him. I didn't have to say anything or bat an eye lash. He politely brushed them away like dust off an AC vent and told them to get a-steppin'! That's what a man does when you let him taste your pussy when you first meet.

That's how you keep pussy on his mind. So when those clueless Ho's tried to cock block they didn't stand a chance. Men hated incarcerated pussy. It was on thing to make a man work and sweat for any clit play. But it was another to act grand, dress grand but have a trashy pussy.

My man loved women who made him wait, sweat and work for the panties and *that* wasn't a problem because my pussy provided overtime in that department. All I did was let him taste a little cunt. Sort of like an appetizer. It'd hold you over until the Main Course was done. Companies with employees couldn't give a man a hefty 401 (k) plan like my clit could.

Excitedly, I had called Be'Anthony when we met and she told me to go for it. That, *hell*, if he had money and was driving a Phantom all over the Beach then I hit the brass ring. She was right. I had good pussy, and good pussy had to ride in style. You didn't put good pussy in a taxi cab, pinto or a car from the early 80's and late 90's. That's a travesty, to say the least. We talked for hours and around four a.m. he let me drive the pricey Phantom all up and down Ocean Drive while he was between my legs eating my pussy. I was bouncing on his tongue, having orgasm after orgasm while the half-dressed Ho's pointed at the car, snapped photos and waved like I was a star and I was just a bitch getting tongue fucked in a $500,000 car.

At first I wanted to put a sim card in his dick (like my cell phone) so I could program it. He was always horny, always hard and normally that wasn't a problem for me because I was a freaky bitch but goddamn. When we *finally* did the wild thing about a month after meeting each other he started to gradually put demands on me. Do it this way. Wear this. Don't suck it like that. Don't call your family. Cut off your friends. I don't want them in my house. Bitch's steal. Talking to Be'Anthony was cool but *that* was about it. I felt like a remote control. I even went in the bathroom, pulled down my panties, spread my dry pussy lips and examined my snatch to make sure the "mute" and "on" and "Off" buttons weren't on my clit. The articulate façade he put up when we met turned out to be an utter mudslide. He was not the same as when I first met him. Then I found out the Phantom automobile was rented and not paid for like he said but *that* was cool because his house was worth three million dollars and was located on Star Island. And on top of that those jealous bitches who took pictures of me driving it could post them on their Myspace page and picture me rolling.

I used to call Be'Anthony every night, complaining about the man with the master plan and she told me, "Gurl, he got you living in a three million dollar house. You better act like Rupunzel and let down your hair; finding, *finding* that golden crystal stair before he turn into Rumpelstilskin on your air-headed ass."

I couldn't help but laugh at her humor. She was right.

"Play the role, remember?" she asked and I chuckled.

He waited until I fell in love with him and quit going to Cedars to drop his high sex drive on me. I swore if his dick was a truck I'd have to buy bags of coffee everyday to keep it awake.

At first I didn't say anything because I loved him…um, yea right. I loved his money. I was a gold digger. Shit, I was a platinum digger and a silver digger, too. I wanted it all. Wal-Mart turned your coins into cash these days so I'll take that, too. When he saw that I was being obedient, he started to get ridiculous. He fired the maids and made me start doing the chores. He had a big ass house and I had to dust, mop, sweep and vacuum and cook nearly three times a day with my titties bare and some Gucci pumps. I did it because of the money but after a few months I secretly hired the maids back when he went to the hospital to work and I made *them* do it. One thing did occur to me when I was cleaning. Not one photograph of him, a flower or a child was hanging up. All the walls were bare. Seemed more like a waiting room then a home.

I got my breasts done. He loved the outcome. I also got a Brazilian butt lift. Men really gawked at the booty when everything came together. I got my teeth fixed and redone. I also got some veneers. I was a gold digging product now. He visited Victoria's Secret more than I did. Dropping thousands. It had gotten so bad all the Victoria employees knew him by first, middle and last name. I heard he fucked them all. Oh, well. I was the one living in the three million dollar house. I was the one playing tennis on the back courts when he was out. I was the one clad in $5,000 tight sweat pants and $2,000 custom-made diamond-and-sapphire high heels, playing basketball by myself. I was the one clad in a $13,000 silk bathing suit, swimming in the Olympic-sized pool. I could piss in the water and enjoy the sunshine. I was the one paying renowned photographers thousands in cash to come over and take breathtaking photos of me. My man was *obsessed* with buying different panties and garments and having me wear them. What truly appalled me was when he wrote out a script and screen play and had me role play. I had to rehearse and learn the lines like I was Diane Carroll. I had to go through all his set ups and set designs. I had to do run throughs and shit. He was serious about it, too. I was a gold digger, yes but this had taken the cake. I was not Anna Mae and he wasn't Ike and I didn't want to eat the goddamn cake, Ike! He had money so I was content with being spoiled, shopping when I wanted and spending up his credit cards. He never protested. I could get anything I wanted. He *never* questioned it or crossed examined me. He always paid the cards off on time, no matter the price. Being with a doctor proved to be heaven sent.

Maybe I was the fool because now he was standing before me with a bag filled with goodies. If you asked me to remember his name I couldn't tell you. He once told me everything about him but

I forgot and we've been fucking all the time. The sex blinded me because it was so good. The only name I referred to him by was "Baby" or "Daddy." I only called him Daddy when he was knocking the brakes off my pussy.

I closed my eyes, inhaled and wanted to fall into a hole. I didn't want to role play at all. It was cool four months ago. But every damn day he came up with a different scenario. Last Friday we must have role played all day. In a twelve hour period I was a Captain saving a Viking, a stripper turned doctor's assistant who fucked herself in the ass with bananas, Hunting for Red October, a Jamaican woman who sucked his dick backward until he came, a gynecologist examining my own pussy in a lab coat while he fucked me in the ass with a thermometer. I was a medical examiner and he wore my blonde wig, dress, heels and panties and I had to eat him out like he was the bitch, and a cruise ship Host turned stewardess who rode his dick backward while fucking my ass with a twelve inch vibrator. By the time my pussy hiccupped I must have slept for two goddamn days.

I heard a thump on the nightstand and from the sound of it I knew what it was. *Another* script. God! Shoot me!

He once told me I was the Olympic Torch that burned in his heart. It's funny he said that because I was the runner with the flame running the opposite way.

He was stroking my cheek. I loved his touch but I wasn't into Oscar-worthy roles anymore.

"Baby," he said and I opened my eyes, stood up off the bed and put on my house coat. I wanted to run like Forest Gump. I was naked but right now I didn't feel like *being* naked. My heart felt naked because this man didn't know four things about me.

"Yes." Barely audible.

He was deeply concerned. "What's wrong?" He was watching me sternly.

I want out of this relationship, that's what's wrong! "I have a head ache."

He set the bag down and went to the medicine cabinet in the bathroom. I looked through his purchases. A garter belt. Panties. MORE PANTIES! *Unflattering* panties. Green with pink polka dots. Who did he think I was? A white woman?

Humming an Xscape cut—*What I need from you is Understanding*—he opened the mirror and pulled out the Tylenol. I was watching him from behind and I actually smiled because he was so fine and I used to tell Be'Anthony that when it came to fine men they could fuck me 'til I bleed and now that I had that I didn't *want* it. I didn't want to be Lil' Kim anymore. The one good thing I could say about him was that he was very into me. He told me that he loved making love to me because he wanted to make me come all the time. Sometimes he didn't come at all. He didn't eat pussy, because he was an island man and he told me that Jamaicans didn't fancy putting their tongues in pussy. I thought it was a crock of shit but it's all good. Maybe he forgot he ate me out twice when we met at the Irish Pub. He brought me the pills and a small glass of water. I pretended to have swallowed the pills. He kissed my lips and watched me.

"Baby. I have a question. And I hope you don't get upset.'

I wound up swallowing the pills, dry. "What?"

He took my hands. "Can we fuck five times a day?"

I was taken aback. "WHAT?"

He was chuckling. "I knew you'd see it my way."

I was shaking my head. *What?* "*Your* way?"

He kissed me and I walked past him. "Baby," he went on. "Look at me."

I don't want you touching me. "No. My pussy is sore right now. This slinky ain't fun for a girl and a boy anymore. I can't handle it *five* times a day."

He shot his cuffs. "My credit cards and bank accounts are sore. You swipe, swipe, swipe three to nine times a day. My bank accounts have become your slinky! Do I *protest?* Do I say anything?"

I felt guilty. And trapped. "No." *I do need his money. I was saving to get that Bug-eyed Lexus I saw on a brochure. He said he'd give it to me.*

He smiled and kissed my cheek. "Then fuck this dick five times a day. Or I cut off the finances you little pricey whore!"

Tears welled in my eyes. *Don't cry now, bitch.*

He thought about it, a finger on his temple. I cringed inside. "…I'm thinking six times day should suffice. Like when I get home from work. I want your pussy shaven, cleaned and perfumed so daddy can give you some dick. I don't care if your pussy has hair or not, shave it everyday. *Military* the pussy, bitch! I'm the First Sergeant and you're the private and I just want to fall in it."

The room was spinning. "I think I gotta vomit."

He eyed the script on the nightstand. "Lay down, baby. The pills are probably working."

I lay down and he rubbed my neck. He kissed my forehead and took off his clothes. He looked so sexy but right now I wanted to run. I didn't have the energy. I wanted to move but I felt glued to the bed. I tried to inhale but my lungs were on fire. I reached for the phone to call Be'Anthony but he took it and replaced the receiver.

"No phone calls until I get some pussy. When you're on my time it's *my* time. Time is money and money is what you spend day and night when I'm at work."

He was between my legs, giving me some tongue. *But Jamaican's don't eat pussy, right?* He ate me roughly. I wanted to die. It didn't feel good at all. I gripped the covers and scooted back but he viciously grabbed my thighs and started biting my clit and that shit hurt and I tried but to scream but my voice failed me.

God—is his house, cars and money worth it? I turned my back on you and dropped outta church for the good life and all I received was hell on stilts.

He started tonguing me and that felt good, thank God. He munched on my pussy like some Bubblelicious. There you go. My twat was Pussylicious. I started to feel the bubbling in my toes and he ate and ate until I had to come.

"I gotta come, baby," I screamed out, tilting my head into the pillow and he stopped cold turkey, stood over me and he began to piss all over me. I was so disgusted I started wiping at my face. He tilted his cock towards my face and tried to piss in my mouth and I started to shake with revulsion. He was laughing, snatching me by the weave and pissing on my lips.

"Open your mouth, Ho. Drink my piss! You wanna spend my money praise this dick until its spent!"

"Please…Please, stop!"

"…I don't want to completely drain the weasel," he said, getting between my legs. He slowly put his dick in me. Sometimes it felt like it was in my belly. He was rough and tough and very aggressive.

I wanted to puke. The smell of piss did a number on me. "Baby, I'm sore. Please," I said, panting. Bracing myself. I had had enough of this. But I wouldn't dare say it.

Maybe I should endure this shit because I also want a new wardrobe. And maybe I should reorganize his closet so I can condense his shit to make more room for my outfits.

"This will only take a minute."

He fucked me for an hour, non stop. I hated it. It initially felt good but after twenty minutes of his constant plowing, it started to hurt. I had to hold his sweaty back and he showed no signs of slowing down. He told me he had to come and I felt it all in me and he pulled out and my legs were still spread eagled and I started to push it out and nothing but piss came out and I sat up, swinging at his face and he laughed boyishly and caught my hands.

"You pissed inside me, man? I can't believe this!"

I was too exhausted to carry on. I got another head ache and it throbbed so bad I had to handle it, moaning piteously.

I started to drift in the blackness, fighting to keep my eyes open but he started to massage my lower thighs and his touch felt good and before I know it the room burst into white sheep and I started to count them and that was that because the blackness swallowed me whole as he slid his dick inside my asshole.

I was in the kitchen about an hour later. He had awakened me and told me he wanted something to eat. In grave pain my loins were on fire. It took a few minutes for it all to come back to me. I knew I had to get out of this relationship, but if I did that would mean no more exclusive parties, no more V.I.P. to some of the most glamorous clubs in Miami, like White Diamonds and Club Mansion. My friends would hate me because I couldn't use his Platinum card and get their hair and nails done or lend them some cash. I already had him thinking I cut my friends off. It seemed my friend list grew on Mysapce.com because I was a bitch with money. No. I was a bitch with a doctor who had money. They were blinded by the pictures on my page. The cars. The exclusive parties. The façade. The unspoken lies. Was the abuse all worth it? Was it worth the money?

I limped down the stairs and into the kitchen. My pussy felt snapped in five places. I was crying, opening the cupboards. I was staring at all the organized can goods. This seemed so Julia Roberts *Sleeping with the Enemy* but he didn't beat me. One thing I could say was that he never forced me to do anything and he never raised his hand to me. Part of me knew he never would. Who was I kidding? I guess snatching me by my weave and pissing on me was a walk in the park. I was already justifying and minimizing his lewd actions.

This was crazy. It's funny how things change when you give a relationship a few months to marinate. You start to see things you should have seen in the beginning. Even though this was doomed from the get go. When you wanted a man's money you never seemed overly anxious. You played the independent role. You told him you hated when people did shit for you. You worked your ass off and you denounced any gifts he gave you. You played that card until the time was right. When he got used to you not accepting any gifts and cash from him you pounced. You started saying shit like, "Baby, I don't have enough for my phone bill. Could you pay half?" and he'd be so happy to do something for you he'd jump at the opportunity. That's how I got in the doctor's wallet.

He smoked a lot and he loved booze. He couldn't go a day without it. And to think he treated accident victims and worked in the ER and he didn't get a clue. He would be next.

The intercom buzzed and he said, "Could you fix me something to drink? A scotch? With cranberry…"

I said, "Sure."

I pushed the "off" button, running my fingers through my hair. A few strands were stuck on something on my hand.

I looked at them and gasped when something glittered from my ring finger.

An expensive ruby and diamond sapphire engagement ring.

He must have put it on me when I was sleeping.

He wanted me to be his wife.

But was I ready?

You better think about it, bitch.

You'll be his urinal till death do you part.

I reluctantly took him a Swiss cheese and grilled turkey sandwich on toasted bread and his scotch. It took me a good twenty minutes to fix it. I had to lightly butter the toast and put the Swiss cheese on the meat after I took it off the little George Foreman grill. If his specifications weren't met he'd throw the sandwich on the floor and make me do it again. Sometimes I would and sometimes I wouldn't. But when I chose not to he cut off all the credit cards and froze the accounts and he fucked me even harder. I didn't want to look silly driving his gold Phantom around my friends and I couldn't fork over the cash to buy them gifts or buy the bar when I did decided to hit clubs while he worked. Money equaled happiness yet I wasn't happy with it now that I had it.

Tenderly, he kissed me and told me to get on his lap. I had said "No," but he took my hand he gently pulled me towards him. I couldn't take my eyes off his towering dick. It's *always* hard, able and willing to fuck me into Z's land. I didn't like his dick anymore. I couldn't *stand* it. But how do I tell him without upsetting him?

So I got on him. He put his dick back in my pussy and he told me to ride him. It took a minute for my walls to absorb him. Jesus, the sensitivity was killing me. I didn't know if I could do this. But I thought of that Prada jacket I wanted and those Gucci pumps and the five hundred dollars he gave me weekly because a) I didn't have a job because b) my man took good care of me and I swallowed my pride and his come and did what he said.

Realizing I didn't love myself, I had tears falling from my eyes. He set the sandwich on the nightstand with his dick still in me. He sipped the drink then decided to gulp it down. Monsters rallying in his eyes he gripped my ass cheeks and he fucked me so good I couldn't stand it. The pleasure mixed with the soreness in my pussy lips was enough to make me go crazy.

I don't love you. I love your money. I need that Prada jacket. And that banging Ralph Laurent dress. I saw some pumps in Macy's that I want. All four colors. The red would go good with my black sapphire dress. But was I willing to keep degrading myself…

He leaned up and took my nipple into his mouth. He was biting it so hard I winced, trying to take it. It'll be over soon. I was praying to God.

Maybe taking his money was worth it. I don't know if I could do this anymore. But I have nothing. I let my apartment and car go when I moved in this lavish ass house with Mr. Horny Doctor.

He pulled out and flipped me on my knees. He spread my ass and opened the nightstand. He took out the heating KY Jelly and squirted it on my asshole, massaging it in. He plummets in the depths and I screamed from the pain. He started fucking me without a care in the world and didn't stop until he pulled out.

And came on my ass.

Distraught, I lay on my stomach, my hole on fire. I was crying so hard. I couldn't do this anymore. He was on my legs. He took his finger and spelled some words on my lips, pronouncing them out.

G-O-L-D. D-I-G-G-E-R.

"That's who I'm in love with. A whore! A gold-digging whore!"

He stood up and walked in front of the bed. I looked at him, trying to sit up but it hurt. He took me by the arm and yanked me to my feet.

He stood before me, smiling.

"Are you going to marry me?"

I said, "No. You have violated me for the last time."

"If I can't have you then *no* one can."

I felt the chills when he said it. "I'm leaving."

"You can't," he said stubbornly. "Bitch, I'll kill you if you give my pussy to another man."

I was weak but I was strong minded. "Watch me leave…"

"I will. And when you do I will make your life a living hell. You can't live without my money."

"*Yes* I can. I have had enough. I'm calling Be'Anthony."

"Be'Anthony. Be'Anthony. Ole Be'Anthony. She *is* a good friend of yours, huh?"

I was defiant. "Yes. She is. I love and trust her."

He picked up his cell phone and he called her. He put it on speaker and I didn't say anything. He put a finger against his sensual lips.

"Hey, Man! How *are* you?" Be'Anthony asked. *They knew each other?*

"I'm fine. My lady just left. She's going shopping."

"Her gold-digging ass. I can't *stand* her."

My mouth fell open.

"Good thing you told me to meet her at the Irish Pub months ago, after she suggested going there."

"I know, right? She said she loved to role play and she told me the only way she'll date anyone is if they had money. So naturally I thought of you. She didn't *know* it was all a set up."

I closed my eyes, holding in my rage. I snatched the phone and hung it up.

"You motherfuckers!" I didn't trust anybody anymore.

"You didn't find it a least bit off she didn't answer her cell when you were at the table, or she hung it up when you came back to the table? At Cedars?'

"*Cedars?*" I was shaking my head. I thought about it.

"Yes. When I met you at the Irish Pub, you told me you didn't have sex for almost a year."

"I *didn't.*"

"But you got fucked the very same night at Cedars. Before *we* met."

I narrowed my eyes. "No I didn't. Did Be'Anthony tell you that?"

"Yes. And no," he said, grinning. "I played the role."

"*What* role."

He pivoted on his heel and opened his closet. He reached up and pulled down a small trunk. He turned the combination lock and it snapped open. He put something on his face and turned to face me.

It was like déjà vu when it all came back to me. The back exclusive room. When I was being fucked by two men. He stood up and walked up to me.

"If you didn't fuck for nearly a year, why did I fuck you in the ass the same night we officially met?" I was shaking at this game. It wasn't very fun. I was backing up, shaking my head.

"I was one of the two guys who double penetrated you that night. *Remember?* The bisexual man who sucked you and your little dick gigolo waiter friend."

"That was *you?*" I asked, covering my face.

"Yes. Joke's on you."

I packed my things and he sat there watching me. He was clad in a very pricey silk suit with gold cuff links. He looked so good. I called Be'Anthony and asked her to come over and she said *sure.* When she got there I opened the door. She hugged me and I didn't hug her. She helped me take my bags to the car and she didn't say anything. I went over to my official ex boyfriend and told him, "You will never see me again."

Be'Anthony was confused. She said, "What happened?"

"You and his role playing days have come to an end. It's over between him and I, and me and you."

Be'Anthony lowered her head. "I'm sorry, Gurl. I didn't…

I took the briefcase and hit her so hard over the head she fell to her knees.

I took her keys, loaded her car up with my things and I left Star Island forever.

I was at a new apartment a few weeks later. Luckily I had a few thousand dollars saved of the doctor's money to hold me over until I found a job. I also pawned the ring. I thought I would get a few hundred for it. But once the Pawn Shop worker put it under a microscope her head snapped up and her mouth fell open. She put $23,000 in an envelope and gave it to me. Cold cash. How much was it really worth?

I lived in Perrine, Florida and I had a date at the career center for job placement.

I stayed to myself, feeling like a fool. I was still in love with my ex. I dreamed about him and thought about him. A few times I picked up the phone and wanted to call him but I couldn't. I couldn't eat or sleep. I cut off all my friends. To go from a rich bitch with a doctor to a cheap apartment in pissy-smelling Perrine was enough to make me slit my wrist.

I was coming home from the grocery store when I saw a few squad cars at the apartment building I lived.

"Damn. Crack heads breaking in my neighbor's apartment again."

I was carrying a few bags of grocery. I would have driven Be'Anthony's car but I left it parked in the driveway. She wouldn't be getting that Honda back anytime soon. I got up to my apartmment and a few cops looked at me. One looked at an open folder and back at me with a smile.

"That's her," he said, fiddling with a pistol.

The taller while male cop approached me and said, "Are you Maxine Moneys?"

I tucked my chin back. "*Yes.*"

"You're under arrest."

My heart stopped. "For *what?*"

"Assault. Grand theft auto. Credit Card fraud. And a host of other charges. Can you put you hands behind your back…"

"You're making a mistake. I'm innocent!"

"Yea, whatever. You're under arrest!"

My world was spinning.

After I was booked, fingerprinted and treated like hell, I was given some clothes and put in a holding cell. Goddamn it! Now my life was over. To go from the lap of luxury to a rundown apartment in the slums to jail was embarrassing in itself. Everyone was going to laugh at me. I was given one phone call and I decided to call Be'Anthony.

She accepted the charge and before I could say anything she said, "So. Miss Thang. You slam a brief case into my face, steal my car and get missing?"

"You lied to me. You better get into it. You set me up with that *man*."

"You said you wanted to play the role. I was a friend for doing that for you. I made close to fifteen thousand off your ignorance."

"I can't believe this."

"Well, believe it. Gold digging isn't always cool. I pressed charges on you. For theft and assault."

"And the credit card fraud?"

"Yup. I'm fucking the cop who fingerprinted you. His name is Officer Charms. He can certainly eat some good pussy. And, oh. Damn. This is the best part. Hope you're sitting down. Your ex boyfriend's name isn't Leonard Phillips. He isn't a doctor. He didn't have credit cards. And that three million dollar house *isn't* his."

I had to close my eyes to keep from screaming. This couldn't be happening.

"Then who is he?" I asked slowly. I didn't think I wanted to know.

"He's a con artist. You were spending up someone else's credit and money. The real owner of the house, cars and credit cards is pressing charges against you for identity theft. You are on store cameras buying this and that all over Dade County. All your online purchases were traced back to you by your computer's I.P. address. You're looking at fifteen years in prison."

"I *won't* get convicted. I will tell them everything, Be'Anthony. You will pay."

Somehow, I didn't believe that myself.

hen the judge dropped the gavel after saying I would do ten years in prison for assault in the first degree, grand theft auto, identity theft, drugging my ex so-called doctor boyfriend with sleeping pills (which I hadn't) and credit card and check fraud, I started screaming. I ran at Be'Anthony and her Gigolo friend and I tried to kill them. Security apprehended me and I lost it.

"I WAS SET UP! I DIDN'T DO ANYTHING! WHY AM I MADE TO SUFFER? I WAS SET UP!"

The jurors were shaking their heads at me. Be'Anthony smiled and my ex smiled with her. They held hands, leaving out of the courtroom.

When I was being tugged past the judge's bench he looked at me and said, "Gold digging doesn't pay, does it?"

And the real Leonard Phillips walked over to me and said, "Don't worry. I forgive you. But what you did was wrong."

"I didn't do anything!"

"Right! Everyone cries innocent when they're caught."

spent about two years in the slammer for a crime I didn't do. I never appreciated my freedom until it was taken from me. I lost all my family and friends. My name was being slandered on the streets. All the money I spent on them and now they wore the gold, jewelry and clothes I bought them, while they bashed me. My own mother visited me and she told me to never call the family again.

I changed a lot as I still tried to put it all into perspective. My actions got me in here, I couldn't blame anyone. I used a man who turned out to be a fake and the joke was on me.

I got a job in the laundry and put out that I had herpes and HIV. It wasn't a lie. To find out I had been fucking an infected man for months, actually letting him piss and come in me turned out to be life threatening. How could somebody so gorgeous and so beautiful have syphilis, herpes and HIV without showing any signs?

The infirmary doctor gave me a bottle of doxycycl hyc 100 MG to take. Fourteen days worth. Little blue pills I had to take once every twelve hours. I couldn't eat two hours before or within an hour after taking it. I couldn't eat dairy products when taking it. It would lessen the effects. They were designed to rid my body of syphilis.

I was depressed. I was sent to the psyche ward for evaluation. I withdrew into myself. Having guards tell me what to do wasn't cutting it. I slapped one of the female guards so hard the bitch flipped over the rail and snapped her neck in two places. She had grabbed my pussy and told me I better let her eat me out or she would put me in segregation. I got a hold of the whore and showed her another way. I was charged and convicted for her assault. No one believed me when I told them she had sexually grabbed me. No one believed me that she was one of the women on South Beach who snapped pictures of me driving the Phantom.

I gave it to God because I wanted to die. Dykes were after me and I had to fight all the time. A few tried to rape me but I fought those Ho's. I had grabbed the smallest one and beat her ass so badly no one tried to rape me again.

It was a little before Christmas a guard came to my cell and told me a lawyer wished to see me.

For what? Who knew!

I had followed the guard to the lawyer, who was in a waiting room. We had privacy. He waited until the guard left and he said, "Hello."

"Hi." I fell silent, chewing on my nails.

"I'm a paid attorney."

"Public pretender, 'ey?"

"No. A *real* lawyer. Someone paid me $23,000 to take your case."

I was confused, standing up. "You got the wrong girl. I don't know anybody with that kinda money."

"Do you know a Leonard Phillips?"

"Yes. He's my victim."

"Well, he hired me. Do you know a guy named George Franks?"

I was racking my brain like crazy. "No." I thought about it deeper. "I can't say that I do."

"He works at a place called Cedars."

"Oh my God! Yes! George! The *waiter*."

"Yes. He uncovered a plot to destroy you. He took the mini tape to Leonard on Star Island and played it. Leonard then called me and said he wanted me to represent you. You're looking at getting your conviction overturned."

"WHAT?" This was the best news.

"Apparently Be'Anthony and her friend Johep Dogma run money rings at Cedars, which is nothing but a classy whorehouse. They are the owners."

It took a minute for it to sink in. "You mean to tell me that Be'Anthony *owns* Cedars?"

"Yes. It actually started from her living room. When she made enough cash she met a Johep, who had just graduated Morehouse College with a degree in business. He runs a drug cartel on the side. The man has money, but he couldn't get a good job because he has four felonies on his rap sheet. He's also a male prostitute. That's how he met Be'Anthony. They linked up and the rest is history. The Feds are investigating Cedars and it has been temporarily shut down. A few politicians and sports stars are being indicted right as we speak for illegalized prostitution."

"So, let me get this straight. Leonard, my victim, is getting me out of prison."

"Yes. He is. And he says he's sorry for thinking you're the one who stole his identity and his money. He is set to help you get back on your feet."

I got on my knees and said, "Thank you, Jesus."

I t took about two weeks for me to be freed. Even the charge against me with the correction's officer was dropped and overturned because this lawyer of mine got her to admit she grabbed my vagina, trying to get me to do sexual favors. Now she was facing sexual misconduct charges and hell, yea I was going to make them stick.

Leonard met me at the penitentiary. He sent me a gold dress and some pumps. A necklace that said NEW BEGINNING and some rings.

I didn't understand it.

He pulled up in a white Phantom. The same one I was driving when I met Johep at the Irish Pub. It wasn't rented after all.

"How are you?" he asked and I shook his hand, tears falling from my eyes.

"Thank you."

"Don't thank me," he said, looking in the back seat.

It was George.

And he looked good.

G eorge was happy to see me. "Hey, Miss Thing."

I hugged him and he kissed my cheek the same way he had when I met him at Cedars. I held him. It felt good to be in his arms. It felt good to be free. It felt good knowing that God gave me a second chance. "Thank you."

"Thank God, don't thank me, Maxine. Just promise me one thing."

I wiped tears out of my eyes. This was overwhelming for me. "What?"

"Learn from this. Gold digging and stealing and taking from people and depending on a man to do for you reaps the lakes of hell. I hope you learned from this."

"Oh believe me, I have."

Leonard said, "I hear you need a job."

"Yes sir, I do."

"Well, I own a few shops on South Beach. I need an accountant."

"But I'm not good with money."

"You're a gold digger. You are good with money."

I couldn't help but laugh. "Ok. I used to be a gold digger. And what ever happened to Be'Anthony and Johep?'

"They were tried and convicted. And with the list of charges, they will be old and gray before they see the light of day. Let's go, so I can show you your new office."

I prayed to God the entire time.

I was given a second chance.

I will monitor my health, take the proper medications and work for my own money from this day forward.

I vow.

K
Ŷ
Ø
©
Σ
Ř Λ

Ř
Ï
GG
Ï
N
S

My name was Kyocera Riggins. I was a 6 foot-3 inch Top brother who lived his sexual life on the DownLo. Sure, friends that were close to me knew about my sexual orientation. They were all on the DownLo as well. Men with wives and families. Men with successful businesses and careers who would never let a hard dick or a piece of ass destroy what they worked so hard for. Some of them belonged to college fraternities and sororities. Their image was everything, as with mine. We had a very tight-lipped, closely-monitored and knitted network that we never compromised for anyone or anything. We ate together, dined together and talked about everything under the sun without having the fear of being snatched out of the closet. We weren't *"clockable"* in public. That meant one couldn't look at us and guess we were bisexuals. And talking with us you would never figure out or guess we were bisexual men and women. Another word I would use would be "Trades." That word signified today's DownLo man who was either in denial about who he was and what he did or he figured that he was still straight as an arrow, no matter how much dick he took up the ass.

My life was filled with promise, research, wasted ink pens, dull pencils, weed, alcohol and good butt booty naked sex. I sometimes frequented gay sites, like blackchat.com and Adam4Steve.com. I participated in the public forums, mainly laughing at all the Beyonce Knowles-looking faggots who defended a singer who didn't know they existed. I swore about a hundred threads on Beyonce or Janet Jackson was posted everyday. Men claiming they love pussy yet they adore Beyonce's wigs and high heels more than her nearly-defunct dance ability. Of course I didn't put my pictures on the sites. It was just a past time. More like gawking at body-revealing photographs featuring sexy brothers all over the country who called themselves DownLo, but had their faces and private information up for grabs. I always called my friend, Shape Clark, a wanna-be lawyer out of Minnesota, and told him to log onto the site and check out my pick of the week.

He never seemed impressed with my selections.

I had a wife, Cortina, a very beautiful, self-employed Mexican woman who loved me beyond measure. Yes, I even loved her. But I had an unsatisfied taste for feminine, bottom men who loved it deep, rough and hard; a burgeoning taste that couldn't remain incarcerated to my mouth alone. Sometimes it liked to roam free. Be what it was. Hook 'em, fuck 'em, nut on 'em then go home to my lesbian wife.

For some reason I didn't want my wife knowing I loved men. I spoke out against homosexuality in a respectful way. I didn't go out of my way to bash them. She loved licking pussy from time to time so that was one of the quirks of my marriage. When she wanted to suck on some titties she told me and we cruised around until we found a willing lesbian who loved a man and a woman sucking her to orgasm city.

Just last week she met up with a pretty blonde who worked at Dolphin Stadium. Her name was Volunteer and she had big, fake titties and the cleanest pussy I had ever seen.

Getting her was a treat because we met at Hooters, when my wife and I grabbed a bite to eat. She was eating alone, cursing at a guy over the phone. Tears fell down her face and she stormed out, barely keeping it together.

My wife was right behind her, offering a friendly ear to a complete stranger.

We shared some drinks and got loose. Next thing I knew I was spreading her pussy in my bed and my wife was riding her face, her ample breasts jumping. I sucked on her clit, imagining Ralph, a one night stand from the week before, sucking my dick until I wiped my name on his forehead with my come. I hated being selfish. Yet part of me loved it, I guess.

Why keep doing the things you hated, right? Wasn't that how the old saying went? You must like it if you kept doing it?

Cortina pulled out a black double-sided dildo and got on her knees, facing the wall. Volunteer got on her knees, facing the foot of the bed. I put one end of the dildo in my wife's ass and the other end in Volunteer's pussy. Their booty cheeks slapped against each other as they moaned into the air.

I was fucking my wife in the mouth while reaching over and slapping Volunteer on her ass.

I loved it. What man wouldn't like kinky shit like this?

I got jealous of the dildo so when they were done making each other come, I went up in Volunteer, with a Jimmy on of course. She had some good pussy, too. Goddamn. It was much tighter than my wife's but I would never admit it. My wife even asked me. "How does it feel, baby?" and I said, "It ain't better than yours," while bouncing in the snatch. I fucked her so long and good she claimed she fell in love with my dick because it was big, long, thick and she never had black cock before.

When I came all over her titties, my wife was expertly licking it up like a good bitch, spitting it in her mouth and swallowing it.

I said, "I don't have a cock. I have a big dick."

We sent Volunteer home and knew we'd be seeing her nasty ass again.

Since I write in a very successful newspaper column, I felt compelled to give back to the community by responding to any concerns they may have about love and life. I published about six letters and my responses once a week. Getting the editorial was a feat in itself, since I was the only black working at So That's News Productions. I also did a radio program for two hours on 78.8 the Jam, an underground station based out of Miami, Florida.

I had to knock some heads and get my knees dirty to open doors. Having an education as a black man, you had to prove yourself harder than the Hispanics, which made up over 60 percent of Miami and the whites. I tried it the old fashioned way: with confidence and class. But everywhere I applied for a job, no matter how seasoned the resume, they always told me one thing: Are you BILINGUAL?

Fuck no I wasn't. Yet half the Hispanics working didn't speak a lick of goddamn English, which pissed me off. Why hire them and not hire me? I figure I could handle the English-speaking people and could handle the Spanish-lashing motherfuckers.

Being that I was raised by a hard-working black woman—with a knack for extension cords and iron thumbs—and father, Kyocera, Sr.—a Jazz singer who had moderate success on Smooth Records, 34 records, over a million copies sold—I learned early on that what you reaped was what you sown. I used to live by that code, build myself up, set my expectations higher and every time I fell flat on my face.

I learned when I did what people said I was a well-behaved child but whenever I protested or didn't like something then I was out of control. That's the psychology adults used to cram in my head and, at the time, I actually believed it.

But as I grew up chopping rejection and reality sunk in, my confidence waivered to getting my high school diploma and enduring stuck up white-collared men who looked me in the eyes with phony promise and letting me down easy with a flat "We'll call you, don't call us" monotone that broke my heart. And I found that Niggahs never helped Negros and Brothers, with their Oreo Cookie-acting asses never helped Da Brothahs.

In my opinion, *Niggahs* were concerned with the trappings of the ghetto, period. They didn't think beyond frolicking with thugs and smoking weed with the Hood Rats while getting their dicks sucked and making umpteen babies. Half of them lived with their Mamas and used the white man for an excuse not to go get a damn job. They owed back child support pay and treated women like filth. They would rather go out with the boys and ride them in their cars four and five deep while their Baby Mama's catch the bus, rearing their offspring.

Negros were high school or college graduates with a knack for a better living and wanted things out of life. Even if they hadn't graduated yet, they were into books, *knew* their history and applied it to their morals and values and knew six things about Africa off the top of the brain without blinking or breathing twice.

They didn't allow anyone to call them "Niggers" or "Niggahs."

Tupac's [N]ever [I]gnorant, [G]etting [G]oals [A]ccomplished didn't fly with Negros. They treated women with respect and treated people in general how they wanted to be treated.

They watched the *History* Channel and *Animal Planet.* A typical black TV show *never* tickled their fancy.

Brothers—I wasn't talking about siblings—were stuck up, *classy* types who only hung around *other* classy types. They were high maintenance men who had a taste for the finer things in life.

They wanted everyone dancing to their marching bands. When they went to grocery stores they wanted eye contact and wanted to be recognized, which was why they *never* shopped at Wal-Mart or the Piggly-Wiggly Supermarket.

They frequented Publix Supermarkets, Safe Way or Albertson's. They wouldn't be caught dead at thrifty stores or the *Goodwill* or wearing anything under 20 dollars. They were into mortgages, expensive watches and driving cars with acronyms: BMW.

They watched their calorie intake and didn't like generic brand anything. They forged relationships with a partner either on their level or above.

They never went to the 'hood and were some of the most biased people on the face of the earth. They had something to say about everything.

Da Brothahs were *my* people! They played basketball in the 'hood and they drank beer and smoked week with peace and respect.

They loved a party and always threw a barbeques somewhere.

They even invited their enemies and had love for them as well. They talked trash and still made it to church on Sundays playing the drums or singing in the choir.

They were very hospitable and very down to earth. They accepted everybody for who they were.

They loved their families and drove their cars playing their music loudly.

They liked to show off their cars during the street parties, slowly driving through with their music thumping over the DJ speakers, drawing their own secret attention.

That's who I was: a Brothah.

ctually, when I was little, I wasn't a very confident man. When I was three years old I tried doing back flips for my father. He would be cutting the grass and I'd call him and start doing back flips.

He'd shake his head, grunt, chew on his straw and continue managing the mower. Mama, who always watched Daddy work (she got off on it), rolled her eyes at me and always tried to make me stop.

I never listened. Daddy totally ignored me and it disappointed me beyond repair. I wanted his attention. He loved playing and writing music, or calling his six male buddies over and they play in the band they called The Goulds Trotters.

So I upped the ante by flipping off crates, hoping that would do the trick.

Again, he'd be too busy doing yard work or playing music or talking, relating or laughing with his band buddies and never focused his energy on me. A ball of jealousy formed in my gut and smooth with my face over time. The only time we spent time together was when we did yard work and I hated doing manual labor.

I loved and looked up to him so much I think I lost myself. But I didn't realize it. It had gotten to the point where I started to annoy him calling his name every five seconds.

He was so anal retentive and so out-of-touch with reality that he finally, after weeks of flipping and embarrassing myself, thrust a guitar at me and said, "Be like the Jacksons and play a tune. We have bills to pay! Doing back flips puts your body at risk for some serious damage! And don't even think about picking up a basketball or football. True wealth was in studying and writing music."

Of course, at 3 years old, I looked at him like he was speaking in Chinese. I didn't know what the hell he was talking about.

Mama always spoke about being independent but she repeated every word Daddy uttered with aplomb and arrogance. Ignoring them, I still ran out in the huge back yard and hit some back flips and he'd storm up to me with the face of a warrior, snatch me by the shirt and whip my ass so bad my ass was too sore to hit a flip let alone sit in the bath tub.

As my fourth birthday approached, it dawned on me that Daddy was serious.

It really settled in my mind with a filthy weight that I wouldn't be able to go out and play with the other neighborhood kids. He would keep whipping my ass until it clicked in my brain that life was about hard work.

Not leisurely fun.

I was supposed to be enjoying life. Not spending time worrying about how a bill was going to be paid.

But my parents didn't care. They figured the younger I learned the better I'd be. In its own little sick, twisted way it was a blessing. Because I thought with the mind of a ten year old. I matured a lot faster. I learned how to look after myself while Mama worked and Daddy strummed his pain with his guitar and his fingers. I learned how to work hard and take initiative.

I was reading and writing on a fourth grade level by the time I was 6 years old. I learned discipline and good character. I learned how to stand tall and walk straight.

Daddy actually gave me speech and walking lessons. "A man walks with his back and shoulders straight, and his chest out. Even under fierce scrutiny, you keep it tight. Never let the world see you cry, whine or sigh. We're men. Men are strong, men control the household and men tell the wife what to do."

Mama agreed. In fact she never spoke against him, which always struck me as odd.

I learned to play the guitar and I learned how to play classical piano. I was the only kid in the neighborhood talking about Mozart and Beethoven while the other black boys talked about basketball and how much pussy they were getting.

Sex became the ultimate bargaining tool.

No matter how up-tight or conservative, people in high places loved a) flattery b) money and c) good sex. I fucked my way through Harvard University and I fucked my way into a high position with *So That's News Productions*. If I had half a brain I'd admit that my desire to fuck men came with my need to survive. I never had gay thoughts. In fact, growing up I had a gay cousin, Bob, who I still loved and admired. Early on, I never ascertained it. But being around Bob and becoming aware of his lifestyle and how the boys chased him on the DownLo, a part of me actually started to become curious. But I never really acted on those feelings.

Now I was at work, putting my editorial together. I was shuffling through legions of letters, but none intrigued me. I logged on the computer and I checked the massive emails I received from black men all over the country. Some people were giving feedback on pervious articles. I wasn't Janet Jackson. I didn't need any "Feedback." Once I write something and hit "Submit," I was done with it.

I moved on to the next write, because I believed in progress and growth.

My brows rose at an email I got from Bigstroke899@yahoo.com

Despite having a wife I had a boyfriend on the Low for ten years. We went to college together and got married together but could never stop touching and kissing and fucking each other. We had threesomes countless times and never frequented the other party after it was over. We remained committed to each other and our wives.

Living a double life is heartbreaking but we don't want to hurt each other or each other's families. In my honest opinion, people have to understand that us having threesomes and cheating on our spouses has nothing to do with selfishness.

Because we both love, admire and respect each other. It's just sex and when you start thinking too much into it, then that's where you get these thoughts of I must not be satisfying my partner.

My husband and I would never end our relationship over a non-emotional sexual encounter.

By the way we have only done a three some about four times in the ten years we been together.

And we are still committed and happy.

Well, I found my first victim. I couldn't believe what I was reading. Part of me knew I couldn't judge him because my own wife and I had threesomes, but to actually hear it from someone else seemed preposterous.

I had to read it again to get the full understanding of it. I actually called up my homeboy Matt and ran it across him.

He guffawed through the phone. "Are you for real, Dawg?"

I pushed some files over on my desk and said, "Hell, yea. Can you believe this?"

"Well, you know you can't really talk. You cheat on your wife."

He got a rise out of me, and I wasn't talking about my dick.

I was wiping my eyes. "Yea, but its different with me."

He laughed. "*How* so?"

"Easily. My name isn't Big Stroke. And my wife knows I'm bisexual."

He sucked his teeth. "You're lying. She doesn't know. She knows you know she's a lesbian but she doesn't know you fuck men in the ass."

I resented that shit. "I don't fuck men in the ass."

"OK, what do you call it?"

I stood up, opening the blinds. "I call it having sex."

"What's the difference?" he asked rhetorically.

I sat back in the chair and poured a cup of coffee. "There is a difference. Gay men fuck each other in the ass. I don't. I'm not gay. I'm bisexual."

"OK, you lost me. I'm gay. Sure, I still fuck women but I prefer a dick."

I was disgusted. "Your *mouth*, Dawg." I sipped the coffee.

"The truth hurts."

"You're not gay. You're bisexual. Gay men want to be Beyonce Knowles and put on her wigs."

I was laughing. "Nah, drag queens are into stuff like that. Gay men don't like women at all. Half of them wish they were women."

"You're stereotyping gay men."

I set the mug on the desk. "Are you sure? I didn't know my stereo could type, shit if that's the case the stereotyping my columns for me would save me about, what, twenty hours a week I could cruise the net and find some new booty to dick down."

"You're so nasty. I'm at work now, and actually we just went on break, even though I take twelve breaks a day. I swear if one more man walk by me with headphones on singing, 'Freakum Dress, Oh-ho-oh put your Freakum Dress on 'cause every woman got one,' I am going to fucking scream!"

I fell over laughing, nearly knocking the hot coffee on my suit.

"Shut 'em down, goddamn it! And my friends wonder why they can't find Top men. Because Top men are secret bottoms hiding in the back of their closets trying to find that Freakum Dress."

"Man, you're too much. Look, I got to go. Got work to do."

"You always got work to do. When are we going to hang out?"

I said, "You know we can't do that. Every time we hang out and keep it platonic my dick always winds up in your mouth."

"You know you're flaw. It's unusually the other way around."

"I don't suck dick, Dawg." I got pissed quickly. "Nor would I *ever*. I am a *Top* brothah. I do the fucking and sticking. And I damn sure don't do no sucking."

"*Right*. Bye, Negro. And call me. So we can catch a movie."

I said, "You're dumb if you think we're going out. Not in this lifetime."

I hung up, shaking my head.

He did have some good ass.

I wrote a response in minutes, and submitted it to my column. Definitely the first I'm exhibiting.

I proofread it then sent it off to one of the Editors.

Knowing them they were fucking off in the break room, talking about everybody they fucked at the office.

They placed bets on who was going to get my dick and no one has gotten it yet. I didn't mix business with pleasure.

Within minutes my phone rang and I answered it.

"Yea, Sup."

"Are you crazy?" asked one of the Editors. Sounded like Mosaic. She always criticized something I read, mainly because she was a straight woman working at a place that was tolerant of gay themes. That's because we only wanted the gay community's money and support. *Nothing* more. You wouldn't catch us dead marching with them at those gay prides.

My brows rose. "Crazy about *what?*"

"You can't run *that* article. Our readers aren't gay."

"*Some* of them are gay, Mosaic. We have straight readers, gay readers and transgender readers. We stretch across all age groups, races and creeds. That's why were so successful."

"You're pushing the envelope, huh?" she asked. "You're *trying* to be different. You don't even *like* gay folks."

I was steaming. "Run the fucking article and shut up. Jesus. It's *my* goddamn column. I approve what goes on there, even after you edit it. I am the most popular columnist on this bullshit."

"You've always been an arrogant prick. I'm not editing it."

"Well, I'll re-write it and send it to you."

"Thank you. At least you have common sense."

"I wasn't serious. I was lying, Girl."

"You're toying with me. I have a three year old who will get his ass whipped if he toys with me. I'm Mama."

I wanted to laugh. "But you're not my Mama you clueless hag and I'm *not* your goddamn child. Bitch if you put your hand on me I will kick your ass all across this office."

"Who are you calling a bitch?"

"I don't hear a third party on this phone, do you Queen Latifah? Don't start with that U-N-I-T-Y bullshit."

"I'll have my brothers come up here and kick your ass!"

I chocked on my spit. "Who? Tiny, Lil Mama and Big Wig? All your brothers are known drag queens. What are they going to do? Chase me down 79th Street into the U.S.A. Flea Market and do my hair while riding my dick? I got a low fade, bitch."

She didn't like that shit at all. "Die, man. Die!"

"Edit my column, Girl," I said, gritting my teeth. I was done playing. We always bumped heads.

"*Whatever*. I am not editing this filth. It's negative. Cheating on his wife with another man and he is justifying it? I actually like what you wrote but *damn* man, you were even being false in the report. You're personalizing a lot of stuff and even suggesting things a gay man would. Now you're pretending to be gay to gain some readers?"

"Yep. Got to make that money. Those dollars making me holler. You feel me?"

"I'm hanging up. Don't send me your column again. As a matter of fact I'm done for the day. I'm clocking out and going home."

"Running from your secrets, 'ey?"

"Fuck you! I don't have secrets!"

And she hung up in my face.

I read over the column I wrote.

Hello Big stroke. First, thanks for emailing me your honest and brutal query. But I must say something. And I hope you don't get offended because I'm being as blunt as I possibly could. That isn't love you and your man have. I'm sorry to tell you, that's lunacy. And it isn't just sex you say? That's what you're trying to tell yourself.

That's low when you sit there and watch someone else fuck your dude, be for real. And to make matters worse you both are married to other people who have no iota you're cheating in the next room.

Both of you are just selfish. You want what you want when you want it. I'm not being disrespectful, but like I said if my dude comes to me with that I would rather be alone. Some people are so afraid of autonomy and being alone that they will accept any and everything that doesn't mean them any good. Something for nothing works for Domino's Pizza, not a relationship.

When you reduce yourself to the seductive waters of "You can do anything to me, I don't care…" then Houston, we have a huge problem a shrink can't fix if you don't want to help yourself.

When you tell your mate, "Baby—I know you're a dog. And I know you're fucking other people. But as long as you come home to me, and share the same bed, then I can look past that.

I just don't want the dinner getting cold and don't neglect me!" then something is seriously lacking in your idea of the perfect, relationship-tight world. That isn't a relationship. That is an utterly low relationshit.

DAPHAROAH69

Stop looking for abnormal things. If he or she doesn't meet you at least half way then your glass is half full, with no room for improvement and half-empty, with no room for progress.

Stop looking for relation-cliques. You don't need anyone to make you happy, all you need is yourself. The idea of a freaking relationship should inspire you to work on your own self-confidence and image before you invite the outside world, a man, a lover or a potential soul mate.

Once you get it that should ensure that you are getting everything you want spiritually, mentally and physically at home.

When something breaks then you go to Home Depot. When a pipe burst then you call a Plumber.

Your mate is supposed to curb your appetite so you don't have the urge to go out and find it somewhere else. Stop making your eyes bigger than your stomach when you're not hungry.

If you're that much of a freak then you two should make love and fuck all the time, not invite someone else. Masturbate if you have to. Buy a toy. Get a dildo. Fuck yourself to your heart's content while your mate looks on. Something is missing if you are continuously seeking threesomes.

You're finding an excuse to momentarily be with someone else. When you give your body to someone it becomes an emotional thing. Whether you are in denial or not is up to you.

Emotions are involved when you're having sex and making each other come. If you're full why would you go grocery shopping? When you're hungry why would you go grocery shopping and get a bunch of herbs and spices you don't need when you could have just gone to a fast food joint? You aren't committed if you gave your body to someone else, I'm sorry.

Just because you feel no emotions are involved when you have sex with a stranger don't mean giving your body to someone else is healthy.

So if he does it behind your back with no emotions involved, is it truly called cheating when you two are clearly not committed?

Commitment means being faithful, period. It don't mean when you feel the need you invite a third wheel.

When I was done reading it, I printed it out and stapled the papers together. Setting it inside a red folder, I re-wrote another edition and when I was done (zonked on four cups of decaffeinated coffee) I hit print and put it in a blue folder.

Getting up from my desk I locked my office and walked to Miss. Editor's office, with her feisty ass.

Mosaic was picking up her purse when I entered her office. She graduated from the top of her class at Harvard. She knew her shit.

Closing the door she was startled, eyeing me evilly.

"What do you want?"

I taunted her. "You can't speak?"

She looked at me for a brief moment, looking good in tight black jeans, a ruffled turquoise blouse and huge bangles. Her hair was done up in micro braids pulled into a loose ponytail.

"No." She turned off her computer and closed her blinds. We were in the semi-darkness. "I am about to clock out and go home for the day."

"You can't go home. You gotta edit my column."

She glared at me, throwing a Styro-foam cup at me. It barely went past the desk.

"I respect gay people, ok. But I'm not a dyke and I have a lot of family and friends who love the paper. They even like some of your work. But this article jeopardizes all that. Straight people don't wanna hear about two gay men fucking each other like an episode of *Passions* while being married to black women."

I said, "Actually, they do. *Noah's Arc* and the *DL Chronicles* are the hottest shows out right now, not to mention *Queer as Folk* had more straight people watching it then anything."

"We're *not* a TV station, we're a *paper*. And Noah's Arc is a Bible story, when Noah built the ark and two of each animal, one male and one female, dumb ass, had shelter for 40 days and for 40 nights."

"All right, Miss Billie Jean, you're trying to be funny."

She stamped up to me and said, "Try me. I am not editing that feature."

"Right," I went on, getting tired of the back and forth. I had a wife and she wasn't Cortina. We were inhaling each other's warm, moist breath. Her breasts were against my chest and my dick had a fit. Calm down, boy. Her tits know not what they do.

She had a piercing glare that intimidated me.

Walking past her, I set the blue file on her desk with a smile.

She didn't look back. "That better not be that story."

I bit her hook. "Read it. I re-wrote it. I didn't even go with the original email. I erased it and picked one more cookie cutter for your fake ass image at this paper."

She turned on the lights and picked up the file. I still held the red one.

She saw the title scribbled on the folder.

"Why didn't you send this to my email as a Word attachment? I don't *do* hard print."

"Read it," I said slowly, loosening my tie. I sat on the black leather sofa and watched.

She opened the folder and sat on her desk. She read out loud.

"She was a woman who was raised in the suburbs but wanted a way out. Sheltered all her life, her Mommy and Daddy did everything for her. She wanted to know how rough life was without the comfort of money." She looked up with a smile and said, "This sounds familiar. Didn't we do a story like this before?"

I was pleased. She liked it. "No, but I did one similar to that one. On the girl who was found dead in Gainesville. This one is fresh…keep reading."

She said, "I'm glad I led a good life. My parents always gave me the best. And I got a college degree because of it."

She continued to read. I nodded my head, listening in awe.

"…So she used to sell her body when she turned fifteen and wound up pregnant by age seventeen. When she lost her baby she got close to a male cousin, who was about twenty five and fucked her senseless just to cover her part of the rent."

Her eyes started to tear up.

But she didn't stop reading. "…Her parents disowned her and she wound up going to college. She had her first lesbian experience when she was twenty. She licked pussy to make the grade because she read on a tenth grade level. She fucked half the professors and by the time she was twenty one she had to transfer from Florida Stare University to Harvard University and wound up graduating at the top of her class."

Jumping off the desk, she ran at me and I jumped up to my feet, holding her in a bear hug. Shaken, she spat at me and tried to stomp my foot.

She was a very strong woman. But I was stronger, mind you.

"You motherfucker! That paper is about me!"

"But you don't have any secrets, right?"

And the winner is…

She pushed against me and we fell on the sofa. She tried to claw at my hands and I held them. She then tried to bite me and I didn't know if she had rabies or not so I held her tighter, showing her that a female couldn't overpower a man.

"I hate you!"

"I got love for you!"

"You had no fucking right, you arrogant motherfucker! I hate you! Let me fucking go!"

"Run my column," I told her. "Or I run yours. It's your choice."

Maybe I was wrong for airing out her dirty laundry. But we all had skeletons; luckily I did a lot of Google.com and found out a lot of stuff about Mosaic.

I wasn't actually going to run her life over the wires, but I did use it as a tool to get her to edit my article.

She still lay on the sofa in my arms, too afraid to move.

I said, "Are you going to be ok?"

She said, "No. I can't believe you would do that."

DAPHAROAH69   167

"I can't believe you would bash gay folks for what they do and in your own life you did some unspeakable things you don't want to ever get out. We all live in glass houses; I don't care how much cement and cinder blocks they use."

"Just hold me for a second."

I held her.

She said, barely above a whisper, "When I was younger I did what I had to do. I never talked about the women I slept with to get through school. When I was a little girl I was sheltered. I had money and the best money could buy but I never had attention, my parents never did homework with me. They never sat with me and talked about life. Maids did that, and they always mislead me. When I started to develop breasts and my body changed Mama was too busy for me. So I ran away from hone and was on my own since…"

"You don't have to say anymore. It's your past. But never forget it. Because you *can't* have a future without it."

She closed her eyes and said, "I'll have your article edit before 6 p.m. tonight."

"And that's all I wanted."

I thought about the advice I gave her when I was driving home. I also replayed in my mind the response I emailed to Big stroke.

How could I give him advice about his life when my wife and I were screwing other people in our bed together?

We were swingers, and at the time I figured this was saving our marriage. We took vows. Didn't they mean anything to me?

And now that I was thinking about it, why would she let anybody other than me touch her?

Why was I being self-conscious now? I didn't know, but something was opening up in me and I didn't understand what it was.

Did I want to live the rest of my life this way? Did I want to continue fucking men behind her back and justifying it?

Did I want to continue sharing my wife, pleasing her lesbian fetishes?

I called a friend of mine on his cell phone, internal issues tearing me up emotionally.

Tears were stinging my eyes. I swallowed the lump in my throat.

"Hey, Man."

I heard singing and instruments through the phone.

"Are you in church?" I asked.

"Yea, Man. And I know you don't do church but maybe you should drop by."

Hell, No! Why should I go to church? I don't believe in organized religion.

I don't believe in going around phony people who sinned more than the sonsofbitches outside of the church.

"I think I will," I said, looking at the Holy Bible on the passenger seat.

What am I doing, Lord? Do I really want to step foot in your Holy home? I am so not worthy and my soul is unclean. I didn't know how I was going to correct my wrongs or change my habits, considering my flesh was weak and my mind even weaker.

But I did know one thing.

I would start with God.

And the rest is up to me, Lord.

H
Ű
Ř
Ŗ
Ï

©

Λ

Ν́

Σ

I turned on the computer and waited a few minutes for the slow thing to boot up. The problem was that I had too many programs running, programs I didn't need. I didn't use Adobe Flash. I didn't really use yahoo Instant Messenger. And I had Internet Explorer, not America Online so I needed to uninstall it. But I was lazy. I didn't feel like fucking with it. Required too much brain power and I wasn't Einstein. I also had a lot of websites bookmarked. I hardly visited the sites, so why did I save them? I needed to do a Spy Sweep. According to the prompt flashing in my face I hadn't done a full system sweep in forty two days. This meant I probably had all kinds of tracking cookies I needed to quarantine. I then logged onto Myspace.com. I used to breathe this site. Literally, I couldn't function once I logged onto MySpace and browsed available people, sent messages galore, listened to up and coming rappers, checked out the latest books and watched funny videos and wrote a few blogs that didn't get any hits so I was like the hell with it.

But ever since I went through the aftermath of love I have lost interest in it.

And Blackplanet.com has lost its luster with me.

I checked my messages.

I know once you see my picture your probably gonna delete this message...but I really hope you read this.

She was right. I deleted her message so fast it should make her head spin. The thought of her killed me because I still loved her but she loved me and another woman. The same woman who happened to be her best friend. So while I was worried about another man taking her…her best friend Barbra was plotting her moves the entire time.

How could that possibly be? How could you love two people? That's like serving two masters. I didn't smoke so I pushed the thought of cigarettes out of my mind. I didn't drink so there goes the beer and liquor. I did like to work out so I pulled out the Soloflex and set it up in my living room so I could work on my abs. They weren't all that great but they were in better shape than they were a couple years ago.

I wanted some entertainment. So I turned on the radio and the phone rang. Since I loved talking on the phone I raced over to it and when I saw her name flashing I took a few steps back and choose to let it ring.

The machine picked up.

You know who it is. And you know what to do. Leave a message and a number and I'll hit you one more time like Britney.

Beep.

I know you're home. And I know you cringed when you saw my name. I love you too much to not know these things. I still feel connected to you.

I didn't feel connected to her. I sat on the couch and folded my hands in my lap.

Anyway moving back home was a big change for me and I have to let a lot of things go and it's so unfortunate that losing you was one of those drastically major things... I have learned so much this past year and a half about myself that its crazy and I just don't wanna deal with anything I've done wrong.

As always. You always run from the pain, you never face them and deal with your faults and your wrongs. And until then you're going to be running for the rest of your life.

But somehow there's no way I can avoid any of my problems. Don't get me wrong—I don't regret anything, but if I coulda changed anything I probably would have but I can't re-write the past. What's done is done! I wish you could see it that way but, as always, you nurse your own hurts and lick your own wounds and you don't care that maybe, just maybe somebody else is hurting.

I really feel horrible just thinking about all that I've done with her and we were best friends and now she doesn't exists to me nor I to her.

Can you believe she won't even talk to me?

Ha, ha bitch. That's what your two-timing ass gets. Served you right! Vengeance! At its finest!

Seriously I wish none of this craziness happened. Now I know there was something I could have done but I only thought of myself at the time.

I know that much. Selfsh.

Even now...

Told you! I actually smiled.

I don't talk to either of you and still I feel like I have to choose.

Choose who? You lost me forever. So the choice has been made.

Don't flatter yourself.

I would have never thought that I would be able to love two people equally and deep down inside I know that I will love you both for the rest of my life.

Honestly do you think we would still be together if nothing started between the two of us? I don't know. All I can do is learn from everything but first I have to DEAL with it!

And dealing with it means we cant be together, I have to learn and move on and to me going back to you means going back to that place I was before and honestly I don't like that person I was. It has nothing to do with you.

You only know half of what went down, down here and maybe one day I will be able to tell you the whole story but for now I just wanna say my love is everlasting and I never meant for any of this crazy crap to happen and I really hope one day we could be friends...

But I guess it's too late to apologize.

I thought you understood that from that Timberland-produced song. It's too late to apologize.

P.S.
I said this without cursing so you should be proud...

Boo! Whatever. Proud of what?

I was in a Catch-22. I loved her but I hated her. I couldn't put it any other way. I still wanted her in my life and I wanted to be in hers yet I couldn't stand the site of her. This seemed a contradictory oxymoron in one fruit roll up of cacophonies.

I knew I'd never forgive her. I could never forget what she did to me. I hated her so damn much I wished she died in her sleep so I could spit on her coffin. I was ugly when I was in pain. I didn't process it very well.

Knowing I should let her be, I called her cell phone because a) she never answered it and b) it always went straight to voice mail. When I heard Ciara's "Promise" song I melted into butter. She first dedicated this song to me when we fell in love. And now hearing it fucked me up inside.

I wasn't a man who was emotional yet I felt emotional right now.

Beep.

You say you left that over-indulged message without cursing and that I should be proud, well I'm not. Because our relationship was cursed by Hurricane Barbra. And I listened to your message, at first shocked that you stopped long enough to put your universe on hold just to remember that I was even alive.

It's funny. A few weeks before, when I found out I was H.I.V. positive and my world was destroyed, I asked you to stop cursing because I thought you were *better* than that and you stopped calling.

If memory served me correctly you even hung up on me and I guess I cut ties then. I was already going through the burden of my health starting to ail. You have to do what you do. Even now, I can't look at your picture online without touching or kissing the screen so I covered my mouth before I did so.

I wound up kissing my hand. To say I feel like a complete, utter fool would be putting it mildly. Its like you completely came into my life and you and Barbra tore it apart without a heart.

You say you love me but all I feel is loathing. When I first met you I never imagined I'd feel this way right now, I still feel betrayed; you can't even leave a message without mentioning that girl.

But you feel how you feel and from this day forward me giving my heart to anybody has ceased. I'll still love life and believe in love but I'll love life believing in love of myself. Being "in love" is overrated and maybe there isn't a person out there for everyone. I wasn't good enough for you. I wasn't sexy enough; I wasn't smart enough for you. Because everything I lacked, things I came up short on Barbra possessed it which is why you turned to her behind my back and wound up embarrassing me in the process.

You left the one you love (me) for the one you liked (Barbra) and she wound up not even loving you anymore. Now you know how I feel.

I will not love again. And I will focus on myself. Maybe it's a good thing we didn't last, because in the back of my mind I already knew we weren't going to last anyway.

All the times I said I wanted you to be my wife has become my nightmare because I know that you never wanted to marry me anyway, and maybe that was wrong of me to ask considering you're young and you have your entire life ahead of you. But I was the dumb ass, I still chose to be with you and that's my own fault. Being with a fantasy.

The Lord of the Rings isn't real and neither was what we shared, obviously.

You made it perfectly clear. I was the little gnome in this relationship chasing "My precious," which was you and you weren't to be obtained. It's not your fault or mine. We both messed up, said things we didn't mean (or did mean) and lashed out at each other.

But faults are made to learn from and I will not be making that mistake ever again and if it feels like I will get in a relationship again I will bite my tongue, stomp my foot to get over it and move on.

I wish you success with your life.

Yea, we'll still be friends (fat chance!). But as your friend, *please* don't tell me you love someone else because that will be enough for me to commit suicide.

Good bye.

Click.

Mama stopped by when I was on my eighth set of crunches. She never knocked. She had a spare key. She waltzed inside carrying grocery bags. I stopped my work out, drenched in sweat, trying to get my ex off my mind.

"Hey, Ma. Call first before you come over?"

"Boy, we go through this all the time."

"And all the time you never listen. Sup with all the grocery. I can buy my own food."

"I'm sure you can. But I was late buying you a house warming gift. So I made it up by buying grocery. You have…" She set the bags on the massive dining table and started taking things out. I stood up, panting and walked behind her.

"Carrots, bell peppers, turkey wings and necks, asparagus…"

She set all the items on the table. Half of those things I didn't eat. But it was the thought that counted.

"Thanks, Ma." I kissed her cheek. I hated that blonde wig she had on. I guess she was having a Marilyn moment.

"No problem. I know you're gonna cook us dinner."

"No, I don't feel like it," I said apprehensively. I was already agitated.

"Why? Where's your girlfriend? Your *fiancé*?"

My face darkened. "I guess she's home."

"Call her over. I miss her a lot. She hasn't been cooking at my house lately. Does she have another job?"

"Yes…"

"And when is the wedding date so I can buy a matching outfit to go with my blonde wig. Hey. I even got blonde lipstick," she went on, taking off her leopard-print jacket and tossing it on my sofa.

"In three weeks," I lied. I wasn't marrying her. She wanted to lick pussy over sucking this dick she could stay gone. I didn't wanna break Mama's heart. She looked forward to the wedding—900 people were expected to show up.

"Oh, good. And never mind, I'll cook these turkey necks. If you noticed I bought things that would be cooked tonight."

"Thanks Ma."

The phone rang. I knew who it was so fuck it, I didn't answer.

Mama started towards it and I said, "No, Ma. I don't wanna be bothered."

"But what if it's your *fiancé*?"

"She'll call back.'

She said, "Nonsense. What if she's bleeding to death?"

Then hurry up bitch and die. "Then I'll call 9-1-1 and watch the news to see what happened."

"Son, something is wrong. I've been married to your father for decades; you can't hide these things from me. Did you two argue?"

"Yes. And we're in love. And we're still getting married."

The phone stopped ringing.

The machine picked up.

"I'm happy you found the one you want to spend your life with."

Bite me, Mama!

You threw so many knives at me but I can't even be mad at anything you said and because of all that... I don't call you because it will only seem as if I'm leading you on and I don't want that.

Yeah I was selfish and now I'm all alone and that's something I deal with everyday...going through this has changed me so much and what's really sad is I can never go back to who I was before and that's all I want.

We're not getting married anymore because I wanted to be with my best friend, Barbra.

I never even knew I was a lesbian until we got close. She was there for me when I needed her the most. You were sort of doing your own thing. So I let you. Why should I have to beg a man to be there for me when he should automatically have my back and my best interests at heart?

Mama's face turned ashen.

She stared at the phone as if her heart failed.

Fantasy...Damn that's sad, but you have every right to feel that way. I can't say I'll always be around but you are the one person I always think about.

Take care.

Click.

Mama glared at me. Yes, I was a liar! Go ahead and say it. I knew your tongue was saturated with the word. Her lips were twitching. She *hated* when I lied. That was her pet peeve. She felt that if you had to lie then keep your goddamn mouth closed. But don't just blatantly lie and know you're lying.

Shamed, I lowered my head and pretended to shuffle through the food.

"You bought hot cocoa. Cool. I hope it's my favorite Swiss kind with marshmallows."

"She left you for a woman?"

"Yes," I whispered.

"She is a rug muncher?"

"Yup."

Tears spilt from her eyes. "My son! Why didn't you tell me?"

"Because karma got me back. I used to be a player, hurting women left and right, remember?"

I looked at her and she was by my side, rubbing my head and kissing my cheek. I felt relaxed, honestly.

"Yes. I did say that. You were ruthless. You hurt so many women. I said you were gonna fall in love. You didn't believe me. And when you did she was going to crush you like you did to so many others."

"Yea, you did say that," I said, overwhelmed with feelings right now. My soul felt empty.

"When you met her and said you were getting married a year and a half later we all thought there was hope for you. You didn't cheat on her like you would normally do and you treated her with politeness, love and kindness. Even your father was proud. He's gonna be crushed."

"Not any more crushed than I am."

"We loved her. How could she do this?"

"I don't know."

"How did you find out she left you for another girl."

"When I went to the doctor and I wound up with H.I.V."

Mama dropped her phone and backed up, shaking her head. She covered her face, stunned. I realized I hadn't told the family yet and when this fell over me I felt like shit. Damn. It slipped out. I fucked up.

"You have what?"

"I was making love to my fiancé without a rubber. I trusted her. I was going down on her, and doing what lovers do. When I turned up positive I knew it was from her. Because I didn't have H.I.V. when we started dating. I got a check up every three months."

"Son."

"She was negative when we started dating. But her girlfriend had it and passed it to her and she didn't even have the decency to tell me. *Now* I have to live with a disease I didn't ask for."

Mama hugged me and said "Everything will be fine. I won't tell anybody if you don't want me to. But I am telling your father. He's my husband. I made a vow to God to forsake all others for his welfare. People live for fifteen and twenty years and longer with this. It's not the end of the world. Your family will support you."

"I know."

"I love you."

"I love you, Mama."

"Have you made another doctor appointment?"

"No."

"I'll make it, and me and your father is going with you. We're a family, and I know we had our differences, but choose life. Choose to live. You can still be happy and one day you'll meet Miss Right. But for right now focus on yourself.

"I'll cook dinner, Ma."

"OK, Son. Live and forget and forgive. Don't hate her. You pray for the best. When you forgive you release her control over you."

What she said made sense. I guess I had to hear it from her to confirm it.

"I'll put the rice on. We'll turn on some music and have Mama and son night. Should I call your father over? You *know* he gets jealous. He's a big baby."

"Go ahead Ma. I'm looking forward to it."

"And what about church? Are you ready to come back to God? Now is the time, Son."

Hell no I wouldn't. "Yes, Ma. I will take it one step at a time."

"God bless you, Son. I want you in heaven. If you atone for your sins then you will be fine."

"After learning I have H.I.V. I am starting to take everything more seriously."

She hugged me and kissed my lips.

"Never put a bitch before your family. And when the worst happens, always remember that God is the way. He'll carry you wherever you want to go. Just as long as it's pure and it's Holy."

I wiped tears out of my eyes.

"I don't need a lecture."

"You need Jesus, Son. But I can't force you. You have to make the decision on your own. I can't do it for you and I won't. When you open your eyes and realize that without God you are nothing then things will start to get better for you.

Until then you will continue to reap sadness,
misery and bitterness."

"Ugh, Ma."

"I know you battle religion internally. I know
you want to duck your head and run. But let go
and let God. Then watch the rewards…"

It's easier said than done, Mama.

†

H

Σ

F

Ï

Ŗ

Σ

M

@

Ń

I unzipped my brown H&M jacket, sweat treading all over my abdomen. I had on a tight Nike halter top, my hair pulled into a loose pony tail; I was driving my Ford F-150, South, on the Turnpike, just passing the Eureka Drive exit.

"Baby, are you home?" I said into the Bluetooth perched on my ear, managing these crammed roads to the best of my ability. I had road rage; I'd cuss a bitch out, quick.

"Yes, sweetness, I'm home."

"Please PLEASE tell me you took out the neck bones, so I can make black eyed peas and rice, maybe back some corn bread."

A few beats of silence. "I forgot."

"Baby, how could you forget?" I slowly braked; there was a traffic accident, a major one. It was cold as hell outside, unusual for Miami, Florida, but this jacket was making me hot. "Fuck!" I punched the steering wheel. "I'm ready to go home! I don't want to be stuck in traffic because these goddamn Cubans can't fuckin' drive."

My husband chuckles. "Calm down, baby."

"You forgot to take my neck bones out; you don't tell me to calm down."

Lil Wayne "The Fireman" song came on the radio. I turned it up a little bit. I loved this Louisiana Rapper; in fact he's my favorite rapper, period. And I think he shoulda won that award over scrawny, need-to-eat-ass T.I. at the BET Hip Hop Awards. That was a popularity contest.

"Baby, just take a deep breath. I know you had a hard day at work. I brought you a sandwich, but your boss told me you were extremely busy."

I was quiet for a sec, staring at the fire trucks speed along the road's shoulder. "My boss didn't tell me you brought food."

"Well, I did. I even gave it to her and told her to make sure she gave it to you."

My devil's horns went up instantly. "Wait a fuckin' minute. Was it a ham sandwich with eggs and cheese and a bottle of Mountain Dew and a couple pickles?"

"Yes," said Lennie, my husband.

"Bitch! She ate my food right in my face!" We were laughing. I had to laugh, because I wanted to fuck the Ho up for eating my damn food. "I even asked her for a piece of her sandwich and she told me to buy my own, that her man bought her the food. She meant MY MAN!"

"It's all right, babe. We can order take out."

"You need to take out those neck bones so I can cook my beans later on. I love you, I'm 'bout to go. Ciao, another call is coming through."

I hung up, digging into my $1,290 Louis Vutton bag, trying to find my little device. I was going to be here for a while so I cut the engine. Traffic was backed up for miles, a helicopter hovered ahead. I wasn't going anywhere any time soon.

Scratching my upper thigh, I put in Gerald Levert's CD. Private Line, I miss his fat ass. Damn shame God took that fat ass fine ass sexy ass thick lip ass soul singer! His voice did a number on me as I heard a phone dialing on the radio and his voice comes Privaaate Linneee. I had tinted windows so the piercing sun, despite the cold air, didn't kill my skin.

Cocking my legs open, my skirt inching up my chiseled thighs, I flipped the "on" button on my...device, and my dildo began vibrating. Oh hell yea. High Way Love. Didn't need a condom for this bitch, didn't need to give it directions, the batteries were the only directions it needed.

I felt lustful, filled with cum that bubbled in my body. I put the tip of the humming toy on my clitoris and I damn near screamed from the sudden pleasure. My legs shaking (I was very easily agitated), tears ran down my face. My titties felt good, I took off the jacket, bobbing and weaving out of it, the toy humming for dear life and I took off the halter top.

The car next to me, with a sexy ass man behind the wheel, dread locks and alone, looked over and stared into my window. The tints I had were very dark, you had to really look at them to see through them and he looked hard, his eyes bulging out of his head.

I was married. But I wanna give him a show. So I rolled down the window just a tad so he could see my eyes, since my husband and I were mad with each other, huge argument last night that resulted in me sleeping on the couch and he locked outside, bamming on the door all night, which was the real reason he didn't take the neck bones out because he called himself getting back at me, and said, "Mind keeping me company?"

He was a happy boy. He didn't respond, he jumped out his car, left the keys in the ignition and hopped in my truck, closing the door. He was fine, tall, thick lips, gray eyes. I loved his ass. I took off the NIKE halter top, my titties full and pretty. Huge meatball type nipples. I had a pretty pussy to match. My husband better had taken out those neck bones.

"Damn, Ma, its like that? You gettin' jazzy on the Turnpike?"

"Well," I began, handing him the vibrator, turning my pussy in his face and watching him stick it deep in my pussy, slow and elegant, licking his lips, narrowing his eyes like he was the one being toy fucked. I had on eight inch pumps. He took one of my heels and started sucking on it, sliding his tongue across the pointy wood. I shook with glee. A stranger. This would be a Strange Fuck.

He massaged my vaginal walls, leaning over and tasting the sweet sugar of my clitoris. Oh my God this was glorious! He tilted the dildo, it vibrated on my left wall, the lips of my being encircling the ribbed damned thing with fierce abandon. He stuck his long, thick tongue in my pussy, the tip of the vibrator and tongue becoming fraternal twins in this Oral Sex game.

I felt the buildup, my titties bouncing, my eyes narrowed, I was leaned against the door, knee on the steering wheel, Gerald Levert singing, this Rasta Niggah sucking my pussy and I started to cum, and he dug that tongue in deeper with the vibrator and I began having multiple orgasms, he swallowed my cum, my pussy walls throbbing on his tongue. He still looked famished.

He sat up, unzipped his pants and pulled out the fattest longest dick I ever saw. That shit sat me straight up. He took the vibrator and rubbed it up and down his shaft, using my pussy juices to highlight the incredible inches and his nuts. He moaned seductively, in a way that was boyishly cute.

I leaned over and took his dick into my hot mouth, giving it enough spit to lubricate it to the max. My pussy tasted good on his fat dick. Yes it did, mind you. I trailed my tongue from the tip of his bulging, mushroom head, put the dick down in my throat, holding my breath, bending my lips over my teeth, held his dick in my throat for about eight seconds, came up for air and took my tongue to the nuts.

"Damn Ma, suck it Ma."

"You like that Daddy?"

His hips began twirling on the seat, nuts dangling. "Hell yeah, Ma."

"Ooh, baby!"

"Handle that dick; let me feel that throat again."

Back in my throat it goes.

"Hell yea…suck it, baby!"

"What you want me to do with this vibrator?"

"Let me suck your pussy off it."

Smiling, slobbing all over his incredible Big Friend, I stuck the vibrator in his mouth and he sucked it slowly, his tongue darting in and out of his mouth. He clutched my hair in a tight fist and shoved his dick in my throat, the way I loved. He told me he had to come. I stopped sucking and threw the vibrator on the floor.

"Ma, *why* you stall my nut?" He was pissed, looking me dead in the face.

"Because…" I straddled his hip and slowly lowered my pussy on his dick. His mouth agape with a stunned look on his face, he grabbed my ass and guided me, controlling my spine. I rode that Horse Dick, it stretched my Pussy Chambers to brand new heights.

We rocked. Back and forth. Body heat rising. I came again and again. If the wind blew I came, it was very easy to make me come.

"You're so sloppy and wet! Feels good on my dick—"

There was a knock on the driver side window. Oh, shit. Forgot to roll the window up all the way, a cop looked at us, a black cop, the worse kind. He

opened the door and I didn't move. I was busted.
He got in the truck, closed the door and said, "You
know fucking in public is against the law."

Me and ole boy couldn't move. Oh, God! I was
going to jail. My husband was going to leave me
when he found out what had happened. I wasn't
ready to lose him.

"Officer...we can explain," Dread Lock said.

"Yes, we can," I went on, nervous, shaking.

The cop looked at us and said, "Niggah tear
that pussy up, lemme see. We're not going
anywhere until you fuck that pussy mah Niggah,
keep this between us." Shit, if it kept me out of jail
why not? He sexed me so good I was singing sob
stories in his ears. The Cop, Officer James,
unzipped his pants and told me to suck him up.
The inside of my truck was huge, so I turned and
slid back on Dread Lock's dick from the side, and
he let the seat back some, watching his dick in my
pussy while I gave Officer James some good head.
He had a somewhat little dick, but big enough to
fill my mouth. Now if my mouth was my pussy
he'd look like a Keebler Elf trying to fuck Naomi
Campbell, Midget Dick.

We all were sweaty and my cellie rung, my
husband's ring tone. Nervous and I had to answer
it; I turned down the radio, told the two Niggahs
"Shhh" and I answered. "Hello." Slurp, slurp.
Shit, suck it quietly!

Dick was too good to just stop sucking. Dread
Lock dug all in my pussy, and I had to bit my lip to
keep quiet.

"I took the neck bones out."

"I have a taste for...those neck bones," I said, necking Officer James's bone. He tensed up, and whispered he had to cum and he came down my throat, I swallowed every drop. "Baby can I call you back?" I asked my disabled husband with a muffled voice.

"Yes, baby." He hung up. Traffic was beginning to move, damn it, I rode homeboy's dick really fast, holding on Officer James's thighs for balance, my ass cheeks clapping all over this beautiful piece of meat.

Dread Lock moaned and slapped my cheeks; finger fucked my asshole while his dick wrecked shop up in the Pink Lounge.

I felt inhibited and wanted, a fire burning in me as he screamed out he had to cum and a thunderous orgasm rocked him quiet.

When it was all over he fixed his clothing, got out of my truck, took my phone and recorded his number, saving it under Dad's Brother. Smoke screen.

He winked, closed my door and I opened my Driver's side door, pushed a half dressed Officer Love out of my ride, hoped in the driver's seat, put my truck in "drive," and I flowed with moving traffic, with the taste of Police Officer cum on my teeth.

"Fire! Fire!" I screamed, rushing into my home, snatching off my coat, trying to ignore the taste of cum in my mouth. I needed to go and attack the Listerine.

My husband rushed into the living room, holding the bag of neck bones. I was jumping up and down, panicking. *"A fire, baby! There's a fire!"*

Now he was freaking out. Dropping the neck bones on the floor he was holding his head, turning around wildly, trying to find it.

"WHERE?"

"A FIRE A FIRE OH MY GODD!"

He snatched me by the arms, wild-eyed. "WHERE GODDAMN IT?"

I started smiling. "In my pussy!"

He dismissed my comment with a wave of his hand. "Ah, shit! I can't *believe* I fell for that."

I wanted to role play. I was hot and horny, despite my little…discreet romp. "Quick, baby!" I said, dropping to my knees, unzipping his pants. He put his hands on his hips, looking down at me with a huge smile on his face. "I need your…fire hose." I pulled his juicy dick out, running my tongue around the head, tasting pre cum. "So I can smother the flames."

"Well turn it on." He always played with his nipples when I gave him head. This was our favorite thing to do. I sucked for dear life. He loved it noisy. He wanted to see the spit, the hand play, the tongue action and the deep throat skills. My man was a thug at heart, even though you could never tell because he was Steve Urkell from

Family Matters at home. He gripped my head, and started pumping my mouth like unleaded gas. I was trying to make him buss a nut to appease him. That way he wouldn't want any pussy. And I couldn't have that, because Police Cop and Dread Locks tore me up in my Ford F-150. I felt like shit for cheating on my man, but I was a promiscuously eager nymphomaniac. When my pussy got hot, I had to fill it up.

"Damn, baby! You're wild today! What has gotten into you?" He was breathy, moaning and cooing. *If you woulda saw me on the turnpike you wouldn't ask what got into me.* His knees got weak so he had to sit on the sofa. I got on my hands and knees beside him, let him smack my ass and I put his manhood back to the confines of my hot mouth.

"Yup." Slurp, sluuuuurp, kiss. "Fireman… my…kitty cat is stuck in the…tree, can you rescue him?"

"Yes…ma'am…I'll chop the tree down."

"Oooooh fireman!" I ran my tongue up and down the length of his temple. I then took it down to the nuts. His eyes rolled to the back of him head.

He got jiggy with it. "Suck dem nuts…!"

I loved talking dirty! "I'm yo' Ho!" He smiled seductively, drove me crazy. "I'm your dirty, filthy Ho!"

"Who's your…daddy?"

"You are, baby."

"Damn, you suckin' it good, Ma…Daddy

wanna fuck, now!"

GODDAMN IT! CAN'T HAVE THAT!
THEN HE'LL KNOW I GAVE HIS PUSSY UP
TO SOMEONE ELSE!

I had a plan. "Sit right here, Daddy! Mama
gotta surprise for you."

He clapped. "Shit, I love surprises."

I rubbed my pussy for a few seconds and stuck
my fingers in his mouth. She sucked me down his
throat.

I backed away from him, rubbing my titties,
licking my lips, gyrating my hips like a stripper. I
winked, disappeared into the kitchen, snatched
open the counter and pulled out the white vinegar.
Rushing upstairs, I went into the bathroom, closed
and locked the door, snatched open a Summer's
Eve douche pack, inserted the comfortable nozzle
deep in my pussy and squeezed the juices
inside.....cleansing myself. Then I take out the
nozzle, open it, fill it half way with warm water,
and filled the rest with vinegar. I inserted the
rubber nozzle inside me once more and squeezed.
There, pussy was like A-B-C-Brand new. I felt it
getting tight.

I ran cold water over my face, gargled with
Listerine and stripped off my clothes.

"Baby get that pussy down here on my dick!"

Daddy called. I went downstairs, through the
kitchen and paused in the dining room, leaning on
the table. He stands up, his pants to his ankles,
muscled legs, gorgeous biceps, corn rowed hair, my
black Justin Timberlake. My hubby looked like

Justin.

I sashayed up to him, got in his face and we stared at each other.

He smiled. I smiled. He said, tonguing me at the same time. "I heard traffic was...hectic."

"It was."

"Good thing I took the day off today."

"Really? This is why you forgot to take out the neck bones."

He decided to ignore my sarcastic remark. "My boy is in town. Old college buddy. He's on his way here. He was stuck in traffic. He told me he saw this white woman he wanted to take out, but he was too scared to ask her."

He stroked his dick, slowly, gripping it tightly, the way he loved. "Oh, yea?"

"Yea."

"Where is he now?"

"He should be here within the hour. I told him my wife was making black-eyed beans and neck...bones."

"I want my neck bones long, juicy and thick." Back on my knees I went, taking him into my mouth. The mushroom head searched for my tonsils...found them. His nuts sporadically slapped my chin. Feeling slutty and adventurous, I lay back on the chair and he straddled my face, tea bagging my mouth. You know. Dig the teabags in the coffee mug, up and down up and dooown. He was trembling.

After an eternity of this, my lips tired, he hopped up, pushed my legs back and dove his tongue into my flesh. I quivered, I loved the way he ate pussy. My hubby ate good twat. I couldn't lie. He sucked the walls and the clit at the same time.

"Hold your legs, baby."

I hold them.

"Pull 'em back."

I obeyed. *After all, he was my husband!* He ate and fingered my desire, moaning for all to hear, telling me I tasted good.

"Rescue the cat, baby."

"Timber....down. come. the. tree."

He slapped my ass, leaned up to me and rubbed the head of his dick on my pussy, teasing the clit. Just the way I like.

"Damn, baby," he said, sliding it in. The head alone swell even bigger inside me and I instantly started coming, my thighs locking up, tears racing from my eyes. My baby put all his weight on me and started grinding inside me, sucking my titty, thrusting deeper and deeper.

"Baby I'm coming so hard."

The thug coming out of him, he pounded me, fast, long and hard, feeling all my extra juices on him. He loved the feeling. I had a good man, funny I cheated on him, but what he didn't know wouldn't hurt him. He would never find out.

The door bell rang as soon as my husband locked up and shot a huge load in my pussy. He was trembling, moaning, cursing. I loved to hear him come.

The door bell rang again.

He put on his clothes; I opened the hall closet and put on a floral dress.

I sprayed Febreeze, the best goddamn invention in mankind. Kill the sex smell out the air.

My hubby answered the door, looking beat and tired.

"Hey, Pat!" He told his friend, shaking his hand. He was excited to see him.

"Sup, dawg! I'm here! Dawg, you will never guess?"

"What, Dawg?"

"I got some pussy, dawg! And she sucked me up."

My hubby's eyes lit up. "The white girl served you up? Shit, where are my manners, come in!"

When I saw Dread Locks come into my home and locked his eyes on me we both did a double take without making it obvious. My heart dropped. I couldn't *breathe*. I had to lower my eyes to the floor.

Dread Locks said, "Is *this* your wife?"

I was so nervous, oh my God what the fuck is going on? This shit wasn't funny.

"Yes. Baby meet my homeboy Pat!"

We shook hands. He kissed it. "Dawg, you got taste."

I snatched my hand back. "Nice to meet you."

Pat said, "Did you cook the...neck bones yet, a Niggah starving!"

I just closed my eyes and wished I was dead.

Ź
Ø
Ń
Ï
Ń
Ğ

L
A
W
S

Hello there. Ahem. Yea. *You*! The one reading this page. My name was Veronique Sims Gregory. I was what you called a dime breezy, a dime piece, meaning I was a Top Notch, High Maintenance bitch.

I stood here, picture this, you could even close your eyes as I spoke to you with this smoky, feminine voice oozing the aura of Goulds, Florida, the Real Nasty Nasty Freaky Deaky Durrty South, feeling horny as hell. My lust burned me up like an unspeakable fire, leaving charred evidence all across my child-bearing hips. My silky hair pinned atop my head, a few weave curls dangle in my face. My piercing green color contacts were to die for as I carefully slid out of this silk blouse.

To my utter delight, Eric Bennet played on the stereo; it's unnaturally cold in my cluttered, need-to-clean-it-living room. Fred Astaire and Billie Holiday framed on my wall, juxtaposed with Martin Luther King...the lights were strikingly dim. I inhaled the scent of floral air freshener as I carefully popped an ecstasy pill, feeling tingly. I down some Grey Goose from the bottle, tenderly grip the neck of the fancy bottle like I gripped dick. Yes, dick! You see I LOVED dick! I couldn't get enough of it. My sex game couldn't be commercialized. I had to issue it out, like standard Military issue. You couldn't give a man all your good loving in one setting. I had more than one serving. There were thirty-seven calories and about two grams of fat in my lips alone. I was a hefty diet plan. Low in carbs and dangerously lean in cholesterol. Some men wanted a full course meal when you only had a tossed salad on the table. This was why I issued it out. I would give him a Kevlar one day. Then the next day a canteen. A few hours later, if he drinks from the canteen without spilling anything over his lips, I might give him some BDU's. Because when he gets between my legs I had a Meal Ready to Eat. Back in my wild days I didn't understand why men damn near knocked my door down to get to my body. Well…I did know why. I held my own in the sack. I sucked it with a purpose and took it like I had a pair. A pair of tits that was. But once the apple fell from the tree and began to rot on the ground I had to move on to the next lay.

Shutting out the outside world, I turned in slow circles, smiling before the reflection in my mirror. I admired myself for just a moment. I loved the way my breasts hung, perfectly created titties God certainly blessed me with.

I loved the sandy-red hair of my pubic region…the way the V-shape dipped into my groin.

The shape of my hips, many men said I had an apple-bottom ass. I was flattered. But I wasn't the type of bitch that wore boots with the fur, like the hit song goes.

I had high cheekbones, a broad chin and a sensually thin nose. It took two nose jobs to get it right. I was satisfied with the end result. And I wasn't going to talk about the Brazilian butt lift I got.

My feet were flat and pretty, I kept them in tip-top shape no matter what.

The Waterfall between my legs feels so WD-40, and it wouldn't surprise me if I had WD-40 pussy, but I didn't.

Meanwhile, the ex pill tearing me up inside, I wanna be touched, kissed, stroked and caressed. And since I couldn't get what I wanted, I danced to Eric's sexy voice. I feel quite...gay.

My hands massaged my huge titties, my nipples erect and ready for the plucking. I have a huge ass.

Or, as my ghetto girlfriends coined it, "Chile, you have a mouth-watering badonka donk."

I slapped it a few times, turning off Eric and putting on one of my favorite club jams called "Look Back At It," featuring Miss Khia (was Khia rapping this?), shaking my ass, like it just didn't stop. Pussy poppin' in the mirror. My weave job glorious.

I was a bit saddened because my father died yesterday. I was suppressing all my pain, all my turmoil, all my grief for a man who used to love me, adore me, buy me the world and treat me like a queen.

He was always there to greet me, smile at me, fix me food; he was the perfect role model, I always saw him reading books or the newspaper, he had an opinion about everything that came on the news; he was respected at his job, working at the Post Office for fifteen years. He always taught me things about life, like how to fight, how to take care of myself in public, how to carry myself, period. He was my champion, until I started fucking.

Let's be real about this shit. When a girl got her first piece of dick, suddenly daddy looked like a pile of horse shit, hoping he was really dog shit so you could step in his mess and keep on a-trucking to the next face and the next lay. When I started having sex, I wanted the whole pie, and I got a cake out of the deal. Sensations flowed through me as I rubbed my sexy, voluptuous hips... licking the lipstick on my lips, tasted like candy, sweet candy...

I brought a tit up to my mouth and I bit the nipple, dancing to this ghetto anthem. When "Take it Back, Ho" came on I went wild, rubbing my neck, humping the air...my hands trailing my neck...down to my tits...the navel...the Rocky Pit leading to my private region...

I broke zoning laws when I gripped my dick, *yes my dick*, and I started stroking, pulling, teasing, and moaning for all to hear. The Grey Goose chasing the butterflies in my stomach, praying for the goose bumps of my arms...my legs quivered, the drugs taking effect, I lay on the sofa, spread my legs and finger fucked my ass while I pulled my dick, tears racing from my face, wishing someone was here to do this for me.

I felt myself climbing the mountain, slapping the fog from my face and getting the moisture…rocky ledges I treaded, passion and I came face to face and we kissed, my hands shaking from the explosions that sounded in the pit of my pussy…I was falling, falling, trying to grab the ledge so I could pull myself out of the abyss.

Tears fall from my eyes and my body begin jerking as I begin coming, my muscles contracting. I couldn't breathe, my toes curled in the pumps.

I cried out for anybody who may hear me to come touch me, tease me or please me. I lay spent for a while, just staring at Billie Holiday, standing up, and taking off the strap on dick. Yes, I was a real woman, I just pretended to have a dick to fuck ya'll up. Glad it worked. Now get the hell out of my house, yes you, reader, I gotta shower, and get ready for my husband to come home and hope I get to fuck him with the strap on again.

Because, come Saturday, I gotta go to my father's funeral, and shed tears over a man who taught me everything I knew. After all, he did take my virginity forcibly, and made me keep it a secret for years.

Then made me fuck him with the very strap on I now put up in my safe, secretly mourning the loss of my virginity, a part of my soul lost forever.

THE
VET
Σ
R
ï

Ń
Λ
Я
Ï
Λ
Π

Frantically, she rushed into my office, closing the door behind her. She startled me and my personal assistant, Wanda from Coral Gables, Florida.

I had no idea who this woman was.

"Sir! You got to help me!" She looked frantic, and being that I was a male veterinarian, I wondered why she was in my place of business. This was not the police station, and the last thing I needed was negative publicity. I wasn't ready to debut on the 6 o'clock news.

I looked her over. She didn't have a pet; all she carried was an oversized Le'Diamond purse made from fake bear skin. She reeked of money, it oozed from her tenfold. "I need help. It's...it's my cat!"

Distraught, Wanda hopped up, and said, "Where is it? What's the problem?"

Wanda had twenty cats, at her trailer home. Her cats were her entire life. They were just like real people to her. And she fought over them like they were her own children.

Ok, *now* I was alarmed. Maybe she did have a genuine problem. I *loved* animals, especially cats. My mother died last year, and she was a cat lover. Did anything for cats. She had about five of 'em, so growing up used to dealing with cats was what made me want to be a Vet when I grew up.

"*Where* is your cat?" I stood up, walking around two metal tables, pausing in front of this sexy, petite black woman with the oversized earrings, the huge bangles, the tight lizard-skinned print pants and matching halter top and the long, flowing weave.

"Can we speak in private, I don't want to talk in front of your assistant, and this is an emergency." Tears started to fall from her eyes. Damn. Lady. *Don't.* Cry. I hated to see sexy women cry, if I could protect them all I would. This was the main reason why I didn't become a therapist or psychologist, couldn't deal with the crying.

"We can talk right here."

She was adamant. "I'd rather talk in private. I don't like telling my business with…" She gave Wanda the evil eye. "Others around, people talk too much these days and I don't wanna have to get stupid up in the Animal House, you feel me?"

"I hear you. But we follow strict protocol in

this building."

"Are you gonna help me or what?" she asked, getting an attitude.

Wanda shot her cuffs. "Is he helping you or your…cat?"

"What is it to you?"

"Where is the cat, ma'am, so we can take a look at it."

"It's a female. Ok, not an 'it.' And I don't like how you're *talking* to me."

"And you are full of complete crap."

The strange woman tucked her chin back. "I beg your pardon? Is this how customers get treated? I should call the board on your ass, bitch butt the fuck out of my business."

Wanda walked up in her face and I stood between them, facing this pretty stranger.

"*Sure.* We can talk. Come to my office." I put my hand on the small of my back and raised the right hand towards the door. I shook my head. "Right this way."

I gave Wanda a weird look.

She hunched her shoulders, whispering, "She looks like a nut case. Be careful…"

I nodded in agreement. But, something seemed very surreal about it all. I had to find out. My untimely visitor remained quiet.

When we walked into my office I closed the door, deep in thought. So far my day had been going good, I hope this sexy vixen didn't mess it up. I didn't like drama, and I didn't have any drama in my life. And I wanted to keep it that way. Kept my blood pressure down that way.

She was shaking, avoiding my eyes.

"Thank you doctor…" She was shaking her head, looking me over.

I was hesitant. "Dr. Ken Fredericks."

She shook my hand, and then I kissed it, cupping it.

"It's my *cat*." She fell silent.

My heart went out to her. Some people were close to their animals like family, I was close to my pit-bull Greg like that, and I would die and kill for my dog. "What's *wrong* with your cat? Did he die or something?"

She looked confused, a little withdrawn. "Well, *no*."

"Is he sick? You know several pet food companies are recalling pet food. Some ingredient is making animals across the country sick."

She looked alarmed. "Oh, no!" She covered her mouth, stunned. "I didn't hear about that."

I didn't mean to scare her. "Some have even died." Well damn, Ken, now you did it.

"No, *poor* things…" She stood in front of me, just as sexy as she wanted to be. It was hard not to try to flirt with her, since I was going through a divorce and my wife and I have been separated for eight months. I had no problem with finding pussy, call me the Pussy Bandit, but I had no desire to get new pussy when I was in love with Miss Old

Booty, meaning my wife. I looked her over while she stood there, trying to find the right words to say. I hoped her cat wasn't sick or dead. The length of the heels on her designer stilettos was identical twins with my dick, nine inches. I didn't need to be thinking about my dick at the office, but there was a stirring in my loins. And I couldn't stop the pleasurable feeling that washed over me.

She looked at me, with Come Fuck Me Good in her eyes.

"Can I have a seat?" she asked. Before I could say, "Sure," she pivoted and sat on the sofa by the door. I leaned against my cluttered desk, a little angry that the cleaning lady from Rhonda's Maids and Company didn't show up this week and dust my office down. I had back allergies, bad sinus problems and I couldn't work around all the dust. Which was the main reason why I didn't open the blinds, because once the sunlight shined through every continent of dust would be revealed to my naked eyes, sending me into a sneezing fit?

She looked at me, sizing me up, crossing her legs. She studied my framed certificates and degrees from school; just a coliseum of accomplishments was some of everywhere. Half of the achievements mean nothing to me because they were fake, computer generated. I used them as props for business, and it had been paying off for three years, since sharing this private practice with Leticia Marks.

"Ma'am, talk to me, because I have to get back to work." I opened my white medical coat and threw it on the desk, rolling up my sleeves, loosening my tie a bit, had it too damn tight, could barely breathe or swallow.

She was measuring her words.

"There's a *cat*...in my pussy that needs saving."

She eyed the look of shock on my face.

She danced in the silence a little longer than I had anticipated. I was still trying to allow her words to register in my brain. Standing up, she slowly approached me like a lioness on prey, slowly, leg over leg, and her hands on her hour glass-shaped hips, her amazingly full breast classically hidden behind loose clothing.

I was stunned into silence, my dick getting hard. I couldn't do this in the office! Outside the door I heard my name, "Dr. Fredericks, you're needed in Room 3." On the P.A. system. I *loved* my career. I took it seriously. It was my bread and butter. I didn't jeopardize it for my wife, so why would I start with a complete stranger?

"So...what are you going to." I swallowed hard. "Do with the cat in your pussy?" I couldn't help but smile. Women threw themselves at me regularly, but I turned 'em all down because HIV drove the human body like the Power Rangers controlling those Voltron-knock-off machines.

She paused in front of me, fiddling with my tie, looking over my chest. "Well, for starters the cat isn't just any cat."

Her lips were inches from mine, we stared into each others eyes, afraid to look away. "Isn't just any cat?"

"Dr. Fredericks, report to Room 3," said the P.A. system again, I ignored it.

Without further delay, she kissed me slowly, my tongue dancing with hers, her breath smelling like Lifesavers candy. Warm and moist, the way I loved for a woman to smell. I was distraught inside, I didn't know where this woman's lips been. What if she just sucked another man's dick? This type of thing was uncalled for, yet I was captured by her spell, her consistency and consistency was an aphrodisiac of mine. What if she gave it up to all men like this, but right now she made me feel young, and when I was younger, in high school, I was more focused on what bitch I could poke and stab with my dick then the school work. Score cards and strikes was the name of the game. The first one cum, wins!

Entranced, I drew invisible pictures on her naked arms, kissing her neck. What was I doing? I didn't know this woman, I could count the number of times I let my little head think for me in my 30 years on this earth, and that would be a total of 3 times. When my wife gave me some trim on the first date. When I lost my virginity with a girl I didn't know was my cousin. And when I had sex with her again when I turned twenty one. After that I have been thinking with the big head to stay ahead now my fingers were keeping abreast as they traced the outline of her erect nipples.

"The cat is a lioness. *Yes*. Wanting to feed the cubs in your nuts, Mr. Grown and Sexy Vet. You see. I been watching you for about three days, when I first saw you I was going into Publix supermarket, to talk to my cousin Tay because his girlfriend slept with Pierre, his god brother, clad in purple panties…and I saw you going into Party City. The finest…" She kissed me. "…thing…" She rubbed my hard on, softly squeezing. "…I…" She sucked on my neck. "…ever…" My lips she taunted. "…seen…"

I was flirty and extremely horny. I had month's worth of build up, just waiting to turn into Mt. Saint Helen. It was time to give the squirrels paid vacation, so they could stop slaving away in my testicles.

"You might have a problem with a leopard in your pussy. Cats hate water."

"You don't say, yet they love to drink from the Lake of Orgasm."

"I'm gonna have to…get that *cat* out of you." The chemistry between us was mind-boggling. I never cheated on my wife, and I loved the Good Book, the Bible, I believed in it, I was church-going and God-fearing, I believed in him with fear and trembling, yet this pussy had me trembling with glee, I wanted her, wanted to be knee deep inside her good pussy.

"When are you going to get started?"

"I'm gonna have to examine you thoroughly."

She challenged me. I loved challenging women. Made life more engaging. "Only if you use a thermometer…to *check* my body temperature."

I was breathless, couldn't believe I was so lucky.

This was every man's dream. "Yes, ma'am." With urgency, I picked her up and lay her on my desk, pushing files on the floor. I picked up the phone and told the secretary. "*Look* my *brother* has been in an accident. Cover for me, please."

"Sure, Dr. Fredericks. I will be praying for you and your family."

I hung up.

"Lying on your brother," she said, sitting up, pulling down her pants. I could smell perfumed pussy, cold mixture.

"I'm an only child, I don't have any brothers."

"*Clever* man."

Very intelligent, pretty lady! "With some good dick."

She kissed at me. "Get out of those clothes."

I saluted her. "Yes, ma'am."

She was duly pleased. "And when you use your thermometer, you got to realize one thing."

I studied her. "What would that be?" I was going to take off her heels, but I didn't. I left them on. Feeling the heat rising. Exploding in my nuts. I tingled all over. Like popping corn.

Her eyes bounced all over my face. "The temperature in my pussy is amazingly uncategorized, so once the vaginal juices get to bubbling from that scrumptious dick I see bulging behind your slacks, it will reach the level I like to refer to as Lava Intensity. I start to get all...rocky, getting 'em off. And turn to boulders when I explode. Might be too much for you to handle."

"Oh, I can handle it." I kissed her pussy,

tonguing her clit like we were long lost friends. Her eyes fluttered to the back of her head, her thighs trembling already.

"It's like that?" I asked her, spreading the pink walls, looking inside, marveling, appreciating and admiring. Looking for the cat, then the leopard. The one with the two cubs living in my scrotum sack mistaken as a kangaroo pouch. "I got a dick that won't quit."

"And...Oh yes, Dr. Fredericks...I got platinum pussy certified through the RIAA!"

I loved her dialogue, turned me on full throttle. "The RIAA, that's hot!"

"*Very* hot. Study the Sound Scan when you're jumping up and down in the softest place on earth."

"With traces of your lipstick across the head of my dick."

I loved this. She held my head and I went to town, using two fingers to penetrate her, and my tongue to torment the clit, the way my wife once taught me. She was shaking uncontrollably, moaning for just me and her to hear.

"Yes, daddy, goddamn baby..."

Feeling on top of the world, I stood up, massaging her shoulders, her arms...I loved the way she looked, a bit exotic, yet she was a 'hood girl.

She said "Where are you from?"

I took her left foot and sucked the heel of her shoe, running my tongue all over it.

"Perrine. Was raised down the street from where Goodfellahs, the Bar, is now. The beige duplexes."

Her hips were twirling all over my desk.

"Hmmm, I heard Perrine Niggahs got good dick." Narrowed eyes, perked lips.

"Yes, ma'am! My wife married me for my dick."

"Wife? Where is she?" She smiled graciously; her eyes telling me the Hell with your Wife!

"Heading for divorce court." I pulled out a thermometer from my desk, small and skinny-looking. I opened the wrapper and tossed the debris in the trash. I spread her legs, stroked the Kitty and inserted it slowly. She moaned sensually, smiling at me.

"What's the temperatures, doc?"

"Hmmm, can't say. Good pussy is sophisticated, requires quite a few...tests."

"What's the verdict of the pussy?"

"Average temperature."

"And the cat?"

"Above average."

"And the leopard?"

"Startling intensities! I may have to admit you into surgery and use my...Ho to shovel your turf."

She sat up, piling her hair atop her head, looking side to side like Marilyn Monroe, blowing me kisses. I wanted to suddenly give her the world but I only had pebbles to offer because my wife was trying to milk me for every penny, since we had two growing and impressionable sons to raise.

"When can we get started?" She took off her bra and wrapped it around my neck.

"After I check your heart beat." I put the cold instrument on her chest, listening to her breathing. She pushed it down to her dripping anatomy.

"And is the heart beat of the cat above average." She looked dead in my eyes, licking her lips. "Or normal?"

I couldn't take it anymore; the lust was eating me alive. I took off my pants, got up on the desk, didn't think about a condom, pussy this good couldn't be plagued with STD's, and I slowly slid up in her.

Her mouth open, she wrapped her legs around my waist, matching my rhythm, tears falling from her eyes. She whispered obscenities, came over and over, she was very easy to stimulate. She built my ego, made me feel beautiful; special...she traced the Goosebumps on my arms with her tongue, causing the butterflies in my stomach to fly through the fire, instead of the moths through the flame.

She was extra tight, my dick fluidly sliding in and out of her, her pussy fitting it like a glove. OJ Simpson's glove, too big...she was sobbing.

"Baby you are too much, feels so good baby goddamn baby work it, yes!"

Bumping sounds on the desk, we were butt naked and sweating, losing air, her hair plastered to her face...

I was licking sweat, pulled out and tasted her pretty pussy, swallowing her dried orgasms...loving her for the moment.

The freak in me now out and about, I straddled her neck and slid my dick in her hot mouth, I smiled like a Rodeo Show, watching her suck her dried passion from it, running her tongue across the head, gripping it, lifting it to taste my balls, humming different tunes every five minutes.

My head leaned back, I gripped her titties and humped her face, my sweaty ass cheeks clapping the faster and faster I went.

I felt it building, rising, Nefertiti was raising from the dead, looking for Akhenaton and Kiya, the Greatly beloved, to rule, to love, to roam...

King Tut was circulating from the pits of my nuts, spiraling like ballerinas past Chad, the Western Provence, searching for Egypt. Basking in the glow of the Sun God Aten...

When King Tut arrived I spurted down her throat. I was moaning so loud I had to stuff my shirt in my mouth, humping her face, she sucked wildly, getting out every seed, rubbing what spilt from her lips all over my nuts.

I was drained. Tired beyond understanding, I fell on the floor, moaning and breathing hard. She sat up, pleasured and appreciative.

A job well done on her face, she stood up, put on her pants and helped me off the floor. Exhausted, about to fall on my face, I pulled her into my embrace.

We kissed. Gave her some tongue. I grabbed her ass and possessed it.

"Gimme all that ass, baby," I said coyly, with a hint of Rico Suave meets GQ Smooth.

"Can we get to know each other?"

I thought about it. This was the answer, so I

wouldn't beat myself up over my impending divorce.

"Yes, we can."

"I would be thrilled."

I walked over by the sofa, putting on my pants. I then slid into my work shirt, drained, and sat behind my desk, leaning back, resting my eye balls, they were tired.

Before I knew it I was in dream land.

The sexy vixen finished putting on her clothes, looking herself over in the mirror, licking the little lipstick she did have on her luscious lips.

At her reflection, she smiled. Victory.

She opened her purse and pressed stop on the small digital camera. She needed to provide his wife proof that he was unfaithful, despite being faithful to her. He never cheated on his wife.

Now his wife's best friend, Myra, had all the proof she needed. Taking out the camera, she filmed him, snoring. She hated lying to him, but his wife stood to walk away with everything with his name on it. She agreed to give Myra $7,000 *if* she could pull it off, and Myra was only all too willing, she needed that down payment on her town house.

After she was done collecting evidence, she pressed stop on the camera and stuffed it in her huge purse. Time to go, she had business to conduct.

Going out into the hallway, she noticed the

lobby was filled to the max. Animals everywhere, all there to see Dr. Fredericks. Parrots were chirping over by an elderly woman clad in a mink, hot as it was in Miami.

She would play a little trick. Walking past the short black woman at the service desk, she turned the Closed sign around in the door, opening it.

"Ok, this establishment is now closed."

Chaos. "What? This place closes at 6 p.m."

"Yea, lady did you fall and bump your fuckin' head?"

"It's only 4 p.m."

Fire in her eyes. "I work for the association. Illegal practices has been run in this establishment, unless you all want to go to jail for the inmates to rape you and your goddamn animals, I would advise you all to leave the premises! Now!"

The people started leaving. Wanda rushed past a couple dogs and got in her face. "What are you doing?"

"Out, now." She pulled fake handcuffs from her purse. "Or I'll arrest you first, bitch now get out! This place is now closed, until further notice."

Defeated, Wanda pivoted on her heel, snatched up her purse and left. Myra watched in awe as her plan worked. Her hand on her hip, twirling the handcuffs, she watched angry patrons and animals leave in silence.

Once the building was abandoned, Myra said behind them, "This place will remain closed until my pussy says it's ok for the cat to come out and presume business."

She slammed the door closed, locking it, drawing down the blinds.

She turned and faced Dr. Fredericks, who was snoring so loud it drove her crazy. His pants half on his ass, his shirt open, his mouth agape.

"Time for round two."

She took out the camera, and went for seconds.

After all, dick that good needed another round.

± Ĥ Ë

Đ
Ï
Š

GUISE

"Baby, how are you?"

"I'm fine. Walking around the hospital. Tired as hell."

"You work too much, baby."

"You think so?"

"I'm your woman. I know so."

Soothed by the sway of tree branches and quivering leaves, I smiled, sitting outside the hospital on a bench.

"And how do you know?"

"Because I cooked for you the other day. When you got home you were so geeky. Sat at the table and asked for a Budweiser. I brought it to you in leopard print panties and matching heels. Tits and ass jiggling. I got on the table, got on my knees; put this pussy in your face. A few seconds later you were snoring."

I was smiling from here to Africa. "Word? I did that?"

"Yes, baby."

"As much as I love your pussy I can't believe it."

"You looked so peaceful. You snored, baby. You only snore when you're extremely tired. I grabbed a pillow from the bedroom and put it on the table. I cautiously laid your head on it, turned out the light and grabbed the couch. Watching my man sleep. You were so at peace."

"You always look out for me. I'll make it up to you."

"Maybe you should cut back on your hours. Our home is paid for, all of our bills are caught up and both of our vehicles are paid off, even though my Chrysler is running hot for some reason."

I was alarmed.

"I popped the hood and…"

I cut her off. "I don't want my lady popping hoods. I got it. When I get home I'll check it out."

A few women I knew walked by, waving at me. I waved back with a smile. I fucked them a few times, when I first started working here. As a man you always had to test new pussy when you were the new kid on the block. You had to find the weakest bitch in the group and make an example out of her. Once you did that she would sing like the famous canary and other women will start to a) kiss up to you and b) flirt. I had it down to a Science.

"I keep forgetting you are a certified mechanic as well as my RN doctor man."

"Funny." I stood up, looking at my watch. My break was nearly over. "I'll call you when I'm on my way home."

"Baby. Seriously. Consider taking some time off or cutting back on your hours. I'm missing you. We do need our time together."

"I promise, Baby. See you when I get home."

"I will." She kissed through the phone. "I love you."

"Same here."

"Say the damn words."

"OK. I love you, Sweetness."

"Bye, Daddy."

I flipped the phone closed, looking at the puffy white clouds differently. I loved her with everything in me.

My name was John L. Hammond. I stood 6 feet on the dot, with caramel skin and freckles all over my face. Long, curly hair I loved the masculine flair I gave off when I walked down the street. I loved the ladies. I didn't care if they were obese or skinny; I found beauty inside of their heart, eyes and smile. Which was why I became a RN? I worked thirteen hours days, six days a week. I didn't have time for anything else. Yes, I had a girlfriend. Her name was Sharonda James. I loved her with everything in me and we just moved in together after dating and getting to know each other for about three years. We had our ups and downs but we were both adults so we learned that communication and empathy were two key factors in making it work. She wasn't the jealous type. She knew I loved women.

She knew it because I told her everything about me. I never kept secrets from her, even though she never really talked about her past. I inquired about it but she'd close up, clam up and say it was too painful to think about so I stopped pressing her when I saw her tears. I loved giving her peace of mind when we curled up together, while Red Foxx entertained us on the TV, before we fell asleep. If a woman called my phone I always put it on speaker. She didn't want me to, but out of respect I did. I never left out of the room to carry a conversation unless I was cleaning up or something, then I was all over the place. She respected my privacy.

I loved how she touched me, like I was the most beautiful man in the world. Never have I encountered a woman with her flair. I fucked women from here to the Bahamas and never have I found a woman who not only matched me in the bed but she surpassed everything I thought I could do by fucking my mind first before she tackled my body. I lost a good thirty pounds since I have been sexed by this woman with the snake tongue and the hot ass.

They way she sucked all over my body, giving each individual spot its own necessary attention. The way she gripped my inches and made them feel like feet. The way she looked in my eyes making me talk to her. Yea, Mama. Suck that. Just like that. Damn, baby. I'm about to cum. Here it goes. Ah, baby. And she'd swallow every drop.

Before we even had sex for the first time we went to the clinic and got tested together. Got our results together. Then we went about two months after that and did it one more time. We were both clean. I hated wearing condoms when fucking my woman and she hated them too. So when the doctor gave us the green light I knocked the red light out of her clit with my tongue and the yellow light came tumbling from those big booty cheeks when I tapped it from the back and she got the intersections that ran wild all over the shaft of my dick.

She set me on fire with her gaze. She had soft ocean green eyes. Being that she was a Jamaican woman, her values and her temper ran deeper than any root I'd ever seen. Her body was to die for. I loved the way she dressed. She turned heads while being dressed from head to toe. She made wearing business suits look divine. She loved those long dresses and she smiled every time she wore accessories. She loved stilettos and getting her hair and nails done. She did her own hair, saved her about $1,200 a year. What I loved most about her was her business savvy. She watched the NASDAQ and the Dow Jones like it was Girlfriends or Martin re-runs. She read the "business" section of the newspaper faithfully. She knew what worked and what didn't. She got

Forbes, Black Enterprise and the Wallstreet Journal magazines once a month in the mail. Her head was always on money. She balanced our bank accounts and kept the receipts for everything. Before she came along I spent money left and right. I was lost and thought I had it all figured out. I had homeboys who weren't about nothing telling me I had something. That kept me stagnated.

I was always in the clubs looking for the next piece of ass. Life back then, when I was 17, 18 and 19, was all about weed, booze and Hoes. My mother told me that one day something was going to happen that would wake me up and see life for what it was: a game of checkers.

I dismissed her comment with a wave of a manicured hand.

Around Memorial Day, I was with all 8 of my boys. We were smoking weed, playing video games and drinking hard dark liquor. My head was spinning so I went into my friend Sammy's room and crashed in his bed. He was playing his PS2. Closing and locking the door, he and I were talking, both of us fucked up. One thing led to another and I wound up popping an ecstasy pill that was shaped like Mickey Mouse. He popped one as well. I started feeling tingly all over, and we were touching and kissing. I was hugging him and the flood gates of lust opened and I was washed with pleasure. Off came my pants and he was doing what he did. I wound up fucking him all night long. When we woke up next to each other the next day we didn't even talk about it. I was so disappointed in myself I called my Mom and told her, "Remember when you told me something traumatic was going to happen that would open my eyes and see life for what it was?"

My homeboy looked at me sadly, putting on his boxers, pants and Timberland boots. We go way back to the first grade.

She said, "Yes."

"Well, last night it happened. I see it now. And I gotta make some changes in my life. If God will forgive me for what I've done."

"Baby," she said, worried. "What happened?"

My boy walked up to me, handing me my shirt. I took it with a faint smile. I had no words for him. How was I to know the effects of that drug? How it would make me feel? The point that the pill and the dark booze altered my memory to the point I had become someone else?

"Mom. I got drunk last night. And I took a pill."

"Drugs?" She was stunned. I heard it in her voice.

I was already feeling bad. But I never lied to my Mom about nothing. That's why we're so close. She was my best friend, my best girl. My boys lied to their parents about everything. Not me. I told my mom the bitter truth about whatever I was doing. She respected me for it.

I inhaled. "Yes. I think its called ecstasy."

There was a mild shriek. "Baby, those things are dangerous." She was crying. I didn't want to

THE DISGUISE

hurt her. "Are you ok? Are you in the hospital, is that what you're…"

My eyes were misty. My boy Sammy touched my shoulder. I walked away from him, his hand falling to his side. I always cared for him. But I never thought I'd be having sex with the boy.

"Baby…" Mama called out.

"No, Ma." Tears fell down my face. I was having a hard time with this. "I'm ok, I'm not hurt or in the hospital."

"Are you telling me the truth?"

"Yes."

Sammy put on his shirt and grabbed his wallet and the keys to his pricey Jaguar he bought with his drug money. He was a big baller here in Maryland.

"So what happened?"

"Ma, I got drunk, popped a pill. And the next thing I know I was having sex with another man."

She said, "Baby. Oh my God. That's why you shouldn't drink and do drugs. But I'm your Mama, mistakes happen, baby. I don't look at you any differently. Give it to God baby and let him take care of it."

I smiled then. She always made me feel better about things I thought were major.

I looked at Sammy. "OK, I'll give it to God."

And I hung up, took him into my arms, fucked him one more time to get the whore out of my pelvic bone and I gave it to God. My flesh was weak being around him. Having sex with him felt good. I couldn't sit here and lie about it. But what was good wasn't always right. It was what it was, even though I had never been with a man before in my life.

And I was never with one again, because that lifestyle was not in my heart. Plus, despite being raunchy with the ladies, I loved God and I didn't want to go before him for anything homosexual. So I cut all ties with my homeboy. Sammy went his way and I went mine and I never told a soul.

That was years ago, and now I was in love with my girlfriend. She really curbed my appetite as far as spending money on dumb shit. I used to buy shoes every time I inhaled. But she taught me to get what I needed first, save for a rainy day. Save some more for the muggy days Mama never taught you about. And have your fun without working so much.

This was why I just turned in some papers to my boss. I was telling him I wanted to work three twelve hour days and have the rest of the week off from now on.

He smiled and nodded his head, saying he'd approve it.

I looked at him, clad in a light blue uniform. My name tag was crooked, been walking around all day.

He was sitting behind his desk. A man of class. Photos of his ten children surrounding him with college plaques and other awards. I had never been in his office before. I wasn't even supposed to be up on this floor but I wanted to see him personally.

"Just like that?"

"Yes. Just like that."

"So it won't be a problem?" I asked, trying to make sure I heard him correctly.

"Yes. Plus there are a few other workers who have been crying about more hours. So I can split them up amongst them and stay within the hospital budget. We are clocking down on a couple things here. And I just hired my son."

"Good for you. As I can see, you got them all on display here in your office."

"I know, tell me about it. But this son I hired I had never knew was mine. I recently took a DNA test and it turned out to be conclusive. He's mine, so I hired him because he needed a job and wanted to be close enough to me so we can get to know each other."

"Sounds like a story there."

"It is a story there. Considering the life he used to live."

"What life?"

"He was a rebel without a cause. A street thug. He shot a couple people and did some time. He has two kids of his own, a cute little girl, Naomi, who is 3 years old and a cocky son who is 5."

"Wow, Grandpa."

"I want you to train my son, if you don't mind. I know how you are with people and I know you'll do a fine job."

"No problem, boss."

"So when you come in to work tomorrow, you'll meet him and get things on the ball."

Damn it, I didn't wanna train anybody! I hated training people because they looked at you like Martians. I ran my hands through my unruly hair. "Got you. Well…" I looked at my watch. "Since its kind of slow today could I have the rest of the day off? I finished the paperwork on Miss Samuels. David is taking down her insurance information that he should have done in Registration. And Mr. George is slacking with mopping the floors around the reception area. Clients are complaining about a stench."

"Sure. Go home. I'll get on Mr. George. I heard he smokes pot in the bathroom. Can't be doing drugs on the job. Kiss that lady of yours, and tell her I said thanks for the brownies."

I shook his hand. "Thanks. Will do."

I snatched up my coat and was out of there.

When I got home I closed the door behind
me and set a few dozen flowers on the
dining table. Turning on the lights, I told
myself I should just open the blinds and let the
sunlight tin but I was tired.

I couldn't get my mind off work. Being in the
medical field was very promising. I encountered
people everyday that made me smile. No matter if
they enter the hospital with an attitude or not, I did
my best to show the clients a good time. I was
known to make even the beast laugh with envy.

I was against a lot of things in life yet I never
pushed my views on anyone else. I loved the gays,
I loved whites and blacks. I loved people from
other countries. I was a people person. Yet with
every culture and every sexual orientation of the

people I knew and didn't know, I set boundaries and they knew what lines not to cross because I verbally tell them with respect and a smile and if anyone tried that boundary, hoping I changed my mind then I modified the time spent with them and the friendship without explanation. I already crossed that line twice in my life with Sammy, thank God that was years ago.

When you saw me at the hospital here in Baltimore, Maryland, I was always talking to someone, asking them how was their day. What was going on in their life? I have been working there for seven months and already my superiors gave me the supervisor position.

With it came a lot of flack from my co-workers. Half of them never came to work, or was always late. Always complained about the work assignments they were given.

But now was not the time to be thinking about work. I worked so much even when I was home I was telling my girl to send off a fax or help me register a patient and she'd look at me cross eyed and say, "Man, you're off the clock. Get a grip."

I went into my bedroom and paused when I saw the photo of Sharonda on my nightstand. She was simply breathtaking. My heart fluttered with happiness, and I couldn't believe I was thinking shit like that.

I remembered how we met. I was just getting off a Hell Date with a fat girl. 'Til this day I will NEVER let a friend set me up on a blind date.

That woman had too many kids, too many problems and had the nerve to keep telling me what I was doing wrong on the entire date. After I cursed her big ass out, I went to a nearby coffee shop and bought a frappuchino. It came up to 5 bucks. I put it on my VISA because I didn't have any cash on me (spent it on fat ass at the Red Lobster) and I didn't feel like going to the bank.

She walked into the place looking fly as hell. I had never seen a woman dress so classy, yet put all the whores to shame who had their cleavage out.

She was behind me and I turned and extended my hand. I didn't care. I told her my name. "I'm Sharonda James." On her side was a portfolio. I offered to buy her what she was drinking. She got a frappuchino, like me. When I paid for it we talked some. She said she was from California, just moved to town because her divorce was finalized.

We grabbed the back table and talked for an hour. I loved the way she thought. I told her I worked at a hospital. She said she worked at an insurance firm. Nice. Before we left she saved her number in my cell phone and said she was single and available. So when I got home I called her and the next day we were on a date and we'd been inseparable ever since. I took her to meet my Mama a few times. Mom loved her from the get go. Sometimes, she checked on my mom for her, taking her the diabetic insulin she needed. I loved that about her. Having empathy for others.

While I was putting a sauce pan on the stove Mom called me. I looked at the called I.D. a few times, debating should I answer. Mama could be overbearing sometimes, especially if she didn't get what she wanted how she wanted.

I snatched up the cordless phone. "Sup, Mama."

I was dancing to some Marvin Gaye, filling the pan up with warm water. It'd boil faster.

"Hey, baby. How are you?"

I turned off the water. "Just getting in from work."

"You work-o-holic."

I smiled. "Tell me about it."

She paused for a few moments. "What are you doing now?"

"About to cook my girl some spaghetti."

She sucked her teeth, which I found rather unusual. "Such the gentleman. Just like your father was, rest his soul. Make sure you bring a plate by here."

Sure, Mama. Whatever you want! "I will."

"As a matter of fact have Sharonda bring the plate by. I like her, son. Do you think she's the One?"

My brows rose. She's probing. "I think she is, Ma. For the first time in my life I feel complete when she is near me. Nothing can possibly go wrong. I feel change in the air, I just do." *Shut up! You sound like a complete goddamn moron! Don't tell your*

I opened the island counter and took out a
huge Wok-looking frying pan to cook the ground
beef. I set it on the stove, turned the dial to "8"
and put in the meat. I took out the olive oil, and
two onions, one bell pepper and a red bell pepper.

"Well, when God is for you the devil can do no
harm. Only when something is lacking in your life
does your past come back to remind you where
you once were. Keep doing the right thing, read
your Bible, go to church and fellowship with
likeminded individuals and you'll be fine, baby. I'm
so proud of you."

"Thank you, Mama."

"Have you watched a program on TV profiling
escaped lunatic patients?"

"No, I don't get to watch much TV."

"Well they had a program on I was watching.
Some individual escaped years ago, from New
York."

"I'll ask my girl if she saw it. I'll look out for
it."

"Well, bye baby."

"Good bye."

"And please don't forget to have my future
daughter-in-law bring my food by."

"Ok. Better yet, Ma, I'll bring it. When she gets
home she'll be too tired to go back out the door."

"I respect that. You always have her best
interest at heart. At least I know I raised you right.

DAPHAROAH69   249

I'm so proud of you, Son. Such the gentleman you are. Muah. Good night."

I hung up and finished cooking my girlfriend's meal.

Sharonda James came home around 6:30 p.m. She smiled, hugging me.

"Hey baby, something smells good…"

I loved her so much. "I cooked for you."

She was in her kitty cat mood. "Really?"

We kissed. "Yup. Spaghetti."

She licked her lips. "With meat balls."

"Nope. Ground beef."

She looked sad. "But I love meat balls," she said, giving me some tongue, squeezing my ass. Electricity shot through me.

"Well…" I looked down. She sunk to her knees and unzipped my pants, pulling it out. Her warm mouth against my soap-smelling flesh drove me crazy. Looking at the ceiling fan, my hair falling behind me, the glow of the light emphasized the freckles on my face as she gripped and slurped.

"You like that, Daddy?"

"I love it."

My legs drumming together she lifts my shaft and took my balls into her mouth, making me moan even louder. So sensitive down there, yet she was gentle and assertive. She was rolling her tongue across them, my dick lying across her beautiful face.

"Yummy. Taste good."

She got up to her feet and went into the kitchen. I started behind her.

"No, stay right there," she instructed. I stood by the dining table, waiting to receive whatever she was to give. How did I get so lucky? How did I find a girl like her?

Her fine ass stood in our kitchen, crawling out of her skirt and jacket. She wore lacy panties and a bra. Those tits and that ass was slamming. Jesus. She opened the pot and put some sauce on a table spoon. Flicking her tongue in it, she held an open hand under the spoon walking to me. She gave me some more tongue.

Getting back on her knees, she said, "I told you I like my sauce with meat balls…"

She used her fingers and spread the sauce on my dick and balls. Some on my ass. She knew I loved getting ate out as well, couldn't lie.

She put it back in her mouth, moaning her approval. Her huge earrings dangling fiercely, she cupped my nuts and deep throats my shaft. I was about to go out my mind feeling her tonsils quiver as I throat fucked her.

She then sucked sauce from my balls, gripping my ass. Her nails dug into the right cheek.

She spun me around and my hands found the entertainment shelf. Marvin was still singing. She spread my ass and dove her tongue all up in there, my eyes fluttering closed.

"You like that baby?"

"I love it."

She stuck a finger deep in my ass and reached around and jacked my pole. I was humping her finger, her tongue and lips occasionally caressing my ass cheeks.

"I love it, girl. Damn. Give me that Jamaican Rum."

She worked me so good my body began to lock up. I saw stars dancing with the spinning ceiling fan blades. My skin crawling, my heart pounding, I could hardly breathe.

There was a knock at the door but we ignored it.

"I'm about to come."

She crawled around me and I snatched her by the weave. I came all across her face while she sucked me from her fingers.

"Damn, baby. Damn…" My chest felt like it was about to explode.

She stood up, wiping my come from her face, sucking it from her fingers. I loved her nasty ass. I pulled her to me, gripping that ass, and gave her some more tongue.

"I love you," I told her.

"I love you, too," she responded, stars in her eyes.

"Will you marry me?" I asked her.

"Yes, baby. I would love to."

Another knock at the door. This time, more rapidly.

"Who's here?" she asked. She was confused.

"I don't know. I didn't invite anyone over. And our guests always call before they come…"

She said, "I'll get it, probably the neighbors."

Her ass bounced as she walked to the door in heels. She answered and it was eight cops dressed in S.W.A.T. attire.

"It's her!" one of them screamed and they thunderously burst into my apartment, apprehending her.

My mouth fell open in shock.

I was repulsed, my skin crawling madly. "It's her, what?" I asked, confused. I was terrified. "What's going on? What did my fiancé do? Her name is Sharonda James, clearly you made a mistake!"

A few of the S.W.A.T. cops came over to me and asked for I.D. I gave it to them.

"This is my apartment. And hers. What did she do? I'm marrying her."

A female cop pulled the ski mask from her face and said, trying to be hard-assed, "You won't be marrying her anytime soon."

I was shaking my head. "What she did, please somebody tell me something!"

My mother walked past them and said, "Son, I'm so sorry."

I rushed up to her and took her by the arms. "Mama, what in the fuck did you do?"

"Son, her name isn't Sharonda James. It's Eleanor Clamps, the escaped patient from the show I watched on TV. She been in hiding for three plus years, disguised as your girlfriend."

My heart died as I took Mama into my arms and closed my eyes as tightly as I could.

My world torn down the side, I felt like crap. As quick as lightning, my heart had walls up. I wouldn't talk to the police; I wouldn't even talk to my own mother.

She was sitting next to me on the back of the cops truck, rubbing my back. I had a cup of coffee. Sipping it as if I was dying. Inside, I was already dead. My heart, once teeming with life now was the golden sand and rubble of the Sahara Desert.

My home was all over the news. The neighbors were out and surrounding me, offering their love and support. They loved Sharonda. We all did. She had us all fooled.

Mama had on her lap a picture of Sharonda's mug shot. She'd been to prison for killing her entire family. She believed they were possessed by demons and she claimed the murders were God induced. "God told me to do it in a dream so I woke up, grabbed Daddy's gun and killed them all."

"No wonder she didn't want to tell me about her past," I told Mama, rubbing her hand. "I used to ask her and she'd clam up and start to cry. I thought she was abused or something."

Mama, opening her Bible, said, "I told you, when something is lacking in your life your past comes back to haunt you, Son. It wasn't your fault. How were you to know?"

"I had asked her to marry me, Ma. She said yes."

She said, "Oh, Son. I know it hurts. But you're strong like your father was. You'll get over it."

I hopped up to my feet, snatched her Bible and threw it towards my apartment. A few cops looked over and a couple news crews were on stand by, talking into their mics, painting my life, my apartment and my ex fiancé.

"Please. Don't go there about God. Please, Ma. Don't. Now is not the time."

"Son, its not God's fault."

"You're right, Ma," I said, eyeing that crazy orange hairdo she had. I closed my eyes, inhaling. "This is incredible. For three years I was in love with a psycho."

Mama had tears falling down her eyes. "…Son…"

"Why didn't you tell me, Ma? Why didn't you warn me?"

She stood up, beautiful in an African robe but right now I was miffed by her.

"Son. I tried to get her to come to my house, where S.W.A.T. were waiting. I told you to have her bring me some food, but you were adamant about bringing it yourself."

"So you lied to me."

"Son." Mama touched my shoulder and I walked past her. I went over to the cops. "What do you need from me? I got a fucking life. Take the psycho, and leave my house. If not I'll get a fucking hotel room, I have to work tomorrow."

They were very sympathetic and understanding. They know what I just lost. My love. My life. The woman who changed my life.

God why did this happen? What was the reason?

They told me my apartment would be on lock down a few days. They talked to their superiors and I was granted to take what I needed for work. With another cop with me, why who knew, I felt like a stranger in my own place. I worked hard for my crib. And this bitch came along and destroyed it. I packed my medical uniform, socks, underwear and shoes.

I grabbed my hygiene bag. My wallet I slid in my back pocket and I grabbed my car keys. I looked at Sharonda's car while going to mine. Damn it! I was missing her already. I walked over to Ma and kissed her.

"Mama, for the next few weeks just leave me be. I'll be fine. I need some time alone. I gotta train some new dude tomorrow so I'm checking into the hotel."

"You can stay at my house."

"I don't wanna be bothered if I do."

"Go ahead baby. I want you with me so I can look out for you."

"Mama."

She was stern. "I'm your mother. Be obedient and you will see the glory of heaven. And before you go do me one favor."

"Yes," I said silently, putting my bags in the car.

"Go get my damn Bible, and get it now!"

I moved like a flash.

I stayed up all night, lying in the bed. I had never cried so hard in my life. My Sharonda. My sweet, sweet Sharonda.

I turned on the computer and Googled her name. All sorts of shit popped up. Her mother was gorgeous. Her father had been a Marines' Vet. She had three brothers and two sisters. Sharonda AKA Eleanor Clamps killed them all. Gruesome pictures were there before my eyes. My Queen. She wasn't even Jamaican. She was half Bolivian and half Black. Her family didn't have any ties to Jamaica what so ever. Her father had his own business. He was heavy into stocks and bonds. Sharonda was his secretary. So that's where she got the knowledge from. Her business savvy she got from her money-hungry father.

He was indicted on several tax frauds, along with her mother. They swindled $56,000 from a major corporation two months before Sharonda killed them.

I was moving the mouse like crazy, reading anything and everything I could on her, trying to understand why she did what she did.

I came across an article from New York. Sharonda was on the front. She looked ravishing, and the breath left my throat. I loved her so much. Something in my heart pulled me back to her and I couldn't explain it. Something was there, something I wasn't seeing. Maybe it was because of the embarrassment she just put me through. But I loved her and I wanted an understanding. I needed to know everything. I needed to form my own conclusions based on my own investigation. There were three sides to every story. His story. Her story. And the truth.

The truth never changed form. People were chameleons. They changed whatever they had to change just to fit in, to feel special. To be liked. To be loved.

Hadn't Sharonda done that? Change? To fit in? To feel special? To belong?

I believed in my heart she truly loved me for me.

I couldn't honestly believe she would kill me or cause me bodily harm, especially after bringing me three years of pleasure.

That told me an innocent soul resided in a sick body, sick because of the newspapers and news shows coloring her life in a sick way.

Should I take their point of view or my very own? Just because someone said it, just because TV showed it (which was the most unbalanced system in the goddamn world), just because magazines screamed it didn't make it right or true.

I clicked the link and read silently to myself. The glow of the screen shining on my face.

Woman says God told her to do it

New York. 2005. Eleanor Clamps, daughter of Marine Veteran James Clamp, was the picture of raw beauty. She graduated with honors from Morris High School in the Bronx. At an early age she loved church, often winning Bible Slams by reciting every scripture she'd ever read. She was labeled a child phenomenon by age 9, having recited 145 verses. Her I.Q. was astounding. Her father and mother praised her. When she turned thirteen she claimed white men pissed on her, calling her black skin a disease. The man was caught and is currently in prison finishing his sentence. She wanted to be an accountant when she grew up so she started reading every book she could on financing, stocks and bonds, money and marketing and making money work for you. She made the Honor Roll ever semester since the fifth grade. Teachers fell in love with her knack for working hard and getting the work done. She set the example of what ever American kid should be before she even hit the tenth grade. Colleges scouted her before she hit the eleventh grade. Offering to pay her room and board and her studies if she enrolled in their schools. She chose a Christian College.

DAPHAROAH69

She was against violence and detested deceitful people. A tenth grade essay paper she aced, she wrote, "If I could rid the world of every bad person I would. The bad has it good and the good has it bad. If I could erase every starving belly from a child and replenish it with love and food I would rob every money-hungry fiend, every greedy cooperation, every robber, every dope dealer and use the money to make sure no one ever starved again…

Could this be the reason why she murdered her family and said God told her to do it? Because her brothers were notorious dope dealers who had enough FEDS combing their activities. Did she murder them because her brothers murdered countless black men and walked off Scott free from the court rooms? The same brothers labeled "The Sick Marine Brothers." The same once promising black men who were smart as a professor yet sold more drugs and killed more people then I knew in recent memory? The same men who fathered children from twelve different women around the globe while serving the Marines? The same men who did nothing for their offspring and publicly bashed the women they once promised to marry?

Did she murder her father because of his crookedness, having a wife who shepherded every crooked thing he'd ever done? Did she murder him because of all the cheating he did behind his wife's back, fathering four kids out of wedlock and hid it from her knowledge? Did she murder her own mother because she lived a double life? She was a very respected interior designer but when the fading sun set she traded in her classy threads for the hooker pumps and attire and she hit the strip with a long blonde wig, thick Bandi shades and fishnet stockings, charging Hollywood-types a leg and an arm (And a couple noses) just to get a whiff of the passion fruit incarcerated by her lacy panties?

Even from the stand, she was an innocently pure young African American woman with her value system set higher than anyone I'd ever encountered in my life. She never cursed and she was passionate about her beliefs.

She said, quote, "…Every murderer, rapist and crooked man should die if they harmed or killed anyone else. I believe in that. God told me to kill my family, its better their bodies die from earth and have a chance at heaven when they're judged rather than their entire bodies going to the pits of hell. I saved them from themselves. All the lives they took, the way my Mama whored all over New York, the way Daddy fathered other children and left the mothers to care for them, struggling.

The way Mom and Dad hid the secrets from each other. The number of people my brothers murdered and they got off without a scratch on their rap sheets. God told me to do what was right. He told me in a dream. Had I not killed them they would still be alive, murdering people, hooking for money, fathering kids, etcetera. I did the world a favor."

Was she right? I agree with some of the things she said. But does that give her the right to be judge and jury, especially after a judge and jury let the Sick Marine Brothers walk out of the courtroom free men.

Later to turn around and murder more people over this out-of-control Drug Game?

She pleaded insanity and the jury found her guilty by reason of insanity.

They dispelled the death penalty, saying she had a chance of being saved. A few call her a murderer. But a

*nation is calling her a Martyr, and she's still living and
breathing.*

Hank Lloyd
New York Chronicle.

I was in shock after reading the paper. I had to read it a few more times to make sure I read it correctly. I knew that deep down, in my opinion; she wasn't the bad monster everyone made her out to be. And I couldn't blame Mama for calling the authorities. She probably thought my life was in jeopardy.

I turned off the computer and masturbated, thinking of my ex girlfriend's face. I swore my fingers remembered her touch. Encoded in the fingerprints must have been her soul because I was on fire. The sweat came in no time. I wallowed in it, tossing and turning in the bed, stroking my stick. My toes curling, I cried out for her and got nothing but air. This was a travesty. How did I break free? I was still ball and chained to her. I still loved her. As weird as it may be.

I focused on the head only, neglecting the rod. I spread my legs so my nuts could have some playing room.

When my body went into spasms I thought I would fall asleep but it didn't quite work out that way.

Deeply saddened, I washed up and set the alarm for 6:30 a.m.

Sleep seemed to zoom by because, before I know it, I was cursing out the alarm clock when it sounded off. I fought to get up. I didn't want to open my eyes but I had to, my heart set on losing Sharonda. Men praised good pussy and Snoop Dog said in a song that his trick had some "killer pussy," but what about "psycho pussy?"

I showered, balling under the warm water. Why it hurt me to find out my love was a lie was crazy. I always told myself I wouldn't cry over a woman and there I was, falling at the seams. I was out the shower and drying off, crawling like a zombie into my clothes. I was out the door and in my car by 8 a.m. I got to work in no time. When I got there I made my way to my boss's office to train the new recruit, his son. I wasn't in the mood. I saw my boss sitting at his desk, looking tired himself.

"Long night?" I asked.
He looked up at me, refusing to smile. I studied his eyes.

"I'm so sorry about Sharonda, man. My son and I caught it on the news. We were watching sports and the show was interrupted with your life flashing for everyone in the U.S."

"I don't want to talk about it."

My boss understood. "My son is here and he's ready to learn."

"Where is he?"

"Behind you."

I turned and had epic heart failure.

"Sammy, meet your training coach…"

Oh, no! Sammy, the only man I ever fucked, the man I was in love with, the man who got high with me on ecstasy and made me come, was my new co-worker. I closed my eyes. I shook his hand, opening my eyes. His skin on mine exploded my lust into horny bitches with tits. My dick was harder than a brick. Images of our rendezvous skyrocketed through my brain, making me moan. My legs trembled and I couldn't think. I loved the way he touched me that night. The way he said my name held me captive. The way he felt was fire. His ass was so good it shattered every piece of pussy I ever had. He knew how to take my dick, how to move and what to say. He built my ego and made me come a hundred different ways. And now we worked together? I knew that deep down I was going to fuck the hell out of him. I wanted the ass again; especially now Sharonda tore my world apart. I needed nurturing…I needed to be held, sucked and touched. And Sammy would do the trick.

He smiled big. "I can't wait to start this training. I know he'll…show me the ropes. And I want to know…the ropes." He licked his lips. I licked mine.

My boss said, "That's my son!"

ĤËẛV¥

CONVERS

A
T
Ï
O
N
S

Indifferent, I came into my living room, disgruntled and a little pissed because my employer tried to cut my pay by twenty five percent. *Bullshit,* I tell you. Two things a bitch didn't mess with, my pussy and my money. Simple. My money, because I was married with children, so unlike Al Bundy, mind you. I had bills, bills, bills and I didn't remember Kelly, Michelle or Beyonce forking over no money to help a Niggah. And Lord knows a Niggah or a bitch better not tamper with my wife's pussy because when I have a good day, bad day, fucked-up day or holiday I take it out on the pussy.

I may seem a bit presumptuous and all that

good shit. I molded the pussy so it curbed to my dick. Seriously. I loved my wife's pussy so much I helped her douche, bathe, shower and take care of it. It's mine! And I make sure its mine, which was why she had my initials right next to it, on her thigh, so if she did creep like TLC (and remember they didn't make hits anymore, feel me?) a Niggah would see my initials and a small colored tat of my face cheesing in his face and that was enough to make any Niggah lose an erection and get gone.

You looked sexy, baby, and I knew you like to "straddle me and be in control" when we did the nasty; but sex wasn't on my mind right now because I put my (our) 401 (k) in jeopardy. Because I had a knock down drag out bout with Boss Lady. I should say Boss Bitch! And my boss, Henrietta's bald-headed ass (who always wore skirts her twelve year old daughter should be wearing) gave me some song and dance about the company (a Cellular company by the way with thirteen million users) losing money and I told her, slamming her office door closed, "You're full of shit. Projections were up twenty five percent last quarter, that's thirty percent higher than the previous year so please don't give me this song and dance about the company losing money when the only song and dance I hear is the H.B.I.C. either authorizing unnecessary vacation times to these favorable Niggahs in here or you're nicking and diming the company to bankruptcy."

She looked whorish with that Lil' Kim-looking

wig on her head. This woman had plastic everything done to her face. She tried to take any image of the ghetto from her very existence. Telling people she was from the East Side of New York, that her Mama and Daddy were lawyers. Running a firm together. Bitch ain't any Niggahs in America doing it *that* big! At least not the people I knew. If there *were*, show me! Her Mama was dead and her Daddy killed her, which was why he was currently serving thirty years in prison without the possibility of parole.

She huffed and puffed but didn't blow my goddamn house down because I was an angry black man, not a pig, who was two months behind on a $1,200 mortgage. That's what I got for trying to splurge in Miami, Florida. I lived in expensive, sorry ass Kendall to be exact, when I was used to snow, chains on my wheels, New York and the assholes it catered to.

Boss Bitch tried to snub a brothah. "I don't appreciate your tone, for one and for two I should have your job."

Her words didn't intimidate me. "Why are you nervous?"

She was shaking something terrible. "I'm not...uh, nervous and you need to get out of my office."

I looked out of the window, loosening my tie. Loosening your tie before you clocked out was grounds for an immediate write up. These bitches were very anal retentive about men looking GQ of the year, which was why our cell phones were up by that percentage because women, lonely women, depressed women, women who needed a man only got the phones hoping to get the Agent's phone number. And it didn't quite work that way...well, not with me.

I was on a mission. Usually, when people messed with me I remained quiet and chopped it up to the game. But sometimes these women got besides themselves, and all of 'em was mad at me anyway because they couldn't get my dick. That's for the wife. And the wife only.

I never cheated on her. Never.

S he was picking up the telephone to call security. I been with this company five years, never missed work, put it before any and everything in my life and she was about to call security? I was their star worker. I was Employee of the Month seven damn times. Seven! The company vehicle I owned, a Chevrolet, was the reward. Did she forget about the dinners they invited me to and the trips? I still have all the awards and the certificates were worth $500 each. I have twenty-four of 'em. Haven't cashed them in yet. I made this company so much money that it was pathetic. And now that I challenged her she threatened me? Something wasn't right and I was going to find out, no matter what.

"It's funny," I told her.

"I don't have time for this. I have a company to run. And you've become very disruptive."

270

"Disruptive."

Her brow rose. "Disruptive."

"You are puzzling the fuck outta me."

"Twenty dollars come outta your check for cursing on the clock."

"Bitch take it all, how about that."

Her hands were shaking, she looked high.

She spewed, "Get outta my office, last warning. Clock out, go home and come back tomorrow refreshed and your old self."

I stared her down, approaching her. She swallowed hard. I felt it.

"Make me clock out. I am scheduled to work until my desired time. And not a moment before." I stopped two feet in front of her, looking her over. I inhaled. "Tell me something."

"What." She hit the panic button.

I laughed out loud, stuffing my hands in my pockets.

"I don't see any earthquakes, so why are you nervous? You're about to drop the phone." A few beats of silence. "Why are you shaking?"

She sucked her teeth and nervously ran her bejeweled hand through her long, curly Queen B wig. Those diamond rings had to cost about a thousand a piece.

"I never seen you like this, and ever since Virginia Tech I have been more guardedly cautious."

I was deeply offended. "Bitch, this is a cell company. Niggahs go 'postal,' not psycho!" I was enraged. "This isn't a college campus. We never fucked. I am not losing a relationship. We're not together. I am not Asian. I would advise you to drop the phone."

I started for the door. I didn't need this, not today. I would clock out and go home and take out my frustration on my wife in bed. I loved Frustration Sex. The best kind.

"…Security…Can you…, uh, come to my office…" She was stuttering terribly, sounded like she was Asian.

I didn't care. On second thought, I paused, pivoted and just looked at her. None of this made sense.

"I remember last year," I went on, approaching her like a lion about to pounce a buffalo. That lion was starving, wanted blood, hadn't eaten for days, didn't care about drinking from lakes because the only stream he wanted to drink from was the stream that led to his pay cut being reinstated.

Stoic, she was watching me, daring me to do something.

I went on. "…On your walls were cheap Big Lots and K-Mart pictures, really cheap shit, shit I wouldn't give my blind grandmother on Mother's day. And now…" I looked around the amazingly crafted and decorated office.

"Picasso…Leonardo…Van Gogh…pricey shit."

I stopped at her desk and moved the mouse 'til the DMX screensaver vanished. The online screen appeared. She needed to lose this "Earth Link" shit and get with America Online.

HEAVY CONVERSATIONS

I clicked on "search." I typed in Van Gogh. Paintings come up dramatically, thanks to DSL. I clicked on the icon matching the painting on her wall. It came up with the speed of light. *Hmm*: $45,000. There was a special serial number under it, letting buyers know if the paintings were authentic duplicates. I scribbled the number down with a pen I took from her cup holder.

She watched me. She said more calmly, "Disregard, false alarm. I'm ok." She hung up.

I walked over with a purpose to the painting. I took it off the wall. I lay it on the Oriental carpeting. Last year she had bare tiles in here. Now I feel Blackanese with all this Oriental shit. Last year she had little tits. This year her tits were bigger than a little bit. Rumor had it that she had $7,000 breast implants.

I shook my head, looking over the serial number. The numbers matched. I stood up, sighed, head to the floor and she paused behind me. I looked up at her with a sneer. She jumped out of her skin. "In a year...you upgraded yourself from a funky muthafucking Mazda to a fucking Lexus coupe. A 2007. It was fresh off the goddamn presses. Cash! Paid for the day you rode out of the dealership. You were flossin'. You got your hair done every week. Van Gogh cost 45 thousand. Your three story home in Kendall cost half a million dollars. You got the bitch seven months ago and already you only have about two more payments and you own it. You make, supposedly, $30,000 a year. How in the living hell are you affording this lavish shit? On *your* salary? But the company is losing money?"

She laughed nervously. "You don't know what you're talking about. I make honest money."

"Whatever. Listen, bitch, if my pay isn't reinstated before the last drop of piss falls from the slit in my dick your job will be stuck so far in your ass the judge is going to say 'Henrietta, that's bullshit!' by the time the goddamn gavel drops, *Ho*. Now get busy before I phone the Feds and have all you stupid bitches probed and investigated for goddamn theft of company funds…"

She laughed again, finding this all funny. I walked to her, glared deep into her eyes, snatched her by her hair and pulled the bitch to my face. The smile died. I meant business.

"…And oh yea, my office loves Oriental carpets, Tiffany lamps, and Van Gogh paintings, whoever that muthafuckah is. And since it's my anniversary today, mail my wife some Gucci silverware and those panties with the vibrating balls. I think I will clock out early."

I looked at my watch, releasing her. She stumbled backwards, calling me something under her breath. I didn't care. She then covered her face, sucking in air.

"Time to go home. UPS better beat me there. I'm going to the gym first to sweat this shit outta my system. Then I might grab a Heineken and then go home to my loving wife."

Without saying another word, I spun on my

HEAVY CONVERSATIONS

heels, snatched open the door, pat the security guard Dan on his shoulder and said, "How do you do?"

I whistled down the hallway, out into the sun, to my simple Ford F-150 truck and out into commuter traffic. I made a stop at the gym but didn't get out. Rolled a blunt and spent a couple hours smoking it, talking on the phone with my brother about his trip to the Cayman Islands…and once I was stoned I stopped by the Citgo gas station, bought two Heinekens, popped the top and drank them so fast I thought I was drinking Kool-Aid. I wanted an immediate buzz.

Feeling good and tipsy, I drove home and through the front door I went. Happily, my wife stood up and hugged me. I hugged her back. She knew something was wrong. When I came home high she knew instantly. But she didn't get lippy. She became very understanding, which was what I loved about her. Her body felt so good against mine. I felt the moisture of her breath on my neck, sent me hay wire.

"Hey, baby." She said.

"Hey baby," I said

"I think you're so handsome, baby," she said, sucking up to me. I knew what she could suck up to. A Niggah needed his dick sucked, it was one of those days but I didn't tell her. Today was special.

"And you're beautiful, my Queen."

"Do you know what today is?"

"Our anniversary, baby."

"My pussy is wet, darling. What are you going

to do about it?"

My flame was ignited, unseen gas seeping from the love in my eyes combusting in my loins where the gris gris and the Louisiana flavor of my heritage explodes in my medulla with a force that pushes me to her lips. It took a minute to realize I was on my knees, dirty little bitches, and was tongue kissing her clit through the panties. I smiled at the rotating little ribbed balls. Henrietta was right on time. I lift her up, her legs over my shoulders.

She faces the front door, in the air holding my head. I face the kitchen, pussy in my face. Hmmm.

My legs shake because I live to pleasure her. She loves those Zane and the King of Erotica novels. I hated both of them...

When I put this dick on her ass, she wouldn't be thinking about the King and the Queen of Erotica anytime soon.

She shivers and shakes. I smile and munch. A delightful burp. I am full. I separate her pink curtains like I am 20th Century Fox. And the red carpet found her passageways. She quivers some more. A kiss on the clit. She says I love you. I say I love you, too.

You say the key to Miss Kitty is in my words. Nah, baby it's in my tongue. You always liked for a man to divulge in heavy conversation. You say something, baby?

Nah, I am talking to your pussy, not you. Didn't Mama tell you never to interrupt grown

HEAVY CONVERSATIONS

people when they're talking?

I could remember when I stepped off the plane in Knoxville, Tennessee a couple years ago and you, the most beautiful thing I ever saw, God's forgotten leaf he plucked, smiled at me. I tried to pretend not to notice you. I was over at the baggage claim a couple seconds later.

My long, resilient hair was freshly braided in tiny micros. Took my mother five hours of stopping, flirting with her husband, who wasn't my Daddy, and drinking her Michelob beer, just to finish. She must have slapped me with the comb a billion times.

I was tender headed. On both heads. My sculpted body waxed, nails and toes in a nice pink and white French Manicure...

I looked in your eyes. I saw your pupils separate to reveal irises that wanted me to see you as Pretty, Hot and Thick. You were Elegant, Sexy and Perfect.

And with all that behind us, and the passionate session that followed, we are now in the present scene, married with children, you are my rock and diamond, my sapphire when I was mad and my refuge when it started to rain and refused to clear out. You are my soul mate.

I love you, and yea, pussy I love you too.

No need to get jealous.

The phone rang and we ignored it. The machine picked up after the third chime. I smiled, my mustache tickling your moist opening when I heard Henrietta's voice.

DAPHAROAH69

You were moaning and silently cursing me.
Yea, baby!
Eat! Eat it good! you said.
I smiled.

*T*his is Henrietta. *Your office is re-decorated with Oriental Carpeting and Tiffany lamps. I replaced your bathroom with something more edgy and high tech. And above your cushioned chair—I threw that other old decrepit chair out—is the Van Gogh painting you wanted. And you just got a 15 percent raise. You start management training Monday. Happy Anniversary.*

I hope your wife loved the Gucci silverware and panties she signed for before you got home. Since it was your big day I put Rush Service on it. Luckily they had a warehouse not too far from your place of residence.

Welcome to the management team.

Looking forward to seeing you.

And when the phone clicked I lowered my Pretty, Hot and Thick wife down to my level and I fucked her standing in place. In love and with a satisfied smile. She felt so soft, my dick curbing her pussy to great new heights. She shivered so much she had to hug me, slamming her pussy onto my shaft, looking me deep in the eyes, moving and rising with me, trying to make daddy cum.

HEAVY CONVERSATIONS

That's right, baby, get that nut outta me. Work it, baby, pull those titties out. Yes. Pop one in my mouth.

I felt my soul building up, my wife and I sweating…rising, I felt explosions in the base of my nuts, I was breathless, breathing her air, becoming one, loving her, needing her…obsessed with her, I loved this pussy, I was about to come, oh God I was about to explode. Boom, it spurted on the inside of her and she began coming with me, both of us exploding together—

"Daddy! What are you doing to Mama? MAMA MAMA MAMA WHAT IS HE DOING TO YOU?!?"

I went soft so quickly I panicked. My son! He fucked off my nut! Damn it! His three year old ass was supposed to be sleeping! Nice time to wake up, Boy! Now see I was mad mad mad! You didn't fuck over a man's money, job, food or pussy. Son or not. I should spank his ass, but he didn't do anything wrong so that was ruled out.

My wife and I hugged each other tight, pausing, not knowing whether to run, jump or hide. Goddamn it!

What did I do?

My little boy was so upset he ran at me and started punching my legs.

"Daddy *stop* hurting Mama! Daddy I hate you! Why are you hurting Mama? Where are your clothes, *ew* Daddy you so nasty oh my God!"

All we could do was laugh. I had never ran into the bathroom so fast. Hell let my wife clean up the mess. After all she liked men who divulged in heavy conversation.

My son was about to give her hell and all the heavy conversations she ever imagined.

I laughed as I turned on the shower.

I laughed so hard tears fell down my face.

M

¥

S

O

N

My first mistake was: Being a thirty-five year old professional man believing everything Envogue didn't sing about in my favorite song of all time: "Hold On." I didn't want too much time. I didn't want him morning, noon and night. I didn't spend my time fighting lies. I didn't want his money and I didn't want a commitment. I didn't want his flashy car (even though it didn't flash a damn thing). I didn't want to meet his loud-mouthed Mama. I didn't want him being a father figure to my fifteen year old son. I just wanted him to do one thing: WASH YOUR GODDAMN DICK!

I mean let's be real. I wasn't a very skinny man. I had more to love. I was sexy and thick. I had to represent for the big men. I carried myself like a gentleman, still flirted with the girls and I didn't do pussy. I once did pussy, years ago and I got a son out of the deal and as much as I loved Peabody, who was developing into a fine man, I didn't want him around my lifestyle so I sheltered him from it. He played sports and he was hardly home. Half of the time he went over to his Mama's house and hung out with his other brothers from the six other men who gave them to her.

I treated people with the same loyalty and respect my heart would allow. But I didn't understand why my so-called question-tell-me-what-you-think-about-me-man Clairvoyance, with his sexy ass, found it cute to come to my crib after his basketball game smelling like a bunch of squirrels ran around in his testicles and left the shells from the nuts scattered about. Wash your dick.

Please.

Take the other day for instance. I knew he played ball on Monday, Wednesdays and Fridays so I had his beer in the fridge and I had the TV on the Clint Eastwood movies. He loved the Westerns. He came home, dripping in sweat. Yea, he was sexy as hell and he had a way with his words. I wound up sucking him off but I nearly vomited.

My Son   284

"You like sucking that sweaty dick, huh?"

Hell, no! "Yes, baby."

He started throat checking me, felt good but I smelled his ass a little and it wasn't pleasant.

"I'ma make you choke from the dick." He opened his legs and his nuts kept swinging towards me so I played with them just to distract myself. As much as I loved giving head I wished I didn't.

"Remember when we met you told me you like the natural smell of your man when he comes home from a ball game."

I had lied about that. I lied just to get him. That was game I was running and now it back fired because my tongue wrote a check my ass couldn't cash. My throat, either.

He hit the wrong spot in my mouth and I grabbed his dick but it was too late. I vomited on him and the floor and he actually smiled, and walked towards the bathroom. "This dick makes 'em choke every time."

He turned on the sink, gloating.

Nah, your funk made me throw up. Don't flatter yourself.

If I could go through the remedies of keeping my ass clean, sometimes going through ungodly measures so when you poked around you didn't get brown paint, then as a *Top* he could do what he do to make me happy. It's just that some of these self-proclaimed King of Sex "Tops" have gotten besides themselves. They are beggars and goddamn choosers. They don't know what a "Bottom" goes through to take dick. It isn't a walk in the park. Sometimes when they fuck you like you're an oil piston the shit hurt and I loved ole boy so much I would bite the pillow and take it like a man just because of those feelings. Yet he turned around, threw that label shit in my face and wound up wanting a nanny, lover, caretaker, dishwasher and waiter and I wasn't with the program.

Just because he got a dick and he threw down in the bedroom (even jacking off with the satin sheets just to come on my face) meant I cook all his meals to his liking? Does that mean I iron all your clothes and color coordinate them when I hang 'em up? Does that mean I cater to his needs when he hardly catered to mine? Does that mean he keep turning this so-called start-of-a-romance into relationshit hell?

I'm sorry. When he pushed his plate back at me like he was Shug Avery from *The Color Purple*, talking about, "I told you I wanted my steak medium rare, not well done," I smiled, picked it up and dumped it all over his ass and he had the gall to get upset, telling me that as a submissive bottom male I need to know my role then slow my role.

I thought about that when he wanted some ass. If you're not going to treat me right then imagine how I treated your dick when you decided to come home from the Club, waking me up out my sleep with your tongue deep in my ass. You spread my cheeks and you suck the chocolate because you know I'm angry with you for not calling me and telling me where you were. I try to tell you but you put your hand over my mouth and your warm, fleshy lips on my inner thighs shuts me up. I wanna fight it but you know just what to do. You know just what to say.

"You still want that $200 Coogi jacket?" you ask. Now I was in a Catch-22. I wanted you gone but I want that fucking jacket because I have been asking for it for months. But you're greedy, wanted me to spend all my money on you first and bills second yet when I asked for something you get offended and tell me that it wasn't the Top's job to spend. It was *my* job to spend my hard earned money on you! I swear. He let those online gay forums distort his thinking. Those messy queens online who spend morning, noon and night gaining Elite and Forum God status on those forums (you get when you make over thousands of posts) aren't a reliable source of information. Half of them are still bitter from a breakup and they mislead you down the wrong path just because you got what they can't have.

Didn't he get that?

Now you look in my eyes and give me the smile I love. Your teeth glimmer in the semi darkness. The glow of the moon turns our bodies into silhouettes. I love the mystery. Smelling Patron on your breath. I feel I couldn't live without you. I love you love you love. Yes I do. I need you need you need you. Inside me.

Next to me. Crawling in and out of me. Painting me with your sticky love and spreading it on my body. If my body could be repainted I would want you to do it with your come. I kiss you and taste something foreign, but what?

I know your taste like the back of my hand and something was off. I start to lick you from head to your navel and I defiantly taste another man's cologne from your skin. My taste isn't that salty or scanty. You wear Fahrenheit.

I tasted something less flaunting. This taste pisses me off more but you pull your dick out and you want me to give you head and I was so turned on I felt like a light switch. You shake it at me and it's so full and gorgeous and pretty and thick that I want to pour into you.

I suddenly get jealous of the little hairs on your body because they are closer to you than I am.

I was jealous of your hand because it's touching you and I am not.

You asked me again to "Suck it, Baby…" and I say "No!" and you say "Please…?" and I say "Why?" and you say "Because you love me" and I say "…What's love got to do with it because Ike loved Tina and he made Anna Mae eat the goddamn cake, raped her in a vocal booth and slapped her ass so hard the Great Wall of China felt the tremor…" and we laughed so hard I had to sneeze and you stroke my booty hole and you tell me "Please, suck Daddy's dick while I eat that phat ass!" and I melt into you because you were begging and we get in the 69 position, since that's my Cancer sign (HEY) and you slap my ass.

The sound of the slap fills the room but you're careful because you didn't like to cause me pain and I was glad my son went over to his mother's tonight so I didn't have to worry about him. He doesn't know that his father is gay and I don't bring gay shit around him. But tonight I forgot I gave you my house keys and I've been craving your dick. And you had the gall to go out without inviting me.

You lean up and soak your experienced tongue in my asshole and you spread your legs and I suck your nuts. There goes that smell again! UGH! Oh my *God*. This time you didn't play basketball so you didn't have an excuse. How did I tell him? Men took these things to heart and my dude was one of the True Tops. He didn't like nothing and no one fumbling around with his booty. Even when I squeezed it he'd glare at me and his unspoken rage told me to tread lightly.

My anger roaring back, I kiss your thighs but I stopped because there's no way a grown man should smell like skunks between his fucking legs.

My eyes shudder because, regardless of how angry I am, you give good tongue. And your tongue slithers across my nuts and I buckle at the knees and I'm moaning your name and I'm saying I want your dick that I want you to crawl in and out of this ass like the atmosphere through the Ozone Layer and you slap my ass and say "suck it first."

And I gripped it and held it and I was reminded of exactly how sexy you are. So I get up, stretch and I turned on the light and I have my back to the cracked bedroom door and I was reminded that I didn't have a sexy body because I was a big boy dating a masculine type male who thought bottoms were put here to worship him. You have on those black Justin Slayer boots and your body was banging baby I loved the way you flaunted it without over doing it. You rub your nipple and you kissed at me and I fought how I felt. I pushed it to the back of my mind and walked up to you, just admiring you because I knew this would be our last night and quite possibly our last fuck.

"I always loved you," I told him, my voice dropping below normal temperatures.

He gave me a quizzical look. "I love you, too."

"Do you really?"

"Yes."

"We haven't exactly been committed but I always put you first." I sat on the edge of the bed. It creaked but fuck it I didn't care. It was mine. I was a big dude and I wasn't going to apologize for that.

"I will do anything for you." He sat up and a soft hand touched my shoulder and I turned to the side and kissed a hand that brought me so much love and life and passion. And now I didn't want it on me.

Yea, right. Your antics aren't working tonight. Put up or shut up will be the game from here on out. "But you lie all the time."

He looked at me more fixedly. "No I don't."

I was getting upset. "You *do*. Where were you tonight?"

He picked up the cigarettes from the nightstand and lit one. He knew I didn't let anyone smoke in my house because I didn't smoke. "At a friend's house."

He's busying himself. Fucking liar! "Really? Who is this friend?"

He blew smoke at me. "I'm not married." He cocked his legs opened, picked up the remote and turned on the plasma screen. His hand was on his crotch.

Figures! "That's usually the first clue in this game called How To Catch a Liar. They evade the question with something as rhetorically challenged as 'I'm not married.'"

He flipped through the channels. "I don't need this." He pulled on the cigarette. "I really don't." He wouldn't look at me.

"Yes you do." I stood up and faced him. "You see your pile of clothes on my floor?"

He pointed at them. "They're there for a reason." He looked at me. "For you to wash them."

Well I never! Now he was being offensive. "You know what? I'm not gonna be taking that big dick in my ass, cooking your food and then washing your clothes. What 401 (k) plan are you providing me? All I'm getting is a bunch of grief." He tucked his chin back and stubbed out the cigarette with an attitude. I feared him a little. But tonight I was one pissed bitch. I went on. "…And you didn't wear that Phat Farm outfit when you left earlier. In fact where is the Sean John attire you wore when you left? Those clothes I don't see. I paid a leg, an arm and an ass for those threads…"

His eyes bounced all over the place. Meant he was thinking up a lie. Wrinkles on his forehead. Meant he was concocting his lie into words. His breathing increased. Meant the lie was about to be executed and I would assassinate his ass if he thought about trying me. I was 290 pounds. He weighed about 190. So who would win? Skeletore?

He stood up and stretched. He'd had enough. "I'm out." *Run Forest Run!* "I don't *do* drama." He picked up his pants and took off his boots. "Plus we all lie in some form. You lied a few times."

"Oh, yea, right! Turn this around on me."

"So you love to give me head after I play ball?"

I grew silent. Damn it. See, now I was mad. "I do."

"You DON'T! You lied. That's why I made you do it. Then you threw up on me. Had me thinking it was because I was so big. Nah. You were sick to your stomach to give me head after I play ball. I just threw that shit in your face."

My mouth fell open. He pointed at the floor and I was looking around. "What?"

"That's your face. Pick it up."

"Fuck you!"

He was enjoying this. "You are dating a woman who is a lesbian as a smoke screen." I withered. "You still haven't told half your family that you're gay. You got them thinking you go with Savannah and she's a dyke you paid to play the role of your girl."

The words stung. "We are not talking about me. And you went to the Club. My friends called me and told me you were in there."

He grinned. "And you believe them over me?"

"Yes. I put on some clothes and put my son in the car. We drove out to South Beach and I saw one of my friends waiting on me. While she watched my boy (he likes looking at her titties anyway) I went to the Club and you were in Twist, dancing up on some sexy man with a big booty and looked like a Gangsta. I waited until you left. You left with him."

He said, "That's the friend's house I went to. And he's a friend of the family. Yea, we are attracted to each other but I rode there with him so it's only fitting that I rode back. I just wanted to have fun. All I do is work, work, work and I don't have a social life."

He was telling the truth. He doesn't.

I walked up to him and hugged him. I knew it was over. Let's be real. I kissed his lips. Felt his power. Died for his fire. Would walk away from his pleasure.

"Still want some head, baby?'

"Shit. Yes. I love when you wrap your lips around it and do what you do.'

He put his hand on my head and pushed me to my knees.

Grinning, he braced himself for the warmth o my mouth.

There's nothing else like it.

I gripped it and said, "But first tell me where this dried shit come from all over it, dumb ass…"

His heart dropped.

He helped me stand up and I pushed him away from me.

"Why do you think I didn't suck your dick while we were in the bed? I wasn't about to suck another Bottom whore from your body. I have tasted his essence from your skin. That was *enough* torture."

He held his hands up. "*Baby*. I can explain."

"What? You went to your friend's house, tripped over the threshold while reaching for the wainscoting and you fell deep in his asshole with your eleven inch dick. Spare me the squabbles, dude. You don't do drama, remember. You do whores."

His eyes clouded over. "Go ahead. Make this about me. I wasn't even going to come here tonight but I got a phone call and I came and I saw you sleeping and I had to have you."

A phone call? I didn't call him. "And you couldn't shower first?"

"I'm a little tipsy. And I smoked trees."

"Whatever. Who called you?"

"You did."

I did? I was raking my brain. "No I didn't."

"Well…if you didn't then who did?"

"I did," said my son, walking out of my closet. His face was on the floor. He'd been crying and his eyes were so red I couldn't see his pupils. My heart exploded from my chest.

"Son…*son.*"

He was shaking his head. "So you're *gay.*"

I wanted to wrap my arms around him and kiss his face and love him and tell him that everything was going to be all right and that we could still do guy things and we could go to the football games and if he told me a girl was pretty I would believe him and…"Oh my God, my boy…"

He was so upset he started to have breathing problems. "My daddy's a *faggot.*"

I reached out for him. "*Son.*"

"I'm *not* your son. How could you lie to me? And to think Savannah is gay also. I really thought you two loved each other."

I tried to hug him and he tried to push me on the bed. I was a big guy; he couldn't push me that easily. I was a mountain. "I *hate* you. Don't wait up. I won't be back."

He ran out of my room.

My heart was sliced down the side.

How could this happen?

A few hours had passed and my son was nowhere to be found. I didn't call anyone because I didn't want to set off any alarms. I gave him some time to think.

In a lot of ways he was like me. When he was upset he would go somewhere and thinks to himself and once his head was pure he would come back home like nothing happened and we would talk about it and we would be best buds again.

I looked at my watch. It was after 8 p.m.

When I stood up my son came through the door, quiet. Looking at the door, he slowly closed it, resting his forehead on it.

He had been crying. I looked down at his shoes. They were dirty. He was sweaty. He must have been playing ball.

He always played ball when something was on his mind.

I walked up behind him, placing my hands on his shoulders. I kissed the back of his neck.

"Why, Daddy?"

"I don't know, Son."

"How long have you been…you know…?"

"*Long* enough."

"Why did you lie to me? I am your son! I thought we could trust one another."

My heart fluttered. "And we can."

"I'm sorry for calling you those names, Daddy. I thought about it when I was playing basketball."

"I know you did."

"How can we get past this, Dad? You being gay is a bitter pill to swallow."

"I don't know. I don't always have all the answers."

He turned to face me. "Can we pray about it?"

His question through me for a loop. Religion and I wasn't really seeing eye to eye because my flesh was too dirty for church clothes.

"I don't know."

"Can we try? You always taught me that prayer changes things. Dad, try. Let's talk to God. Maybe he can help."

"Help do what?" I asked hesitantly.

My son took my hand and said, "Help rid your soul of unclean spirits."

"I can try, Son."

"No, Dad. Just do it. If you *don't* do it you will lose me forever! I am serious! Try me if you dare."

"Don't say that, Son. I will die without you."

"Dad. I feel the same way. But try to change."

"I can't do it overnight. And what if I don't want to change? I love you. Yes, you are my son but I made you. You didn't make me. So as much as it'll hurt you don't put ultimatums on me young man."

I can't lose my son, Lord.

He handed me the small Bible from his back pocket.

"Thanks, Dad. Thanks for at least *wanting* to change. Even if it's only temporary."

"I didn't say I wanted to change. Honestly, I will be lying to myself if I try to change right now. It's not in my heart to do so."

"I understand…"

"I love you, Son."

"I love you too, Dad."

M

á̊

M

Å

DËARËST

y momma was a mess. She never
actually walked in on me having sex
with another man but she damn sure
liked to play games. You would think
older people was mature enough to act like
civilized adults. But not Mama. She was cut from a
different cloth.

Today, she told me she had to go to work to
get some overtime so I was like, Cool. I knew she
had a ton of bills to pay and my child support
check could only stretch so far. I mean Daddy sent
me a hundred and seventy bucks every two weeks.
Wow. I'm rich! He could keep the shit. He lived a
few blocks away from here and he refused to talk

to me. He hated Mama that much. I walked past him on the street and didn't acknowledge him or his new wife. Every time I saw him hugged on that ugly ass woman I feel abandoned and betrayed. Growing up, I used to hide my true feelings about my father, my sperm donor. If the man died tonight I wouldn't give a rat's ass. Maybe I was bitter. Maybe I wasn't. But part of the reason I turned out bisexual was because, as a teenager, I searched for a father figure in my football team. I looked in church. I looked and looked until one day the captain of the basketball team became my best friend. And a few months later we were fucking all over his mother's living room. He said he'd be my father figure and I welcomed it. I was attached to him. We talked on the phone daily and we hung out. My mom adored him, but we had to keep our affair quiet. After my 16th birthday I walked in on him servicing my friend Paul in the gym's bathroom. And that was the bitter end to my first relationship. I have been fucking and keeping my heart under wraps ever since. Shit, I figured that if my own Daddy didn't want me why should I expect any other man to take his place?

I wanted to be home alone. I was twenty-three years old and home on college break. I went to Louisiana State. For some reason when I ate some oysters I got extremely horny and I kept looking at the lotion bottle but I was tired of beating my stick and shifting gears because the clutch in my nuts wasn't revving up properly so I called over this dl

MAMA DEAREST

dude, who was fine as all outdoors and told him to come through.

"Your Mom there?"

I was cleaning up my room. Putting some clothes in the drawers. "Yea, dawg. She knows about me, but she's the only one that knows. You're cool."

He released a large gush of air. "I don't *know*, Man. We're talking about your mom. When I fuck I talk a lot of shit."

Um, ok. "Sure you do."

"I'm serious. I don't like whispering. I'm a grown man. Why should I hide it?"

"You don't have to."

I put on some cologne. I had on a pair of basketball shorts, no underwear, a wife beater, long tube socks and flip flops because I was a country boy.

We chuckled.

"So are you coming over?" I asked, brushing some dust off my Tupac poster, hanging on the closet door.

"When I get off work in the next five minutes I'll drop by. But if your Mom is there then I am not coming in."

I lift my wife-beater T shirt and checked out my abs.

I made my dick jump in the shorts just once for effect. "I'm telling you dawg, you're good."

"OK."

He hung up and I got cleaned up.

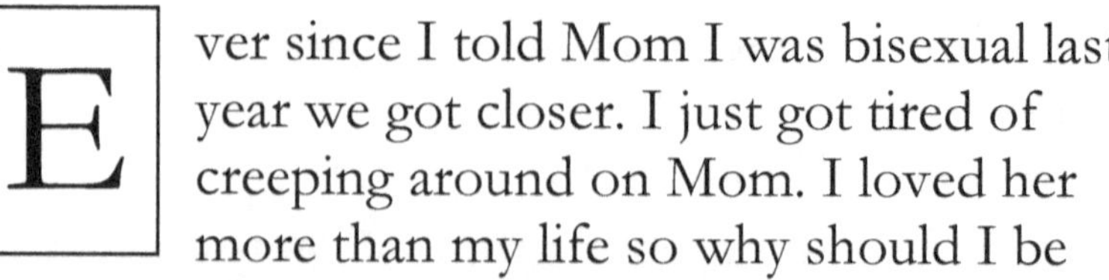ver since I told Mom I was bisexual last year we got closer. I just got tired of creeping around on Mom. I loved her more than my life so why should I be honest with my dl friends but lie to a woman who gave me life? God wouldn't bless you and he records every lie you tell. THOU SHALL NOT LIE.

I didn't see why people trusted their friends over their mothers. My Mama slaved for me as I grew up, got me what I wanted, taught me the value of money, taught me the birds and the bees minus Adam and Steve and she was always there to tuck me in at night, making sure I was full three times a day and kept money in my pocket. She made sure I attended church.

I was very religious but I was spiritual and I believed in God and that Jesus died for my sins. Who else lined nine planets to orbit around a sun that doesn't move?

Damn sure wasn't the white man. Something put it there. Everything came from thought. Nothing was just there. And now she was paying out of her pocket to put me through college. Why would I lie to her?

So I stopped and I was glad I did because she told me, "I already knew you were gay, baby. Yea you get the girls and yea I know you're fucking them but I knew you were gay ever since you were thirteen. I watched you beat off to an all male magazine I just never said nothing. I politely closed your door back and let you finish."

I felt like a fool when she told me that.

I never met my Daddy so he's oranges with these apples right now. She accepted me for me and was thankful I didn't come out the closet to the entire family. She really thanked me for not disgracing the family.

So when my Homie dropped by Mama opened the door. He was nervous and she took his hand and said, "Boy come inside. I don't bite."

"How are you?" he asked, his voice stuttering. This was hot. A real life mixed, light-skinned thug niggah shaking from Mom's voice. What kinda thug was he?

He was mixed with a lot of shit. Japanese grandfather. Russian mother. Jamaican father who had done twenty years in the Army. But he was sexy, though.

You know most DL niggahs aren't having it with company over. They like to be alone with you. And it was all over his face. Mama was dressed for work and was about to head out. She tossed me a condom, grinning and ole boy like to had heart failure.

He waited until she went in her room to grab her purse.

"Is she for real? Tossing you a Jimmy?"

"Oh, yea. We're adults. She knows we're about to fuck. You cool, man."

DAPHAROAH69

Mama kissed my lips and hit the door, locking it behind her.

"Are we in the clear? No more surprises?"

"We cool." I take his hand and go to the bedroom. When he got inside I kissed his lips and he closed and locked the door. He smelled so good and felt even better in my arms. He was very aggressive, biting my bottom lip and grabbing my plump ass.

So we're doing our thing. I was riding his dick, sweaty, naked and everything. He was slapping my ass, filling me up to the depths of my limitations. As soon as he told me he had to nut I had to nut. We were about to come together. There was nothing more beautiful than that.

I held his chest and gave him some tongue. Our heat combusted into a gyrating cloud of love and I was falling over the cliffs, towards the Come Lake.

Lovingly, he looked at me. "Ready to come, baby?"

Panting and heavy breathing. "YES!"

So as he said, "I'm about to nut..." and started fucking me harder, the headboard smacking the wall, Mama started pounding on the door so hard I froze and he froze and we held our breath. DAMN IT! This bitch yelled, "What are ya'll niggahs doing in there?"

She had never caught me before. She was always playing games. I crawled off him, telling him to be quiet. She scared the nut right out of our asses. I was sweating so hard I couldn't see and I tripped over my own feet and fell on the wooden floor.

"Why ya'll so quiet? Can't talk? Why was the headboard smacking the wall? Huh? Can't talk to me? Couldn't get a room?"

"I thought you said it was cool?" he asked harshly, shaking as he put on his pants. He was about to vomit, the look on his face had gone pale. He didn't even buckle them and his dick was hanging as he put on his shirt.

I was laughing.

"She's just fucking with you, Dawg. Why you think she threw me the condom. I think she was toying with us about going to work."

"This is some Twilight Zone shit."

I kissed him and he turned his face. When he put on his shoes he opened my window and tried to crawl out. I opened the door and Mama came in and saw him. She got a visual of his dick and she started pointing and laughing.

"What are you running for? You man enough to fuck my son in my house you're man enough to face his Mama. With your little dick ass."

I was laughing so hard I fell on the bed. "…Why do the little dick men always run for the hills?"

He fell on the ground outside the window and I had never saw a thug run so fast.

That shit was funny after he left.

I looked at Mama, who was grinning. "I hope
you didn't fuck up my wall. Shit cost me thousands
to have built from the ground up and you need to
stop fucking in my house because you aren't paying
any rent."

"Mama, you messed up my nut. Don't be doing
that shit."

She pats my shoulder. "I couldn't help it. He
was so scared. And why can't you find a man with
a bigger dick than that? That little thing had the
headboard banging like a Maxwell song?"

I loved my Mama.

"No. Me riding him and trying to imagine it
was bigger than what it was caused the headboard
to knock like that."

"Something for nothing when you all
Domino's, huh?"

We giggled into the daylight.

P

ǻ

ǂ

Я

Ø

ɓ

Øŋ

Đ

Ë

©

K

R eynard Trevor called me. I was happy to hear his voice.

"Sup, Playboy!" he said. "*What* it do?"

"Hey, partner. I'm chillin'. Where are you?" I asked, sitting on my couch, butt ass naked.

"I got my Patron on deck right now, watching my girl shake her ass and make her baby daddy mad."

I sipped my concoction of Hennessy, Hypnotiq, and cranberry juice with light ice. It's called "What's Love Got to Do with It." You chill your Miami Dolphins beer mug for three hours before usage.

"You are her baby daddy, *dumb* ass."

"OK, Sherlock. My dick is her Baby Daddy and he's getting mad because she's been saving the pussy for some reason."

I looked at the TV. "Women are unpredictable."

"Tell me about it."

"You're the pussy bandit. Hoes love you. I wish I had some of that."

"No you don't," I said. "It's not what it's cracked up to be."

"How do you balance all those females?"

"Keep a rolodex, and a cell phone. Three different cell phones. And you also keep an index card file. Put the female's name, birthday, favorite singer and color. How she looks, her likes and dislikes. It's like studying for a test. Once you learn Hoes you're set."

"That's hot. I love you, Dawg. We've been cool for a minute. I could always count on you. I trust my girl and my family around you. They think the world of you."

I smiled. I felt good. I sipped some more of the drink.

"Well I'm about to hit it. Gotta get out of here and go do something."

"Are you hitting the club tonight?"

"Nah. But I heard it's gonna be popping at Gusto's."

"Yea it is. The Mary J and Jay Z after Party is tonight."

"That's right. Well, I'll get at you Renard."

"See you later."

"Bet that up…"

PATRON ON DECK

I loved females. I love them to death. When I meet a broad I automatically wanna hit the pussy. Let's be real. Who wants to commit when the world was full of females? Everyday a different face I encounter when I go to work. My job is irrelevant. My description is irrelevant. Just know I'm a fine ass man. I love getting head. Oh my damn. There's nothing sweeter then a big booty bitch sucking your dick and actually knows what she is doing. She understands that the flick of a tongue on my swollen head and a tug of the nuts don't do it for a man like me. She gotta stroke it, work it. Spit on it, massage the saliva into my skin and slowly jack it while sucking it. Look in my eyes so Daddy can cuss that ass out if she doesn't do it right. Time was money and money was time. I didn't have time for the bullshit and I damn sure didn't have time to school a grown woman. Which reminds me of the last "shone" I was with. A shone is another word for "Ho" down here in Dade County. She was short, light skinned and had big titties and an ass to match. She smelled of a fragrance that was strange to my nose and walked like she had good pussy.

Being the pimp that I am, I took her hand and pulled her to me. Looking deep in the eyes with a shit-eating grin. She was a sucker instantly. I told her my name and she told me hers. *Precious.*

"What made *you* so precious?" I asked.

Licking her lips, she said, "Let's cut the bullshit. Are you *packing?*"

314

DAPHAROAH69

"Like a sausage factory."

She looked over my ride. The black Chevy with the butterfly doors. Black rims with the purple light under the front bumper.

"You like that?" I asked giving her a hug. She felt good in my arms. Her weave was a little on the "take that shit out" side but it was ok.

"Damn, Pa. You feel good. I can feel your heart beat."

I saw she wanted to take it to the next level so I took her to the Blow Pop Phase.

We got in my ride with the dark tints and she pulled down my zipper. She dropped her huge purse on the floor and she crank up Soulja Boy. Leaning my seat back I pull out my shit. She looked it over and smiles. Pushing her hair to the back of her head she puckered those lips and I knew it was on. I hadn't come in about four days and I had built up like skyscrapers.

`She goes down on me and I jumped out of my skin. Bitch teeth were so sharp I felt like a chopped onion.

I tried to tolerate it, swallowing my pride because Shorty was a ten but as the seconds ticked away and she got worse I told her, "Ma. Hold up, Girl…"

I hadn't realized I was sweating. Hot as hell in here. She looked at me, squeezing my upper thigh and I didn't want her touching me.

"What's wrong?"

I looked at my cell phone and said, "I just remembered. I gotta work later on today. It's already after 3 a.m. Late."

She leaned over and tried to kiss my cheek and I lay back. She stared at me.

"Something I did wrong?"

"It's what you didn't do right. Now it was nice meeting you. Leave a niggah your number."

She picked up my cell and typed it in. I already had formulated in my mind that this shone wasn't on deck like I had thought. On deck meant she was supposed to have her shit together.

She opened the door and didn't tell me goodbye. I didn't care. She strutted over past a group of young niggahs with red bandannas hanging out of their right pants pocket. They howl at her and I opened my glove box.

She got in her car and I turned on mine. I drove over to her and she rolled down the window.

"I knew you'd come back. Miss my head game already?" she asked, licking her lips.

"Your head game is on the bench right now. Too many technical fouls, homegurl."

"You so crazy, niggah…"

"I know. Getting crazier by the second." I reach into my glove box and pull out a bag.

"So are you gonna call me?"

"Yea, *sure*. Right after you *do* something for me."

She checked her make-up in the rear-view mirror and said, "Do what?"

I threw a full bag of assorted Blow Pops at her and it hit her in the face.

"What the fuck?"

I grinned. "Practice sucking on those. Learn to bend your lips over your teeth because you turned sucking dick 101 into hell on earth."

She started to curse and I rolled up the window. She got out of the car and I put it in drive. She kicked my wheel and punched my window and I grabbed my strap, put the car in park and hopped out. I rushed around the car and she started to scream and I snatched her by the weave and shoved the pistol in her mouth. I was hot headed. What my car did to her? All it did was sit there and look fly.

"If you ever hit my bitch again I will give your car the tonsils special."

She shook her head feverishly. A few niggahs were laughing, telling me to gut the Ho. I wasn't that homicidal. I just wanted to scare her up. I hopped in my ride and drove home.

When I pulled up in my drive way I saw Frederica sitting on the hood of her car, parked on the side of my house. I was a little annoyed because she hadn't called before she showed up. I got out and closed the door. "How long have you been here?" I asked her with an attitude and she hopped her fine Asian and black ass off the ride and walked up to me. We embrace and kiss. She felt so good and she loved my

PATRON ON DECK

swagger. I held her ass and she pressed her pussy up against my stick.

"Feel like being naughty?" she asked me.

"Depends on your definition of naughty."

"Naughty. Being bad." She gives me some tongue.

"What's wrong?"

"I lost my job. Dealing with my boyfriend. He is such an asshole."

"You should leave him."

"I can't."

"Why?"

"Because he's the father of my child."

"That's not a reason to stay."

"Yes it is."

"Says who?"

"I was raised like that. Mama stayed with my father because they had three kids. She didn't love him and he didn't love her but they loved me so they stayed together and made the family work. So I carried this with me into adulthood."

"I still think you should leave him. I'm tired of sneaking around on him."

She started to feel guilty.

"You're not sneaking around. Plus he's a big boy."

"He's my homeboy. I love that dude. He is always there for me and I'm behind his back fucking his lady."

"You can't fuck what's not his. I am only with him so he can care for his son. I can't imagine

318

tearing my son's tranquility apart for my own
selfish needs."

"You should make it right with him."

"He'll never know."

"You're right," I said, feeling queasy about it
all. "Renard Trevors will never know. At least I
know I still have my job."

"Pains you to look your friend and boss man
in the face knowing you're tagging this ass. He
trusts you with his life. You're all he talks about…"

I closed my eyes. My heart burning.

"It makes me feel like shit.

Maybe I was wrong for what I was doing.
But like most Niggahs, we were so weak
in the mind, we could only take what we
could get. I lived my life this way. I always took
another man's prize. I didn't lose no sleep about it.
Throw some good pussy into the mix and *viola*, I'll
take that shit, too. Loose or not. Pussy was pussy
and it made a dick do the same thing. Nut. That
simple. I would wait until he did the dirty work,
paid off the bills and dusted off the furniture and
once he sat on his ass, content with his conclusion
I would move in and snatch that shit. I was a lazy,
crummy asshole. Yea, I know. But my parents
never worked for a damn thing in their lives so
naturally, since your parents were your first
teachers, I became a chip off the ole block.

I never thought about going to him and
telling him what I did behind his back. If I had half

PATRON ON DECK

a brain I'd realize that I was a grimy Niggah for
what I did and if a Niggah shot me it would be well
justified. I was a man, a real man. I would like to
think so. But the longer I deceived my friend, then,
tell me, what kind of man was I really? I didn't
know. I didn't want to know either. I took down
every mirror in my house. I wasn't man enough to
look at my reflection. With that in mind, I picked
up my cell phone and made a quick phone call. I
had to handle business so I could go on and do
what I had to do with my life. Taking a deep
breath, Reynard Trevor answered the phone with
an enthusiastic, "HEY BOY!"

I cracked a smile. Could I do it? Could I tell
him? We were friends and I couldn't do this
behind his back anymore. "Hey, Dawg. I have
something to tell you."

"What's that?"

I cringed. Oh, God. My lips turned to sand. I
closed my eyes. "I've been seeing your baby
Mama…"

He said, "So what. We're old news. Have
fun. I do appreciate you telling me. It was fun
watching you smile in my face and squirm and I
already knew you two were seeing each other. She
told me initially and I didn't believe her. I was just
waiting for you to tell me."

I felt guilty. "Damn, Dawg. I'm sorry."

"It's no thang, bruh. Let's go out for drinks
later."

"Drinks are on me."

Dapharoah69's brown paper bagging his erotica. All the Old School Playahs know what I'm talking about. Here. Take a sip. It's just Old English. Drink responsibly.

L
U
S
C

I

O

U

S

When the New Year started I told myself I would make affirmations I could live up to because last year I hadn't lived up to one single expectation I'd set for myself. And that's me. Always doing something I wasn't supposed to. We all had our days and we all had our nights but lately my nights seemed like muggy days and my cool days seemed like frustrated evenings with a touch of aggravation setting me off at any given moment. A few affirmations I made this year went as followed. I will get to work on time. I will treat my friends with respect. I will treat my best friend like royalty. I will love my girlfriend. I will. Love. My.

Girlfriend. I WILL LOVE MY GIRL. FRIEND. Hmm, maybe I shouldn't have made that one. Reason being was simple. Um, yes, I'm bisexual. *So what!* It's *my* goddamn life. I will do what I want to. In fact, I thought about climbing out of the window of my girl's house now. I always did, to go see a different niggah. I didn't do it a lot, though. Probably twice a month. Why didn't I go through the door? She got a new alarm put on it and when you opened the door it made that soul-lacerating buzzing sound that made me jump. It'd wake ay Charles up from the dead and I didn't know the code to the alarm to cut it off. She went behind my back and had the codes changed because she claimed that she felt vulnerable when I used to turn it off. "I got it in place so I know when somebody is opening my door."

"But I hate it, Boo."

"I know you do. But I like it. I have to be aware these days. Don't need anybody creeping up in here while we're sleeping…"

I thought about my sex romps with the fellahs being compromised. "Nobody is going to come in here, Boo."

She hugged me and put her hands in my pants. My dick took a while to get hard. She didn't turn me on as much as she used to. Was it because I lusted after the fellahs? Maybe. Maybe not. I looked in her eyes and saw the love she had for me. And she always did this. Tried to give me some Shut Up, Its My Way Pussy to get me to go

324

along with her request. And for the most part, since women were too emotional, I went along with it.

Now I lay in bed, wide awake. The clock tells me it's pouring into the wee hours of the morning. Her arm is over her face and she's snoring. She always slept like a brick. I could slide my dick in that pussy and she'd still be snoring.

I'm too slick with my shit. Plus Karma was on my side. I will never get caught up. I shouldn't creep out of windows, a bit childish if you asked me. But a Niggah called me I hadn't fucked in ages and I wanted him. I looked at the side of her face, stroking her cheek. I thought about him instead of her. I knew I was wrong but damn, he used to give me the best orgasms of my life. She used to tell me that she took our sexcapades as something utterly sweet. That she allowed our sexual union to strengthen our relationship. Didn't she understand that I said whatever I had to say (in the beginning) just to fuck her? I just didn't imaging that I would develop feelings for her air headed ass.

Knowing full damn well I was wrong for creeping, I slowly slid out of bed and cautiously walked across the room to the armoire. I opened it. It creaked a tad. She stirred and I held my breath. Watching. Observing. Good. She's still sleeping. She turned over and her ass is tooted in the air, her lips flapping like a horse.

325

DAPHAROAH69

I took out a pair of black sweat pants. I took off my boxers and kicked them under the dresser. I put on the sweats and then a long sleeved black shirt. A black hat and black socks. I closed the doors of the armoire and went to the closet and put on some all black Jordans.

I looked at her, telling myself that I shouldn't cheat on her. But she was always nagging. Always doing things that pissed me off. Always going against what I asked for. Never cooked on time. Always bought shit outside of our budget. Stepped on my manhood. Thinking about it all upset me and I just had to act on it. There's no way she could keep getting away with treating me like I was her brother instead of her lover.

I walked down the stairs and looked at the alarm box. What was the code? I went snooping through her bills and letter son the dining table. Nothing. I then thought about the password to her cell phone. It was her birthday. I walked back to the alarm box and typed in her birthday and hit "Enter" and the door chime turned off. YES! Bingo!

I tip toed out of the front door and was careful when I closed it. I left it unlocked. She'd be safe for the time being. I speed walked to my car, trying my best to will my nervousness back to where it came from. My hands shook as I fumbled in my pockets for the keys. I was looking round, surveying. Making sure no one saw me. I finally found my keys and they nosily dangled as I

LUSCIOUS

unlocked my ride. I didn't have an alarm on it nor did I want one. If someone stole my car they'd be doing me a huge favor. I could then call my insurance company and get another one.

I got in the driver's seat and put the car in reverse. I got out and pushed it back, the crickets chirping. When I got it in the road I turned it on, got inside and hot-trotted to his house, which was a couple blocks away. He told me he owned his home and I was happy that he did because my money was funny and I didn't have enough to spot a hotel room.

I wondered exactly how long he lived in my neighborhood because I hadn't seen him until a few days ago and it was like old times when we locked eyes. Every thing I thought I would never feel again came flooding back like I was Moses crossing the Red Sea and I couldn't keep it together. I wound up fucking him in the stall at Wal-Mart as an end result.

When I got to the impoverished home he opened the garage and I parked next to a SUV. Looking at him brought back so much. I am not giving my name or description. That's not important. What's important was the nut bubbling in my testicles, which wanted to be all over his handsome face.

With lust in his eyes, he opened my car door looking like a young Shemar Moore. He gives me some tongue and I am rubbing on his big ass. It was plump and soft. Just the way I remembered it.

327

DAPHAROAH69

I had a quick flash of the red thongs he used to wear for me. He hated wearing anything on the feminine side but he had did it just to make me happy. Coyly, he unbuttons his shirt and takes it off and the soft glow of the garage lights bring out the beauty of his eyes. He pushes a control in his hand and the garage door closed with a noisy thud.

Gently, he pushes me on my car seat and gets on top of me. I felt so good. I had to make it quick. I looked at my watch. I really had to get a move on. Hit this booty hole and get home before my girl wakes up.

I hated to treat him like a whore but any man sucking my dick in the wee hours of the morning either had a habit or a problem. Either way it wasn't my problem. Looking as sexy as he wanted to be, he unbuttons my pants and pulls out my dick. He doesn't waste anytime. He started to lick on it with a fire I'd never seen before. Like he hadn't had dick in ages. Like he was hungry for it. Famished without it. Like a seasoned professional, he takes it to the tonsils in ways my girl wish she could. He slobbers all over it as I try to forget that I proposed to my girl a few weeks ago. We were set to marry and her cousin was supposed to be coming to town to be in the wedding and to help plan it. Some dude named Elroy Joseph who I had talked to on the phone but had never met.

This Niggah still sucked a mean dick. Nothing has changed about it. I gave him time to enjoy the incredible inches. But now I wanted something

LUSCIOUS

more. I wanted to feel his tight asshole on my stick. I really needed a shot of ass so I slapped his booty and told him let me out the car. Like a little bitch he turned around and pulled his pants down. He knew what I wanted.

I got on my knees and admired his gorgeous ass. I spread his cheeks and used my index fingers to make that hole say "*Aaaah.*" I started to feast, slowly munching in his chocolate, my mustache tickling the hairs on his ass. Booty cheeks were on either side of my tongue. He moaned and I slapped his booty again. Smack. Smack. I stood up and slid in him. Fuck the rubber.

This one time wouldn't hurt. I called him "Luscious."

When I first met him at the mall he told me his name was George Samuels. I fell in love with him in nearly a day, but we had double lives so that was that.

I rummaged around in the ass, making him squirm. He could barely take it but I didn't care. I pulled out, slapping his ass cheeks with my dick. He gyrated that booty, loving it. I spread the cheeks and spit on that hole, tasting him. He died.

He told me he wanted to come so I let him sit on my seat and beat off while I pushed his legs back and ate him out like he was my girl. He loved it. When he had to come a few minutes later it squirted on his chest and I licked it up, swallowing him on impulse. I wanted some more ass so I went up in him again, not caring if it hurt him or not.

He was the bottom. Take this dick, handle it. A true bottom could take dick with his eyes closed while bungee jumping towards a tight rope in a tutu. I looked at my watch and decided I had to get back home. It was 4:45 a.m.

My girl's alarm was set for 5 a.m., and she loved waking up and sucking my dick and I loved head so I strained my muscles and I caught a nut instantly, coming inside him. I put on my clothes and hopped in my car.

"We can't at least talk?"

"I gotta get home. We'll hook up later."

He lets me out and I burn rubber. When I got home I cut the engine and rushed through the front door, closing it. I put in her birthday and the door chime activated without making a sound. I inhaled, getting high of his scent on my top lip. I loved the way he smelled. I loved him. I wanted to be with him again. Fucking him opened everything I had suppressed.

When I got to the room I was happy that she's still sleeping. I take a quick shower and dry off. Brushing my teeth, I then crawl in bed beside her, looking in her face. I felt guilty, but at the same time if she learned how to treat me better I would treat her better.

I loved watching her sleep. I sat there until the alarm sounded and I pretended I was sleep. She fumbled all over the sheets and her hands find my dick. She gripped it and I held my breath. She pulled it out and sucked on it, it started to grow in her mouth. Her warmth was pleasant and I closed my eyes, imagining she was Luscious. In contrast, she used her tongue to form circles on my rod. Luscious used those very same circular motions but he deep throats in ways that blew my mind.

She smiled at me, trying to fully awaken. "I can't wait to marry you," she said, making me feel good. I didn't want to marry her at all, but I'm on the Low, I have to do this.

Damn it. "I can't wait, either."

"My cousin should be in town. He's staying with a friend of mine. Elroy Johnson…he just bought a house not too far from here."

Ask me do I give a fuck! I held her head, loving her moist mouth and the way she pulled on my balls. "Oh, yea?"

She started to slowly kiss my nuts and that felt good. She took the left nut into her mouth, humming a tune. "Yes. He's been having bad luck. He got HIV and he is in denial about it."

I didn't want to hear about this.

"Sorry to hear that."

"Damn, you taste good, baby."

Can you please hurry up! "Thanks."

"I'm going to see him later on today, do you wanna come?"

I tensed up and I curled my toes. I was about to come and my girl loved to swallow.

DAPHAROAH69

I was stuttering. "Sure…anyways, what's his name?"

She sucked on my balls, giving me a head rush. Come spurted from my dick and in the air and she started wiping it up and sucking it from her fingers. She put some in my mouth and I tasted it.

"His name is…" Slurp, slurp. "George Samuels."

My dick went soft in her mouth and I had heart failure.

Yes. He's been having bad luck. He got HIV and he is in denial about it… Oh my God! And I swallowed him. And my girl just swallowed me.

We're now infected…

I can never tell her. I will take it to my grave.

ÞUSSɎT

ЯØꟼICS

His Marlins baseball cap was turned to the left, like he was from New York. "Sup, Baby."

I held my breath. He was fine as shit. His voice was full of smoke and caramel. "Sup, Pa." My eyes scanned him like a document at the office. Black slacks, nice leather boots and he wore moderate jewelry, which told me he wasn't a show off. He had a nice dick print behind the slacks. Oh, yea! *You got the Green light to give it to Mama!*

He smiled, perfect white teeth. No fillings, and believe me I was looking for them. "I'm good, about to go to Denny's."

"Hungry, 'ey?" I asked, patting my weave because my scalp was itching something fierce. And let's not talk about these heels. I grabbed the pair that was a size too small on my way here and didn't realize it until the corn on my right toe was like, "Bitch, act like you know!"

His magnificent eyes sparkled. "Yea. Niggah gotta get some grub. Hopping in this club got a niggah tired and shit. Had one too many drinks. So are you here with anybody?" he asked, taking my hand and kissing it. I loved when men were men, engaging in conversation. I guess my pussy loved him too because I was wetter than a wet fish. And these were my good panties, too. Which goes to tell me that I was already losing money with this dude? Preposterous.

"I came with a friend. His name is Sammy. He's around somewhere." I looked around for him. There were so many people out here on the South Beach streets that it was virtually impossible to find his tall, fine ass.

His spirits dropped. He squeezed my hand. "Damn, Baby. I was hoping we could grab a bite to eat. I know I wanna bite on something…"

He was looking me up and down and I was smiling. I would love for those lips to connect with my bottom lips and make some type of rapport but right now I had to find Sammy because he was my ride home and I was on South Beach, thirty miles away from my house and I didn't feel like being

PUSSYTRONICS

stranded. And knowing this niggah he didn't live down south.

"Oh, yea. Well, Sammy is a friend, like I said. Nothing special. In fact he's married to a female I can't stand and every time she kisses him I am laughing on the inside because she doesn't have a clue that she tastes another man's come."

Ole boy covered his mouth, wide eyed. He looked grossed out. "He's…"

I lowered my voice, looking around, gripping my purse. I didn't normally talk about my friends with strangers but I liked this man and quite frankly I wanted to do what niggahs did: chase the prey.

A few Hood Rat types walked by me, trying to get ole boy's attention and he only had eyes for me.

"He's bisexual. Wifey doesn't have a clue. He only sneaks out to get some dick then he creeps back home and cuddles with her like nothing ever happened."

"I don't disrespect those types of people but damn, why get married if you know your heart isn't right?"

I smiled. I loved how he carried on a conversation.

"He was a little suspect of being gay back when he was in school. So he got a girlfriend, ate her until she fell in love, married her and produced three kids and played the family man role to get rid of the doubts. He is miserable. I know he's miserable. You can see it on his face when he speaks."

"I bet he is. I feel for ole boy. Me, personally, I'm not gay. I don't disrespect their community. One of my good friends is bisexual and he knows what lines not to cross with me."

"I appreciate the honesty."

"I'm a grown man, got nothing to lie or hide. So, can I talk you outta leaving with Sammy and getting with me?"

"He's my ride home."

He pointed at a shiny Yukon. Wow. Nice. "That's mine over there. Where do you live, I can take you home."

"Down south."

"Where about?" he asked, tugging on his Florida marlins Jersey with *Uggla* on the back in huge black letters.

"Perrine."

He grinned. "I stay by the big park."

"Get out of here! Are you serious?"

"So ride with me. I don't bite. Unless you want me too."

I pulled out my cell and phoned Sammy.

"What's your name?" I asked ole boy while the phone rang in my ear.

"Jesse."

He took my hand again.

"Nice name."

He wouldn't take his eyes off me.

"And your name?"

PUSSYTRONICS

"Bernadette."

Sammy answered with a gruff, "What, woman?"

I smiled. "Hey, Sammy where are you?"

"I left. Couldn't take those ghetto acting cunts in the club."

I was upset. Ole boy was alarmed. "You left me all the way up here with no way home?"

"You got the hottest pussy on South Beach. Some dude would love to take you for a ride."

I was disgusted. I slammed my purse on the ground. I heard my compact mirror shatter.

"Sammy McCall you get back here and you pick me up!"

People were looking and I started clicking. "What the hell are ya'll looking at, goddamn. Find another statue to gawk at."

Ole boy picked up my purse and handed it to me. He was finding this all funny.

"I'm about to go, Girl."

"Sammy!" I was nervous. Someone tapped me from behind and I snapped again.

"Don't touch…"

Sammy stood there laughing at me, hanging up his phone. I slapped his arm.

"You tricked me."

Sammy eyed Jesse. "Sup, Man."

He shook Jesse's hand. Jesse was a complete gentleman. The majority of men in

339

the world cringed when they shook a bisexual man's hand but not Jesse.

He was cool and confident, which further told me I had nothing to worry about.

"Sup, how are you? Sammy, right?"

"Yea, that's my name. Look, I'm going home. My wife is calling me left and right."

Jesse nodded and said, "I will take Bernadette home. I like what I see." I put his arm around me and I felt safe. He was a rough-around-the-edges man and I loved my men rough with hairy legs and asses. I loved running my fingers through chest hair. That was my fetish.

Sammy looked at me, his hands in his pockets. "You cool with that?"

I said, "Sure. Go ahead. Love you, bruh?"

He kissed my cheek. "Love you, too."

And he was gone.

Jesse took me to a fine restaurant. Very familiar place. I come here all the time. I loved the menu because the restaurant wasn't inside an expensive building. It was in my bedroom. Wearing a baby bib, T-shirt and boxers and unlaced leather boots, he was eating my pussy the way it should be eaten. I could barely stand it lying naked in front of this fine man. He was pulverizing my black silk sheets and my toes were alert. I hadn't gotten any head in ages, because all I do is work. Deal with people all day. Meet sales quotas. Talking to

PUSSYTRONICS

customers on the phone. Dealing with attitudes. Shunning men who wanted to bone me and hadn't a chance in hell. I couldn't wait to get his dick. He already told me it was the best, that girls called him "Deep Stroke" in high school.

"Something is missing," he told me, Jill Scott singing on my radio. He was snapping his fingers, clearly taking his time with me. That was refreshing because I truly enjoyed his company. He was rubbing his nipples, and I used my right hand to squeeze his thigh. God's most beautiful man.

"I'll be back," he said, telling me he was going into my kitchen. What for? I smiled, very comfortable with him in my room and in my house. When you had tongue as well as his I might just make him a spare key.

Surprisingly, he went into my kitchen and came back to my bedroom with a small bottle of Crystal Louisiana Hot sauce. Taking off the top, I was curious. What was he about to do with it? I loved the hot sauce. I put it on everything I ate. It was that good to me.

He started rubbing hot sauce on my dripping anatomy and I loved the pleasurable sting. Yummy. I shivered under his magnificent touch. He slowly sucked it off, his tongue separating my pink walls and substituting nothing but tongue. No fingers. He didn't use his hands at all. He had them folded behind his back as his head bobbed and weaved. I put my legs up in the air and opened them, my heels catching the glow of the lamp.

DAPHAROAH69

He pushed my legs behind my head and told
me to hold them there. My arms trembling I did
so. He then used a butter knife and fork to spread
my tight pussy and his slick tongue made me feel
like butterflies.

"I love the baby bib you got on," I said and
he smiled, sucking my clit, the butter knife holding
my left pink wall so it didn't connect with the right.

"You like that?"

"Hell yea."

"I don't wanna mess up my good T-shirt.
Sometimes my money is funny." He set the
utensils on my belly and slapped my upper thighs.
Make it hurt, baby.

He put hot sauce on his fingers and inserted
two into my mouth. I sucked for dear life. "Play
with that pussy," he told me and I went to town. I
wanted to come and I wanted to come now,
goddamn it.

I was massaging it and he was in my
nightstand. He helped himself. He found my little
leopard-print dildo.

He put some hot sauce on it and began
sucking it, leaning up to my lips and making me
put my legs down. I licked it with him, both of us
sucking the dildo and this turned me on.

He started spanking my pussy with his left
hand. "You been bad?"

"Hell yea…"

"Ready to be punished?"

"Yes! Discipline this pussy!"

He inserted the dildo, which was about seven inches. It felt so good falling into my pleasurable folds. I grinded on it and he licked his lips and enjoyed his new video game. Pussy Tronics. The Bitch Edition. With the leopard-print dildo/joy stick.

"You gonna come for Daddy?"

"Hell, yea!"

"Work it, baby. Aren't you glad I came home with you?"

"Hell yes! Oh, shit Pa, work it! Turn my pussy into the Amazon Rain forest."

"Want some wood in your forest?"

"Yes..! I want my beaver to chew through that…wooden log!"

"I want you to come on my tongue." He pulled the dildo from my softness and began tasting it. He swallowed my essence and buried his tongue into my pussy. His tongue was looking for something, sent out an APB because my clit robbed my ass cheeks and he wanted a search warrant to search my dark tunnel.

He was aggressive. He gripped both my legs and pulled me to him.

"Don't run from this tongue."

Hell yes.

"Yes, Daddy." Tears raced from my eyes and my tits bounced like balls. I started to gyrate faster, his tongue so far in me I felt foreign.

"You ready to come, baby? I feel those pussy muscles tensing on my tongue."

I was holding his head and he slapped my hands. "Don't touch me, I'm touching you."

"Talk that shit to me."

"You're my bitch?"

"Hell yea."

"You want me to taste that pussy?"

"Hell yea?"

"Can my tongue taste the pussy until it cries?'

I shivered. "Oh, hell yea. I'm about to come!"

He tongue fucked me long, deep and fast and I had heart failure as I came out what I felt.

Open wide, I wanted round two so I got on my knees and said, "Fuck me from the back Daddy!"

"I thought you'd never ask."

I just know this is about to be good!

"**O**h, yea baby. You are working it." He slapped my ass, getting it from the back. My face in the pillow, fucking up my make-up. I paid good money for that make-up.

He growled, with his sexy ass. "You like this dick?"

I rolled my eyes. *Damn shame your tongue felt a hundred percent better!* "Yes, Daddy!"

He leaned into my face. *Damn it! Don't do that. Now I can't fake it.* "Tell me you like it!"

I hate it! "I love it! This is the best dick. I. Ever. Had, shit!"

He gripped both ass cheeks and started slamming my pussy on his shaft, pleased with his hard work because I wasn't. I needed Vitamin Water. I couldn't believe I was burning calories on this stroke-less wonder. "Who this pussy belongs to?"

Me, damn it! "*You,* Pa."

He pushed my booty down towards the bed, and put an arch in my back. "Pa or Daddy!"

"Damn I feel it in my stomach." Bullshit, I barely felt it in my pussy. In fact it was drying up and his dick was starting to feel like sand paper on a paper cut.

I was very disappointed. This man had a huge dick and it felt like a huge commercial flop.

Now I know how rapper Lloyd Banks felt when his Big Apple CD fell off the charts.

‡ Ķ Ø E 3

Un/sin/sored

sneak peak

F
R
A
N

C
I
N
E

THE WEDDING CONCLUDED

rancine looked at her mother, the woman who gave her life. The woman who controlled her, the woman she could *never* please. *She's a jealous bitch*! She thought about Chandra and what she was going through. A sweet woman thrown into a nightmarish game of lies and betrayal by two people she trusted most in the world.

Chandra was vibrant and colorful. Full of life and God. She cherished church and family. She loved her friends and was a darling. People loved her instantly when they met her.

Now she's a manufactured heroine addict with no idea on how to save herself.

Now she was pregnant with Samuel's child. She chain-smoked, didn't keep herself up and she bites her nails. She hadn't an iota of God or religion in her mental frame of mind.

And Francine had to rectify that. She owed her best friend that much.

"I don't want you to be my Maid of Honor anymore," Francine said, waiting to bash her face in. She was counting from ten to one in her mind, keeping her wits in check.

Mama was furious. "What?" She huffed, snapping her fingers like she'd gone crazy. "I have on this fabulous dress and I called all my girlfriends, Chile. They are here and want to see me sport my Dolce and Gabana pumps, Chile. *Please.* You must have gotten drunk or something." Francine tucked her chin back. "Girl, give me some of what you're on so I can act out of whack with you. Ain't nothing and nobody stopping me from modeling this amazing dress."

"This is a wedding, not America's Next Top Bitch. Tyra Banks isn't the emcee and fuck that ugly ass dress!"

Mama tucked her chin back. She just about had it. Image was everything to her and Francine just destroyed it.

Dangerously, she said, "You will not talk to me…"

The little girl inside Francine called out to her.

Don't upset Mama! She will whip you. She will talk down to you. Please, Francine…she will lock you in the closet again when she doesn't get her way! She will call all

352

your friends and tell them you're a bitch and tell all your business.

Francine held her stomach, bile rising in her throat. Frightened, she stood her ground.

Francine, don't do it. Don't talk back to your mother.

Exploding inside, Francine walked into her Mama's face, her hands on her hips.

"Don't look at me like that, Ma. You don't fucking scare me anymore."

Francine! Please! PLEASE! She is going to lock you in the closet! And leave you there all night to fight the darkness! Like she did when you were nine year old!

"Ever since I was a little girl I always tried to make you happy. I did whatever you said. You used to lock me inside the closet for hours. If I didn't clean your house right you locked me in the closet. If boys talked to me you'd whip me until you drew blood. I remember when your cousin called you and said I had lost my virginity…"

"Your point…"

"SHUT UP! And you snatched me by my braids and shoved a hot sauce bottle up my pussy! What kind of mother does that to her child? I couldn't piss straight for weeks. I lied to the doctor for you and told him I tried to masturbate with said bottle just to keep you out of jail. And it turned out that your cousin lied. I hadn't lost my virginity yet…"

"Grow up. You're still singing that sad OH GOD LIFE IS UNFAIR song and quite frankly

353

you remind me of Patti Labelle trying to will another hit. *Ain't* interested."

Francine gritted her teeth.

"I'm sick of you…"

"Take some Advil."

"I'm no longer scared of you."

"Whoopee!"

"Go to hell, Mama! Burn for an eternity. I can't deal with this anymore."

"I should have had an abortion. I was sick of you years ago…"

THE KING OF EROTICA 3
COMING IN DECEMBER

Letter to everyone:

Hello, how are you all doing? I hope this letter reaches you all in good health. I have a confession to make. But before I talk about it I want everyone to understand something. I don't say this to release steam or for your opinion. Do me a favor. If you have rebuttals for what lies beneath this sentence then save it. Don't waste your time or your breath because you will hyperventilate before I give a shit. These books are written for a reason. They exist for a greater reason. I write the things I do for a reason. When I die these books will belong to my nieces, sister and God brother. I write what I want and what I desire. I am not happy. In fact I haven't been happy in a very long time. You know why I'm not happy? Because family wants me to pretend I'm not a bisexual man. They want me to write the things they want me to write. They want to control what I do and what I say. Don't do this. Don't wear that. Don't go there. And I'm tired of being a robot. So I've stopped. They want me to be a puppet and they wanna be the strings and if I don't dance to their tune or march to their marching band then I'm being disobedient, then I am a selfish asshole, then I am a piece of shit. When I dance I have to be crazy. Don't hate me because God gave me the talent for words and movement. If God didn't want me to dance he wouldn't have given me the gift. So when I'm dancing at the bus stop or in an abandoned alley I'm dancing because of one thing: to save you from my wrath. So let me dance. Trust me the day I stop dancing is when you need to worry. Family want me to wear masks and dance at the parties with the ladies and pretend to be in love and walk around with a noose on my neck and *pretend* because of what people say. Fuck people! Fuck what they have to say. People don't pay my bills or fuck me. I've been "pretending" for a decade. I can't pretend anymore. Over the past few months I have been through so much. Successfully getting off parole for a crime I never committed eleven years ago, pretending just to live in my mother's house, putting people before myself, doing things for others before I do for self, giving my last dollar to selfish motherfuckers who had the world in their living rooms, shunning public opinion and scorn for my own saneness. My own mother called me things to my face a mother should never tell her son. And even though I love her and I will never bash her, I don't trust her anymore. I don't pick up my phone and I don't check on anybody anymore. I don't trust *anyone but my nieces*. Literally overnight my soul has darkened. It has gotten to the point where I don't care anymore. I don't care about church. I don't care what people say, and if they or you or them or family don't like Larry C Wilson, Jr. then everybody can kiss my ass. I am no longer living my life for you, us, or them. I am living for me. Because if I don't stop pretending, all of you will be preparing for a funeral. And I don't want any of you there if you were one of the people who want me to pretend for your sanity. I don't need people. I need God and I love God and God is all I want and need. After all, I trust God whole-heartedly.

Pharaoh

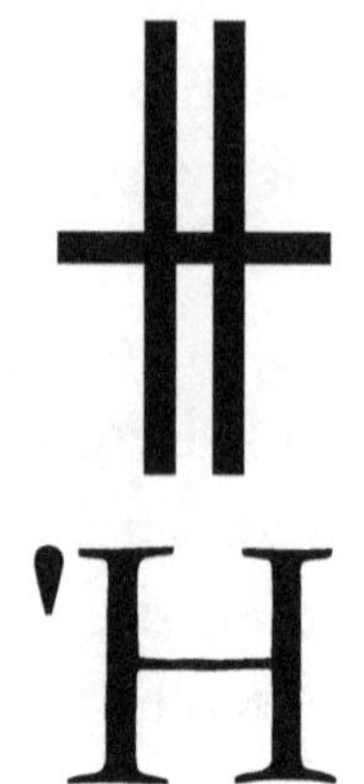

'H

Å

ɒ

K

Ɏ

Ø

Ű

ACKNOWLEDGEMENTS:

If you want to doubt my power as an author, if you say I'm writing for nothing and if you say Larry Wilson AKA D.Phar.69 hasn't changed lives then the reviews below from buyers on Barnes and Noble should push your hate elsewhere. These fans extend African-Americans. These stories have brought different races of people together and given them something to take with them, long after I perish. I decided to publish about 20 of the fifty plus 5 star reviews my books garnered.

Pharoah69

The King of Erotica 1:
Special Edition Reviews

Most Helpful Review ★★★★★

Posted September 27, 2008, 9:20 AM EST: He rose from childhood tragedy to being a rebellious teenager and no one knew he was nursing four years of abuse. He acted out. Reading these things about him, reading that he rose from prison to where he is now shows us that this young black man has seen some things, been accused of some things and his head is high on his book cover and the beautiful part about it is that his book isn't about him. Reading this book was invigorating, to say the least. I'm 50 years old, and yes, I've seen some things, but the onslaughts he's lived through shape his writing ability to the legendary

strokes it has become. No one can match this book.
His short stories are outrageously real. Candidly real.
He digs deep into the character and you wonder why
they do the things they do. Why did Melissa Jackson
attend a 60 plus member orgy in the back of her
church while the corrupt Pastor Troy lead an
organization straight to the tithe's baskets? Why does
Clever want to live out her dreams? Why does Jadish
have horrible nightmares, being that she's a virgin and
never had sex with a man? The answer will stun you.
This book is like the Lord of the Rings. It ends on cliff
hangers leading into Book two.

6 out of 6 people found this review helpful.

<u>Young Dro23</u>

**Hmm: Dapharoah69 is just like his name:
PHARAOH!**

★ ★ ★ ★ ★ **Rating**

Posted October 23, 2008, 3:07 PM EST: I'm a straight
male. And seeing this book on my sister's dresser lured
me to pick it up. How could I not? A nice-looking
brothah doing his thing was to be desired. I sat on her
bed and thumbed through it. I tell you something.
When I read in its entirety the Purpose of the Book
ALPHA AND OMEGA, I was hooked. I bought a
copy for myself. He tells you bluntly that his book isn't
a straight book. It isn't a gay book. It's a book about
REAL PEOPLE! Its understanding why people have
the type of sex the way they do. I love the book. And I
look forward to reading Book 2. Dapharoah69 is one

of my favorite authors now. I urge you all to get a
copy.

<u>JasonJL</u>

I love this book

★ ★ ★ ★ ★ **Rating**

Posted October 21, 2008, 1:17 PM EST: What's not to
love about the King of Erotica. What's not to love
about how personal he gets to his readers? Even
though the short stories are fictional, he gives a huge
piece of himself throughout the book. The first half is
stories. The second half is poetry. And what an
amazing poet he is. The book's opening has the Oath
of the Freak that you must read and sign, and when
you do be prepared to be taken on a rollercoaster.
Rayne in the Bedroom completely blew my mind. I
have never read a story like this. A sexual Dr. Jekyl and
Mr. Hyde. Overall, I give the book an A! He is in a
league all his own.

The Book Lives up to the Hype!

★ ★ ★ ★ ★ **Rating**

Posted September 26, 2008, 8:39 AM EST: He name is
making the rounds baby. And I am not one to do a
review, but after reading the book I just had to.
DApharoah69 writes things that you don't read
everyday in a book. His characters are so mind-
blowing how could I walk away the same as I was
before I read it. This book has it all, a testimonial, The

Oath of the Freak. In the beginning it reads like a sexually charged Chicken Soup for the Soul, detailing the Alpha and Omega and why he wrote an erotic book. He is clearly more than just a pretty face and sex. And slapping himself on the cover lets the world know that the King of Erotica has arrived. And there will never be another one.

THE KING OF EROTICA 2 THE CROWN:
FROM THE FANS

I'M IN LOVE
Someone in Miami, A reviewer, 09/24/2008

I'm in love with his writing, his image and the fact that he has risen from the lowest of low points in his life and created an entity called the King of Erotica. I enjoyed every single page.

★★★★★**I have one thing to say...**
Roberta, A reviewer, 09/19/2008

AWESOME! This man is a work of art and only GOD could have made something so gorgeous! Brilliant first book. BRAVO! Can't wait for Part 3 in December. And rumor has it that it's an 800 page shocker! Zane who?????? There's a new kid on the block and he's taking NO prisoners.

★★★★★**His Mama should be PROUD!**
True Reader, A reviewer, 09/11/2008

The man is a legend in the making. Take a look at the next Big Thing. The book is spectacular. Who knew sex was this invigorating? And the best part is that he's more than sex. Zane need to dump half of those boring authors she promotes and get this man on her team. Impressive!

★★★★★Jaw-Droppingly GOOD
Richard, A reviewer, 07/16/2008

I have one thing to say. If you haven't bought this man book or been introduced into his elite world then I got a suggestion for you: BUY IT!!!!!!!!!!!!!!!!!!!! It is well worth the money! He is on Zane's level. In fact, his writing is on par better than any erotic writing I have ever seen. It borders literature.

★★★★★A reviewer
Adonis, A reviewer, 07/08/2008

When I read a book I am looking for something. I am looking for something I hope the author can give five pages into whatever he or she is trying to convey. By the time I read the first paragraph, Dapharoah69 had me as a fan forever. Each page is a very encouraging trek into his mind. His mother and father could not have raised him, because the things he write about extends family. It is struggle. It is pain. It is a young man who took charge of his image and published a collection of stories. Each story has book potential in themselves. I could see PH Balance being a book. Smoke and Mirrors would probably win him a NAACP Image Award for literary brilliance. Smoke and Mirrors is a harrowing tale of a man who is connected to a little girl he once saw at his dead mother's funeral. And the twist was so upsetting I had to close the book and wipe tears away. He had me…

★★★★★**A reviewer**
De'Andre, A reviewer, 07/08/2008

He is a fantastic Writer. Gifted poet. And from the look of him on his book cover he can be a breathtakingly successful Model. Not bad for a 31 year old erotic author who is so much more than sex. He looks good and his writing is better. If you think you are going to get the typical stories from other authors. No. You're not. I want to give my opinion on his fabulous book. For starters, the Introduction into the book is poetry in itself. You get a glimpse of letters from his fans, emails from his fans from as far as Germany and what other authors thought of his book. From the looks of it, they are applauding him for stepping outside of the box and giving you pure entertainment. His topics are such a taboo in the black community but he doesn't care. He writes with a take-no-prisoners attitude. The poem "What is Africa?" is a lyrical gem on Langston Hughes' level. I will surely show my English teacher. The Poem "Barbra Streisand" eloquently touches on his displeasure for being racial profiled because he doesn't relate to the singer's music. It's both a testy and angry rant about showing self-love, and why should he care about a woman who never walked a mile in his shoes through the ghetto and find out what it feels like to be deprived of a chance at life. I read this three times over. The Short stories are a treat. Booty-Do, a prostitute who, throughout the story, goes from selfish to self-love, touched me but it ends on a very mind-boggling, twist-of-a-cliff hanger, leading into Book 3, which I heard he's releasing in December of '08. 'Freaky Deaky.' Let's just say don't read this with another person in the room. Your hands might be able to take the heat. 'Invading MySpace' doesn't have one sexual episode in the story and this proves amazing because this shows he can carry a story without including sex and still leave you satisfied and wanting more. 'Purple Panties 2.' Again. No mention of sex, but the way he writes with a prose that will make you smile and touch your neck, he shows off his smarter side. The story is about two lesbian women who got caught up in their deceit and lies to their husband that turned deadly, but for whom? I won't give it away. 'Rayne in the Bedroom 2.' picked up where Part 1 left off in Book 1. My Dapharoah is a master storyteller and he has the talent to make you feel things for people emotionally, people you wouldn't normally feel any empathy for. He writes from a man and woman's point a view with accuracy. I duly hope you all get his book. You will be sweating for Book 3. And I can't wait.

A reviewer
Dominick, A reviewer, 07/08/2008

Must I say I am thoroughly impressed...I saw this man walking around and catching the bus everyday to go to work and school and I had no idea he was an author with such a hot book and fans. I had no idea he lived in my neighborhood. He put us on the map again with a very well-written and risqué book. He doesn't talk about what other erotica authors talk about. No. He is daring and I get the sense that he doesn't care if people

like it or love it. He just wants to tell a story and his
lyrical word play is astounding. He is average. He's
even more gorgeous in person. The photographs don't
do him justice. I ran across his Buy my Book now
banner on Myspace and was directed here I was
shocked. So I bought it just because. Who is this man?
He blends in with society and he is very intelligent.
Getting the book was a treat. No one knows what
Goulds and Naranja is like. Utter slums. It has its
newly built suburban side, but to know Dapharoah69
didn't succumb to violence and selling drugs, he
decided to use his deadly arsenals: his pen, keyboard
and brilliant mind. I loved the book. I must get book
one. Dapharoah, thank you for setting the example
and showing brothers that are in the struggle a
different way out that don't involve basketballs, ESPN
or guns and violence.

***** **A reviewer**
Ayjay, A reviewer, 07/04/2008

I call him Dade County's Finest Secret. I'm a Hispanic
male who don't really read anything. But I heard so
much about this new writer I decided to buy the book.
I mean I had nothing to lose. I just got through
reading the second book. I love it. Every line and
every story. His metaphors will stun you. The way he
writes digs into your emotions. Right on Dapharoah69
for putting GOULDS and NARANJA on the map
showing the world that we have talent down in the
Forgotten City.

***** **Electrifying!**
Sandra, A reviewer, 07/02/2008

What can I say that no one else has said? The man has a very bright future and he will be a household name. I'm glad he didn't get published by those huge publishing houses because they would have tried to change him and his work. He did it himself. That means he's in control. And control the reader he does. Congratulations the King of Erotica. I bought the book again as a gift to a friend. I love it. And I'll be sending links to all my business associates to get this book. Its a must read. If you're tired of watered down erotica and typical fiction then consider getting his books. I promise they will stimulate and educate.

★★★★★HE IS DESERVING!!!!
Bishop, A reviewer, 07/02/2008

The KING of Erotica has arrived haters. I love his work. The entire book is golden

★★★★★I am in Awe of his Talent
Jason, A reviewer, 07/02/2008

Wow. Wow. And wow. This was the first time I tried to read erotica. Erotica isn't what I'm in to. But one read of the King of Erotica the Crown was well worth my $14.95 and then some. I read this book twice, and got from it what I missed the first time because I was too excited about reading it. From cover to cover the book is well formatted. He included tidbits of himself in the Testament portion. A college student from F.I.U. wrote a paper on his writing and he published it in the book, which I thought was very nice of the author. His poem 'Adolescence II' blew me away, as he talked about the brutality of being raped at a young age. His metaphors and the way he drew the picture made me shudder with tears in my eyes. Each story pours into the next. I made the mistake of buying Book 2 before I bought book 1, as some of the stories are sequels to what's in Book 1. His poem 'What is Africa,' in book 2 and 'Barbra Streisand' gives a look into the mind of a young Negro facing racism in America. The short stories are the standouts. Each and every last story 'especially THE KITTY CHRONICLES' were hilariously funny and very well written. Smoke and Mirrors blew my mind. You want to know what true family deception is? Dapharoah69 writes it in a way like no other. You will never guess the ending to his work. I recommend this book to anyone who wants erotica and who wants something more in return. I can't wait until book three. I must know what Melissa Jackson will do with the Golden Mask.

★★★★★The next E. Lynn Harris? Nah. He's the next thing, PERIOD!
Very Impressed, A reviewer, 07/02/2008

To stuff this magnificent man into the box with other authors is incredulous. In fact it's demeaning and it takes away the man's struggle to be known in the literary world. A lot of people have been following him. I loved him since Trimaxx Publishing had him on their site. I watched them stab him in the back. I watched them write a Blog on him on MySpace saying he is a plagiarist. The man IS NOT. He had thousands of fans come through and defend his honor. He wasn't even published yet. He's very humble. He stood his ground. They could not produce the proof. Because there wasn't any. Then he came harder by putting out his book himself and it sold over 6,000 copies. I became a fan then. Poem after poem, story after story he has shattered the competition. Now he's on the Barnes and Noble site. WHAT AN ACCOMPLISHMENT!!!!! His books are named The King of erotica. Not him. He's Dapharoah69. He has built from the ground up his legacy. He may not be a millionaire and he may not be on Eric Jerome Dickey's level as far as success but he darn sure writes better material then Eric does. He has GOD! He has heart. He writes better books than Eric Jerome, in my opinion. He's raw and uncensored. His writing is in your face. He's fresh and he owns his own publishing company, TKOE Publications. Which means one thing: He does his books HIS WAY! He uses his image to market himself. He uses every medium necessary to put himself in everyone's faces. Newspapers, magazines, you name it he's in it. He does what he does without apology, as the back cover of the King of Erotica 2 suggests. I bought the book a few months ago and I am just now writing my review. I read the other reviews on here. And they are absolutely right. He writes for all people. Gay, bisexual, and straight people love this man and I can see why. Can you say HUNK?????? Can you say one of the most beautiful and sexy men I've ever seen? The gay community loves him. The straight community loves him. If you wanna understand yourself and explore why people have the type of sex the way they do, buy the book. My favorite story...I don't have a favorite. They are all very well written and slowly unravel into a ball of entertainment. Yes, SEX

COLORS THE BOOK!! But, guess what? There are hidden stories within. You are going to uncover some family secrets in each and every one. Dapharoah69, my hat off to you brothah. You are the epitome of young black excellence. And your star will continue to rise. Kudos!

Also recommended: James Baldwin Giovanni's Room

★★★★★OH MY GOD! I HAVE A NEW FAVORITE AUTHOR
Andre, very impressed, 06/30/2008

I am a gay male, a 49 year old man in his prime. I have read a lot of books in my life. But none comes close to the brilliance of Dapharoah's brilliant mind. If I ever met his mother I'd kiss her hand and thank her for his life. His name is vastly and rapidly making the rounds. I saw a friend with his book a couple weeks ago and she told me where I could get it. Of course I was a skeptic. I went to Barnes and Noble but they told me they didn't have it so I logged on the net and bought it. I wanted to find a reason ANY REASON to tear his book down. I am sorry. I could NOT find one. I love this man. I could not put it down. Each story slowly and viciously pours into the next. The way he writes about sex is more like poetry in motion. This is what an erotic book should be and I am so thankful to God for this man!

★★★★★BELIEVE THE HYPE!!!!!
Danielle, A reviewer, 06/27/2008

I was buying a Zane book when I saw the pop up for this erotic book. Since I'm a woman I was drawn to the handsome man on the cover. I was happy to see that it was the actual author. So I bought his book as well. I read it in a day. I was done. You get a sense of Timelessness when you flip through it. He put it together and you can feel the heart he put into it. I could not stop flipping the pages as each story slowly unfolds into the next. He's more than sex people. YOU HEAR ME? He's more than Erotica. He has stories for the straight, gay and bisexual community. He writes it ALL!!! Giving the reader insight to the character mind. I couldn't help but look at myself in the process. If I could find one thing wrong with this book it would be how late we all found out about this incredible man who not only wrote an enlightening, thrilling fictional novel but he has included things in his book no other Erotic other has: pictures of himself. Standing behind his work. The book is called the Crown. And in it he has pictures representing that. On a Basketball court with the goal above him as his 'Literary Crown,' challenging his peers. Every story, from Freaky Deaky 'which will have the bedroom walls sweating and the beds shot of breath' to his knack for writing from a female and male's point of view with accuracy left me mind-boggled. I look forward to Book 3.

★★★★★**Outstanding. Totally Impressed**
A True Critic, A reviewer, 06/27/2008

I am woman. And I love to read. I will give my brief rundown of the King of Erotica, who is clearly a man on his way to greatness. He can't be touched. Frankly I love the man better than Zane. Better than Eric Jerome. Why? He not only writes well crafted, gritty, in your FACE literature but he borders perfection in the process. His poem 'Barbra Streisand' touches on racism that he experienced in his classroom. Very touching. 'What is Africa' is another magnum opus college professors seriously need to PRINT out and give out with lesson plans. Every black man should read this poem. The boy not only writes good fiction but he is a very well-versed POET. Rayne in the Bedroom 2. Pure genius. And the twist is so good it left me shocked and breathless. FATE WILLIAMS. Was so shocking I was left in tears reading about the abuse she endured at the hands of her own mother. BOOTY-DO. The title was comical but the story of a reformed prostitute who bangs her best friend's husband was such treat I read it twice. FREAKY DEAKY. Melissa is back, from Part 1 of his book. This time she gets freaky with candle wax, and her own selfish pleasures that left me panting and desiring her myself. Dapharoah has been touched by God with the gift of GAB. Dapharoah will always get my last twenty bucks. He is worth it. SHAME on publishing houses sleeping on this magnificent writer.

★★★★★**headline**
A Dude, God, 06/15/2008

This book is so amazing. You should buy it, you should see the girls around the way. They love this stuff. Not to mention its literature that makes you think.

xiv

★★★★★**Freak of Nature**
A reviewer, A reviewer, 06/14/2008

I was looking around the internet and came across this book. I was a big fan of Zane and his books so i wanted to check this guy out and then later on learned that he knew Zane. The thing i like about the book is that incorporates safe sex and it turns on all your inhibitions and makes you wanna throw them out the window. I look forward to another book in this series like this. I love this book

★★★★★**Ladies and Gentleman He has Arrived**
Quincy, just like you..., 06/14/2008

I am a straight male. And I never thought of getting into trying to understand the gay lifestyle or entertaining lesbianism. But a friend girl of mine had this book and I read it and I am hooked. I wound up buying the book myself. I didn't realize that he had Part 1 out as well. I bought that one, too. I am a fan. The King of Erotica is so much more. He is a cornucopia of everything you want to understand ABOUT YOURSELF.

★★★★★**HE IS HE KING OF EROTICA...AND MORE**
A Changed Woman in Dade County, a business woman working Downtown, 06/14/2008

He's known as the King of Erotica. And he's from Dade County (Miami). But homeboy embodies guts, strength and beautiful writing. His in your face literature is just what the world needs. Call it curiosity or call it me being bored. But I got an email from a friend a few weeks ago about some new writer named The King of Erotica. I was like 'Yea, ok.' I took a chance and checked him out. I am so glad that I did. I read some of his stuff on Myspace. I was impressed. I read his life story. How he was raped and abused from age 6-10. I was taken aback that this beautiful man battled everything from family back biting to his sexuality to publishing his book ON HIS OWN! So I bought part 1 of the book. I got it a week later. Must I say from cover to cover of his well-put together book he took me up and down and left me in tears and breathless with his short stories. The sex will make Zane blush. But they are SO MUCH MORE! He has me as a fan for life. I didn't think Part 2 would top the first. It did.

That should shut the haters up.

Dapharoah69

THE KING OF EROTICA 1

THE KING OF EROTICA 2: THE CROWN

AVAILABLE NOW
AMAZON.COM AND BARNES AND
NOBLE.COM

THE KING OF EROTICA 3
COMING SOON
D.PHAR.69

www.ingramcontent.com/pod-product-compliance
Lightning Source LLC
Chambersburg PA
CBHW020653110726
47901CB00001B/172